Exhaust from the Tin Woods

Written by **Erik J Kregel**

With *Inevitable Unicorn Press*

With *Amazon*

I0544241

Exhaust from the Tin Woods

ISBN 978-1-988327-41-9

With Inevitable Unicorn Press

We would like to acknowledge the following for their contributions:

Editing by Donna Shumaker
Cover art work by Conner Cantelon
Cover design by Rusty Knight
Revisions and feedback, Kenneth Shumaker, Aria
Produced, published and distribution by, with marketing and
promotions contributed by Rusty Knight with Inevitable Unicorn
Press

Exhaust from the Tin Woods

For Catherine

Table of Contents

Exhaust from the Tin Woods

A Note from the Author:

For this to make sense as a book, which you are now reading; it must be known that I am not the author.

This is listed as a novel, as a work of fiction: I think that would be the safest category and certainly would be the least upsetting to people.

But it isn't.

Two years ago, I attended a family camp just outside of Edmonton. My kids were chasing the other kids, my wife was busying herself making apple pies, and I was, well, bored. A group from the camp knew of a family-owned antique store near the camp and invited me to come along. I obliged and went shopping: the sport of the bored.

I bought a doctor's bag, my only purchase. I thought it was a novelty and it was a rather worn out leather casing. I thought nothing of it until, that night, I found the lining frayed and the weathered case revealed a small book.

Its print date was 1910 and made in the capital of Grouard, Alberta. For those unaware of the geography of Canada, Alberta's capital is Edmonton. It's never been Grouard. Alberta, a western province that stands over the state of Montana like an older brother, has never had another capital other than Edmonton.

There's also dates that are askew. Charles Babbage's inventions never made it into the mainstream, yet his difference engine seems to be as popular as Graham Bell's telephone in this story. H.G. Wells is a little too popular in this world as what I understand him to be and his books, from some of the quotes, are out of chronological order.

And then there's the word "glitz" – not an Edwardian expression and its etymological history is a lot more current.

As I read the book – this book – it intimated that the United States was split into three countries – Mexicia, the Union (or "The State"), and the Confederation of States. The civil war, according to this author, ended quite different than the one I learned about in High School.

Alternative historical fiction? I wondered. I hid the book

Exhaust from the Tin Woods

away, believing that's what it might be, and enjoyed the rest of the camp. Only two weeks later, when I brought it to a rare book dealer near my office, did this book become an even greater problem.

The bookseller – an amateur archeologist of ancient text – ran some tests and confirmed the age of the book to be printed around 1910.

Really? I thought to myself.

So, we have here a manuscript either written by someone who is pretending a different history and the world is much different than the actual one or … it's an artifact from a place much like ours, only with differences – subtle at first – culminating into an alien artifact.

I'm not sure. Let's say it's a work of fiction. Why not? If that helps you sleep better at night. However, I have my doubts and yet I know I cannot say outright this is from another world. You decide.

I did my best as an editor, to supply footnotes and a map and any descriptions that might help you – the gentle reader – through this artifact from a world not ours but close to ours. This book has its own vocabulary to which I sought to make guesses and suggestions as to what they might be. I hope it helps in clearing this book up.

I hope there are other books out there from this world. I'm not sure and drop me a line if you find any. There's important lesson in all of this: whenever buying antique luggage, always check the lining.

Dr. Eric J. Kregel
Edmonton, Canada

Exhaust from the Tin Woods

Chapter One
January 1895

"This is Grouard, the heart of Alberta," says the handsome coachman. He is an old, withered man who looks to have spent most of his adult years under the rule of a Monarch. He looks out to the frozen river and snow, with crippled, withered buildings burping steam, mist, and smoke. "This is as far as I can take 'ee." He turns to face Brambely. "Dinna be fooled by the trees and snow. It be a real Tin Woods[1] out 'ere."

"A map," Mistress Sorrows says to the coachman. "I understand there ought to be a map."

"Aye," he says. He rifles through his long coat for a few seconds and then produces a folded piece of paper, held together by a seal made of bee's wax. "Thar be the map. Careful, now. I speak to you as Londoners: Alberta has a lot of phantasmagoria to it."

"Duly noted," Sorrows says and gives him a sovereign for his troubles.

The pair – Brambely and his much older traveling companion, Sorrows – steps out of the warm, still air of the coach into the blustering, screeching wind of the Woods.

"I'm still getting used to the Commonwealth," Brambely says as the coachman hands him his duffel pack. "It looks … uncombed."

The coachman burgles a throaty laugh, baring his yellowed and steel teeth.

"Canada be rough," the coachman says as he tips his hat made of coyote, like a proper gentleman. "Welcome to the heart of the Tin Woods."

He climbs up to his coach and his horses rumble to life, like that of an obsolete gas engine. With his snowy wake firmly

---

[1] 1) An environment where nature is combined with humanity combined with technology 2) An expression about Northern Canada.

Exhaust from the Tin Woods

upon the road, Mistress Sorrows turns to Brambley. "Have faith in our God, Master Brambely. Take courage. The last leg of our journey is before us. Be a true, as you young people say, Dreamer[2]."

"'Tis not Africa or Mars[3], M'Lady."

"It is Canada. Mine as well be those places most civilized people read only in the rags," Sorrows says as she clutches her long purse containing her clothes, medicine, Bible, and spare parts for the past three weeks. The purse was standard carrying for most women of London, yet it stands out of place in Alberta.

The pair walk westward, by-passing the town completely. They come to the cusp of the town, with nothing but the trees and flat of the frozen eddies before them.

Brambley studies the folded map. His eyes betray an expectation for the map to unfold itself, dance, and sing their way to the desired location. The seal is of a beautiful maiden all toggled[4] by a team of prattlers into an iron hand, with a hammer working out a rainbow of metalmancy[5].   Pure glitz[6], without a smack of Luddmunstering[7].

"Our magic carpet is on loan to the Sultan," Mistress Sorrows says. "Allow us the privilege of an opened map so we may complete our trek by foot."

"Right," the young Brambley says. He opens the map and

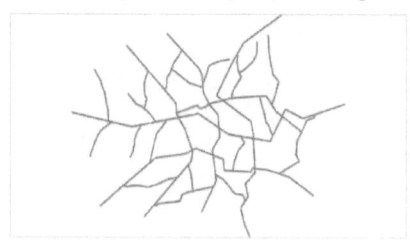

---

[2] An explorer; a scientist with a really big curiosity.

[3] I guess there had been space exploration, expeditions to Mars and Venus.

[4] Cybernetics; a human body augmented by robotics

[5] adding style and flare to machines

[6] There's that word! Okay, the closest idea I can find is something terribly fashionable or incredibly vogue

[7] Favouring something anti-technology, that is closer to a gas station than a steam engine.

sees:

"This map is seeing gray," he says with a start. "It's the maddest thing given to us. How, under Heaven and Earth, can we use this?"

Sorrows looks at the map. She grunts. "It's a joke from Allbrung. A riddle. Best use our wits or we shall become ice sculptures of Londoners."

Brambely walks to the face of the forest, studying the map. They walk to a bare opening to the woods. "Let us pretend, then, that this is a road map applied to the forest. The streets are natural paths, made by run-off and deer. And this," he says, pointing to the opening in the woods, "Is this," he says, pointing to the road leading out on the west side of the page. "Keeping our wits, we follow the map against the natural shifts and holes of the woods."

"Are you sure, boy?" Sorrows asks.

"No, I'm sherlucking[8]. But it stands to reason: the trees are the buildings, and the natural pathways are the roads." He smirks. "I could be wrong."

"We shall soon see," Sorrows says as she extends her hand to Brambely. He takes it as he leads her through the woods. With the prompts from the map, they turn and charge down the paths. The trees grow tightly together, so there is little guess. After fifteen minutes, the two fall into a pattern of trust with the map, making their way with little error or dead ends.

"You shall like Allbrung," Sorrows says. "He is much like you that I sometimes think you to be cousins. He is mad as you, I should think. The only balm in our departure is that you shall be with Allbrung."

"I am quite anxious to make a name for myself in the Empire, but I am ill at ease in leaving your home. Mistress Sorrows, your kindness is worthy of a tale told by all Holy books."

"Holy books are quite Luddmunster in our new and liberated era," the old woman scolds. "But thank you. No matter what the progress might befall us, I hold firm to the fraternity of humankind. Fraternity begged us, originally, to take you in and

---

[8] When someone makes a deduction not based on reason or science.

Exhaust from the Tin Woods

raise you at our school. It became a sheer pleasure to raise you, Master Brambely."

Brambley blushes, and it is a true blush, a case of his biology catching up with the rushing of his thoughts.

The pair continue into the woods, turning and weaving around the poplars and pines. A brisk, sweet wind blows through the trees. The frosted air stings in their nose. A crackle of chill sounds in the distance. Another fifteen minutes' pass, with the small town dissolved into their distance.

"Allbrung," Sorrows says to break the silence. "Shall show you a trade. You are anxious to make your way in the world, and yet you have no station, so you need a trade. Allbrung shall teach you."

"It is good you mention this now," Brambely says. "For this is the one thing, in all of our weeks of travels, you have not mentioned: where, what and why am I to live in Canada."

"But we have talked about a good many of other important things," Sorrows says, tightening her grip in his hand. "No, I have kept the profit of our trip to Canada a mystery." Her free, robotic hand pushed away the loose, gray hair that fled her weave of proper braids. "Allbrung is a great and wonderful scientist. Few know this in London, but there were only three men who created our modern age. Allbrung was one of them. Think Wells, think Babbage, and think Edison. And with all of these, think Allbrung who knew and inspired all of them."

"So my apprenticeship shall be at the hands of the Grandfather of all Prattlers[9]? All glitz[10] and steam and steel?"

"Nay," she says. "Allbrung is a bit more crushed, and I say that in a good way. He apprentices ... students of everything, yet his particular genius is of the vaporous exhaust."

"A man must be specialized," Brambley quotes from almost everyone in London.

Sorrows chuckles. "Indeed, studying under Allbrung shall be an education. He might change your thinking in today's trend in education."

---

[9] steam scientists
[10] street punk style decked out in the latest fashion

Exhaust from the Tin Woods

Quickly the quiet of the woods ends. In its place is a growl. The two look at each other and then march through the woods to a nearby clearing. Once in the small hole in the expanse of the tight, constricted woods, they look down to see a descending bluff.

Another growl.

An ice fog rolls and opens, like curtains rolling back to reveal an opera. In the center of the clearing marches a creature. More like an obstruction, an intrusion – not a creature.

A brown bear. It stood with a steel hull and a right, ribbed metal leg. A yellow light shoots from where his left eye should be. Marching, huffing, and grumbling. Brambley studies the mismatched creature. His brain does not allow what his eyes tell him: the bear has a human face, sad and unstable and seemingly drunk. The bear slouches, full of fur and robotics and anger. The face twitches. Gray skin of a bear shaved, yet … human.

"That is wrong," Sorrows whispers.

The steam of the bear, so hot and rich, it cuts through the snow and turns it to vapor. The whole ground seems to bend to the will of the creature. A path now is set behind the bear, as the pistons and pumps and pipes create a solid gray parade pluming behind him.

The human face of the bear changes. From stupefaction, it turns to wonder, still keeping the severe narrowing of his eyebrows. His black nose crinkles to a sniff.

"Do you think he sees us?" Sorrows whispers.

Steel, serrated claws shine in the dull, winter sunlight. A snarl opened the bear's mouth, revealing a spring loaded trap – ironically for bears – as teeth. Brambley deduces, with a simple swat, the creature could knock them over without breaking any stride.

"If it knew we were here, it would either flee or attack," Brambley says, stepping in front of his elderly godmother. The young man, quite tall, hides her completely in his cover. "Nay, he does not see us."

The bear stops, smelling, he closes his eyes. Opening his mouth as if to yawn, the bear cries a deep, sonorous lament that shakes the fabric of the forest. He stops and opens his eyes. And continues his march.

11

Exhaust from the Tin Woods

Once the bear marches on, disappearing northward away from where the map is to lead them, Brambley turns to Sorrows. "That was a half-man, half-machine, and half-bear: one too many 'halves' to be a safe and secure equation. Is that the work of this genius Allbrung?"

"Suffer the thought. The good doctor would never do something so foundationally ... klownish[11]. That is a monsteration[12], in direct defiance to the Lord's creation," Sorrows says and makes a face as if to spit. Brambley knew she would not, for such a rude action would be beneath her etiquette.

Brambley looks at the map. "This way," he says with a point eastward. "According to this map, we are just across the bay." He takes her hand and walks her across the field. They come to the path recently made by the bear; the grass and dirt are still hot from the creature's steam. "I fear I'm not used to these kinds of wonders, Mistress."

"No, we at the Academy, kept away from all of this ... science." She laughs. "I almost wasn't hired by the foundation because of my hand."

"Is that from Allbrung?" he asks as he points to her robotic hand.

"Yes," she says. "A snake bite turned infected while doing missionary work in the Congo. Allbrung was visiting the settlement and severed my hand before I was to expire. With my consent, he forged my new hand and my body received the hardware. I have always owed him. So I guess my delivery of you shall be payment."

"But this an imposition, is it not?" Brambley asks. "He is to tutor, train, and apprentice me for two years? For free? How is that a fair payment for saving your life?"

"Dr. Allbrung has his own weights and measurements." Sorrows pauses and stares at Brambley. She smiles and pats Brambley's hand with her silk-gloved hand. Always a lady, she wears gloves, and embroidered gloves even in the stark, cold

---

[11] to intentionally be irritating or disturbing for a greater purpose, based on European clowns that street perform in England despite the steampunks hating clowns

[12] cybernetics done wrong

woods. "You are coming into his very capable hands, and your future shall be secure."

They walk through the woods, crossing the expanse of white on the map. With their entrance back into woods, another fifteen minutes draws them to the line that takes them to an X. "Like a labyrinth," Sorrows says.

They rounded their last corner to find a great manor, made of ageless stone and defiant poplar beams and brightly shining bricks and sprawling rooftops. The great house looked part castle, part estate, and part school: again, too many halves to be reasonable.

"What a nounschwanstein[13]!" Brambley shoots out. His eyes widened, and his jaws open as if to gobble up the sight of the great house.

Tudor, Regency, Gothic, Classical – it stood a mix of every housing design from England. And yet, it fit within the woods. The colors matched the woods as if it is a seamless blend of a lady's scarf with her bodice. Despite the matching woodwork, the shapes of the wings and towers look as if pulled from villages and neighborhoods all over the continent.

He counted five towers, connecting together by a three-story stretch of a brick and mortar hall. The entire building is in a tetrahedron shape, with some deviations with its outer wall connecting to a mammoth, square building against the woods. The windowpanes crisscross over the multiple windows. Tudor boards cross wherever the windows aren't. Every rooftop is some semblance to a cone, to a triangle. Tiles drape the roofs in a dizzying array of lines and blocks.

As they approach, they are no longer cold. Soon, Brambley feels quite hot, so he takes off his wool scarf and unbuttons his long tweed coat. Brambley feels his longish hair – in the style of a gentleman – turn to curl around his ears and sideburns. Brambley is proud of his sideburns, able to grow them three years ago, a week after his thirteenth birthday.

The pair make their way to the front gate. The word "*Veritas*" stretch across the top, in place of a family name or crest.

---

[13] a really neat looking home

Exhaust from the Tin Woods

They reach the front and use the doorknockers in the shape of hammers.

Quickly, the door opens to a tall, young man who appears to be from the islands of Japan. His face is without expression. His suit denotes that of a butler with the difference of the traditional uniform as his is out of solid, black leather. Brambley looks a bit closer and sees that the young man has long, luxurious dreadlocks, tied in the back.

"Yes?" the servant asks.

"We are here to see Dr. Pieter Van Allbrung," Sorrows says to the butler. "Might we come in?"

"You are expected. Welcome to Grouard," the tall Asian says, towering over the very petite Sorrows and the average height of Brambley.

They walk into the house; first to cross the atrium made entirely out of colored copper, favoring earth tones. A soft brush lines the floors, providing comfort and an acoustic barrier to their steps.

Brambley immediately notices the house possess a pulse and breadth, made up of ticks and grinds and buzzes of a thousand motors. Throughout the house, exposed sprockets turn, and pendulums swing, and hands click and a steady beat of gears sound. The house is alive, the sounds of a thousand and one clocks connected to a single rhythm. A clock rests against the odd wall, so the army of time devices must be invisible – Brambley reasons.

The butler takes them to a very warm sunroom with an expansive blue tinted window displaying the gardens, with the greens, and the snow-dappled forest. There is a solid perimeter around the house absent of any snow. The walls drip, condensation collects over the windows.

And there, Brambely sees an old man painting with oils. He is nude.

The butler exhales a breathy sigh as he charges out to the greens. Sorrows stifles a shriek as she turns away. Brambley, too, turns away but then returns to see a silent pantomime out in the gardens. First, the old man hears something the butler says, and then he jumps in the air, arms waving. The old man turns towards the house, looking excited. Then the butler grabs his arm and

Exhaust from the Tin Woods

gestures to his lower body. The old man realizes something and runs to fetch his robe.

A few moments later, the older man enters the sunroom. "Ah, Madeline," he says and smiles down to Mistress Sorrows. "It has been a decade, at least. How are you, my dear?"

Brambley notices the old man speaks in pitch-perfect English. Brambley cannot think of when he heard his mother tongue spoken without an accent or regional expression. Every word is exact, without an emphasis on a particular consonant.

"Well, my dear Dr. Allbrung. Quite well. The Foundation has new staff, and we are able to take care of a lot more of our orphaned youngsters," she says with a deep grin. "And you?"

"I am blessed. I have never been so blessed. Mercyminster has been so good for me, yes. So good."

The old man is fit, like a career soldier who lives on the airships that chase Napoleon's troops. His age is impossible to place: 49? 78? 63? His jaw is angular and strong, with a head of full, long gray hair. His eyes blue, the color of a rich fabric or the screen of a Difference Engine. Broad shoulders are an athletic build.

"And you are Mistress Sorrow's reward?" he asks Brambely.

"Brambley Williams is our finest student, excelling in science and literature and all of the aspects of a classic education. He speaks Latin, Greek, and German. As well, his chief interest is the study of religion. Brambley is quite religious."

"Will that be a problem?" Brambley asks.

"No," Allbrung says slowly. "Our world is quite religious. I think you shall find a home in reality. Science is quite religious too." He points with his eyes to the ironwork of the ceiling, showing the room with reflective light. "So, what do you think of Mercyminster?"

"Quite posh, toggled to perfection. A real nounshwanstein," Brambley says.

"You are generous in your praise," Allbrung says. "So, what would you like to learn?"

"I'm not sure. Everything, at some point," Brambley says and then chuckles as if to explain his joke.

Allbrung studies the young man, painfully long and

thorough. His blue eyes rarely move, surveying and drinking in the sight of the youth. "You must have warmer gloves, my boy?" he asks.

"I have some great gloves, but they're quite wet. Our hotel in Edmonton sprung a leak, and I stopped up the drain, while I fixed the plumbing. I fear they're still soggy or packs of ice."

Allbrung smiles at the butler. "Suk, welcome Mr. Williams," he says. "The boy just passed our entrance exam. Welcome him aboard "

"Glad to have you," The butler says with a bow.

"Suk rarely lies, so you've made a good impression on him."

"How?" Brambley asks with his hands in the air.

"The key to harmony is watching, is studying. Our god is in the details, which is terribly Mexician[14] of me, I know. Still, the holy and the divine and the true things are in the details. You gushed over my home; a proper gentleman would be economic with his praise. You fixed the plumbing of your hotel; a nobleman would just ring for a servant. You figured out a map; a standard toggled prattler or common sense Dreamer or a Posh Pony[15] would just throw up their hands, say they were lost because the directions were difficult. You are prodigal, charitable, and innovative; while the rest of the world is miserly, useless, and easily dismayed. Welcome to Mercyminster."

"Is this a school?" Brambley asks.

"Depends."

"That isn't really an answer, Dr. Allbrung," says Sorrows.

"And I am entirely happy with that," the old man says, looking down at his feet with a slight chuckle. "Suk, please show Brambley to the other children in the playground. I wish to have tea with my very old, dear friend. We shall have supper and ..." He looks to Sorrows. "... then shall you be staying –"

"There is a dirigible that shall be landing in Grouard," she says. "I plan to leave on it. It leaves tonight. I must get back to the Foundation as fast as possible. We travelled with a slow pace

---

[14] Mexico that owns California; lots of religion
[15] dance hall girl or professional escort

Exhaust from the Tin Woods

worthy of Jules Verne, but I intend to fly back across the pond."

"The Foundation, the Foundation! It sounds like some sort of mythical, secret society. And I should know, I've worked for a few. It doesn't sound like what it truly is, and that is an orphanage, a place that loves children."

"The title is fine," she says.

"I'm sure it is."

Suk offers his hand as a direction, pointing out of the sunroom.

Brambley bows to Mistress Sorrows and leaves. As he exits, Suk leads but hesitates upon the first hard right. Why would the staff hesitate? Brambley wonders. Hasn't he been down these halls a thousand times?

Gathering speed, Suk marches down the hallway through the copper atrium and out the doors. The warm, humid air blasts them as Brambley sees the deep snow and frost and cold of Alberta before him.

"Our work produces so much steam and exhaust, it makes the area around Mercyminster almost ... tropical," Suk says. He is in full stride to the large, brick building connecting to the manor. "I'm a great judge of character. In fact, I'm never wrong. You, Mr. Williams, I like. Please remember that. I have the habit of sometimes suggesting the opposite."

"How?" Brambley asks.

"Your suit. It is from a haberdasher, is it not? Good style, strong cloth and well made. Yet it's worn, suggesting that it is your only outfit. Clothes say a lot about a man. You are quality, Brambley. And modest, almost frugal. I bet most of the adults around you would say you embody what is best about Victoria's London."

Brambley winces. Suk continues, "No modesty, my friend. If you haven't deduced yet, we're all punks. Every one of us. We are not made by Victoria's London; and, for that matter, as an orphan you have not been manufactured by London's social machine. You, instead, are a by-product."

Brambley feels hot in his cheeks and opens his mouth to rebut the insult.

"No, I'm right. And please remember, I like you," Suk

Exhaust from the Tin Woods

says. "And I'm never wrong about my read of someone."

They trudge through the steaming, cobblestone walkway to the square, windowless building. A large beast of a building, resembling a Kraken laying on its side in repose, ready to rise. Everything is brick or mortar, except the thatched rooftop. Brambley would expect to find it in West London or on the docks somewhere in Wales. Not here, not in the middle of the Canadian woods. "I know for a fact, in less than a minute, you will find yourself overwhelmed, and it will have nothing to do with technology."

The pair made their way to the front of the mouth, an imperfect square of double doors befitting the opened mouth of a beast. Steam wrecks out the corners, exhaling to the cold of the snowy land.

Suk swings the doors open. The building is one, three story room. Metal shelf levels hang made of iron sheets and chains. Gears and sprockets and chains, too large for any single mortal to wield, roll and swing and turn around the platforms. Hoses and tubes and levers and furnaces proliferate like mushrooms in a darkened world. The steam and the heat is hellfire, causing every pore in Brambley to immediately flood with sweat. There are the pulse returns of a thousand clock parts running.

Suk shuts the door.

Brambley peers upon the tabletops, strewn with goggles and tools and boxes and pans and gadgets and pails and wires and tubes and pieces of machines. A prattlers afterlife, their paradise.

A zip of rope sounds overhead and cascading downward is a nearly nude young woman. She wears a white bodice and a slim undergarment and nothing else. Her legs and feet and arms and some of her bosom is bare. Brambley, before thinking, spies a glance of her uncovered ankle. He turns away, averting his eyes.

"Is he the new bloke?" she asks.

"His name is Brambley Williams, and he's proving my point," Suk says.

Brambley offers his hand in the young woman's direction. "I don't mean to be rude, M'lady," he says. "It is a pleasure to make your acquaintance." His strength strains to keep his eyes away from her and to return to the sight of her naked ankles.

Exhaust from the Tin Woods

"You look it," she says in her thick Welsh accent. "You look full of pleasure."

"I am sorry; I am not used to seeing a woman without the aid of clothing."

"Clothing doesn't aid a body like mine. Look at me, I'm amazing," she says proudly. "You're a real Luddmunster[16] before the world was Babbaged[17]."

"Sorry," Brambley says, almost shaking. "Old religions take a long time to die."

"I'd almost be insulted if you weren't such a Charles Dickens[18]." She reaches out and grabs Brambley's hand. Her hand is small, moist, and gentle in the shake. She leans in and whispers. "Look at me. Just my face."

He turns and faces her. She is beautiful, and it scares him even more. Her nose is long but upturned in a pretty point. She has light blue eyes, like jewels of impossible worth. Her chin is pointed, but not like a man's – a fine point with a slim dimple. Her hair, cut to a man's length, is so blonde that it's almost white.

"I am human. I am a girl. I have a story, and we're going to be mates. Get used to me, for steam and heat tends to take off a lot of clothing," she whispers.

Brambley closes his eyes and thinks a single word prayer: chivalry. "Like Suk, I also aspire to read one's character. And I should think, your story cannot be bested and shall be worthy of most memories."

"Good," she says and then takes a step backwards. "Get used to the body."

He studies everything but her ankles, hoping to turn it into a mechanical collection of parts without any lure or lechery. His intention is to liken unto a surgeon, full of science and without judgment. This lasts only for three seconds, as his study is suspended on her torso.

"I, fear, am hopeless," Brambley says.

---

[16] Luddites and those who favored gas powered technology who lost the argument

[17] based on Charles Babbage's first computer, it's when something human has been replaced by a machine

[18] a good looking man

Exhaust from the Tin Woods

"Don't worry," a male voice erupts from behind him. "In a weeks' time, you'll be near naked along with the rest of us. Rolling around with Cat, searching for parts."

Brambley turns to the author of the male voice. "There is little assurance in what you have just said." He sees the young man, close to his age, wearing wool trousers, canvas gators, and clogs. Shirtless, yet he still has his fob watch and chain.

"Patrick is the name," he says, extending his hand. "That is Cat. And the rest shall be coming on your heels. Tonight, mainly. And you must be Brambley?"

"I must be, although I don't feel as much that I am." Brambley looks around. "This place is really special, a joywig[19] factory."

"It's all of my dreams come true," Cat says. "Not with a thousand dollars and dating Henry the VIII could I land a place as special as this. All the glitz, metalmancy, granding[20], and the shine ... it's all here." She winked at Brambley. "I'm back to my workstation. I haven't yet figured out how to make my engine earrings come alive. Patrick, be extra kind to this one: I like him." She says, and Brambley only figures out, soon after, she is pulled up by her repelling apparatus.

"Are all of Allbrung's students like her?" Brambley asks.

"Like Cat? In what regards?" Patrick asks innocently.

"I mean, look at her. She is amazing. A full figured woman with the face of an angel. Yet she is more scantily clad than most dancing girls. She is perfect in appearance, yet trollops around like a Pony[21] from the streets of Cardiff. I say, how does anyone get any work done around here?"

"I can still hear you," Cat says from above. "The acoustics in here are amazing."

Brambley begins to shake, face turning beet red. '*Did I just*', he begun to think. '*Did I just ... no, she did not hear ... I mean ... I am so flustered I'm stuttering in my thought life.*' "By the way, thank you. I can already tell you have a tremendous backside ... and

---

[19] absolute happiness, beyond the usual good mood
[20] something made amazing by technology
[21] dance hall girl or professional escort

that isn't a metaphor." A thud of her feet sounded as they struck her hoisted platform of a lab. "Patrick, be kind to him. Please. He's precious, if not entirely too Mexician[22]."

Patrick wraps his arm around Brambley. "Let us try to recover from that one, shall we?" he says as he leads Brambley over to a long, lone table in the center of the building. "So, your family name? Williams? That is quite common. Are you the Williams from Scotland? Bentonshire?"

"No," Brambley says. "My parents are both deceased orphans and met and fell in love at the Foundation. Ironically, it's the same Foundation that raised me when I was then orphaned by them."

"Did your father die in the war?"

"No," Brambley says, the red shame washing from his face. "My mother died from the pox, and my father is in debtor's prison, paying for her treatment. I lost them when I was four."

"I am so sorry. Mercyminster is mostly orphans. I may be the only one who knows their parents," Patrick asks brightly. "Say, what is your specialization? Everyone needs to have one. Say you're not crushed[23]. What is yours?"

"I fear it is nothing handy. It is science, but nothing practical. And religion."

"Ah, we have an awful lot in common. I'm a book smart child as well. Everything I know is theory. Wells, Verne, Babbage … everything is up here." He points to his temple. "All up here." He points to his hand. "None here. That's why I'm here. My hands and my head need to talk."

"And what about Cat?" Brambley asks.

"She's a metalmancer[24]. And, from what I've seen so far, she's one of the best. Give her an engine the size of Piccadilly Square, and she'll turn them into cufflinks. Function, form, and style: she has it all. You met Suk, I suppose?"

Brambley nods and looks around, seeing the Japanese man is gone. "He used to be a metalmancer, but he started spending

---

[22] someone who is very religious
[23] a negative expression for integration
[24] one who adds style and flare to machines

more and more time with the good doctor. Now he's into, I think, computation. He's hunting for really big numbers. From fashion to zero, literally." Patrick picks up a gear. "We're one, big, happy family here, in Mercyminster. The problem is, we have to be. Nothing but us woodland creatures."

Brambley bit his tongue, feeling the compulsion to speak of the monsteration of the cyber-bear in the woods. He holds back and remains silent.

.....

Mistress Sorrows cries. Brambley knows she can't help it. She stands in the brass atrium, clutching her bag and trembling. She shakes, placing her right hand over her mouth. "I promised I wouldn't do this. I mustn't. You see, I loved your parents. We all went to school together. All friends. I loved them. I promised I would take care of you. I did out of duty. Then you got the love I had for them. Had to go somewhere. Cruel, horrible world. With its steam and machines and factories and robots. It killed them, this world of oil and grime."

She coughs which shakes the tears from within her. "Tears have afternooned me. Sorry. And now, I must say good-bye." Tears stream down her face.

Brambley's arm wraps around her.

Allbrung sits on the staircase, and it looks like he is crying.

Up the staircase is Cat, pretending not to watch.

"I shall seek to make you proud. The Foundation shall be proud. I'm a second generation student," Brambley says.

"That isn't right for an orphanage. Bad math, that's what it is."

"But it's what my present sum must be," Brambley says and whispers to her. "Thank you for adding to my value, Sorrows." He kisses her on the forehead.

The sobs now end. "Do not kiss me. There is little propriety in a young man kissing an old woman like myself. Stop it!"

"I think my reputation can survive such a moment."

They hug, and Mistress Sorrows leaves, as the handsome cab waits outside the gates of Mercyminster. The door shuts behind her; the sound of the clockwork manor fills the silence of her

Exhaust from the Tin Woods

departure.

Brambley stands as if made of ice. Nothing further comes through his face as he stares at the shut door.

Dr. Allbrung lingers in this silence for a few more moments. "My forte is orphans," the doctor says as if to wake Brambley from his frozen stillness. "My expressed mission is not to care for orphans, but I get a lot of them. Who knows why? Business has been snatched up by those who have families and connections; politics is in the hands of the few, and any other trade is too inbred. Like the Dreamers[25] who set off to explore Venus and China, I offer a leveled playing field. And nothing draws orphans more than equality. So, I tend to attract orphans." He rises. "And out of all the orphans who show up on my doorstep, you are, by far, the most loved."

"It's a lot to live up to, being loved by Mistress Madeline Sorrows and all of the Foundation," Brambley whispers.

"Let's make that status a little more light." Allbrung looks up at Cat. "My dear, come with us. It'll make your eavesdropping a little less strenuous. Plus, you need to rehear the tour of our estate."

"Why? Are you afraid I might forget or disagree?"

"No, my dear. I'm afraid you agree and need to hear it again, especially since you've lived in a world that vampidly disagrees with me."

Cat stomps down the steps wearing a brown corset strapped over a frayed gown full of flowing sleeves and a severed bottom. Brambley feels relief, for she's wearing button boots to cover her ankles.

"This is the speech I give to all of my incoming members of the community. Do you know the three things I value in students?" Allbrung asks as he walks down the hall. Brambley and Cat follow. "Of course you don't, Mistress Sorrows just dropped you off without explanation. And that was my idea, not hers. I didn't want to fill your head with anything until I could see you personally. Then, I can fill you all the way up." He chuckles. "Three things: harmony, innovation, and grace."

"Harmony – our technology must work with other people

---

[25] explorers

23

and things and the land, not against it. Innovation – let's not make what is always made because it's what we make. No, no: we are true artysams[26]. Grace – we must embrace everything with love, including our failure. Failing is the greatest form of innovation and is the best of all teachers."

He grins.

"Do we understand ourselves?" Allbrung asks. Then he throws up his hand. "Of course not. This is all abstract and boring and full zeitgeisted[27] notions." He grins. "Now, practical detail. Down this hall are the breakfast and lunch rooms. Make all meals. Every third week, you shall be in charge of cooking; every second week, we'll be in charge of doing the dishes; and this week, we'll tend the garden in the greenhouse. We make most of our own food here, and you will cook."

"But a gentleman –"

"– will learn how to cook." Cat smiles. "Now, in addition, we shall begin the morning with breakfast. Rule #1: make all meals, unless you are dying. After breakfast, if your duties give you free time, study. Lectures begin at 10 am and go to 1 pm. Then a light lunch. Afternoons are for prattling. Dinner is in the dining room, which is on the other side. Ties for the ladies, gowns for the gentlemen."

Cat chuckles.

"Reverse that, although I'm not sure I should. That might be a good idea. You know," Allbrung turns to face Cat, trailing behind him. "The one weakness is Gentlemen courting ladies might be? They don't know what they're courting." He smirks at Brambley. "For your education, you might be wearing a gown."

"I daresay –" Brambley begins.

"You will dare more than just that around here. Integration, integration, integration! That is my virtue. Unfair, is it not? I insist that you keep three virtues and I only have the one: integration. So be it!"

Allbrung's voice is steady, consistent despite the flash of

[26] an artisan, someone who is creative with innovative technology
[27] before the steam revolution, the religion of Europe when it was believed

his eyes and hands waving in the air. For this older man, all of his exclamation marks are on his face.

"It is key that you do not have dinner where we have breakfast or breakfast where we have dinner. The library is available to you only in the evening; there is to be no studying where we do our lectures."

"Why?"

"The house will not allow it." Brambley hears the tone in Allbrung's voice as if when he speaks of the house, it is his spouse. "On Saturdays, you can visit Grouard. On Sundays, we all go to church and have one, giant meal in town. We are a family. We plan to learn from each other. Many teachers say this, but you shall really, really see it here. Like –" He pointed to Cat. "What are the words over my gate?"

"I don't recall," she says.

Allbrung points to Brambely. "Veritas," the young man says.

"Good. Now, Cat: what is so terribly wrong with this new invention the Godiva Glockenspiel?" Allbrung asks.

"It is a device a woman wears around her wrist that reads a woman's biles and tempers, to ascertain her health and when she shall become sick," Cat says. "The problem is that a woman must keep it on herself the entire time. She cannot dance, run, or do anything active, for fear of breaking the expensive equipment."

"So?"

"It's made for Ponies in training, and the only ones who would use it are inactive women ... who are more prone to get sick."

Allbrung smiles at Brambley. "She is a professionally trained pony, former pickpocket, and child of London's wharf. Her pedigree, my friend, is far better than H.G. can ever offer us." He points to Cat and her eyes widen. The old man leads the pair up a twisted, slightly crooked, spiral staircase. They ascend into a great room with towers and towers of bookcases. Tracks and springs and motors cover every corner of this great library.

"This library is made up of Dewey Decimal books. Most libraries are filed by the Dewey Decimal system, demanding the patron find his or her own book based upon some cold, strange number. Here is the reverse."

Exhaust from the Tin Woods

The trio goes to the filing cabinet, and the old man draws out a card. "Ah, 'The Anatomy of Melancholy'. Fantastic," Allbrung says as he displays the card. The card is punched with a variety of holes of various sizes. He then slips the card into a mighty machine, breathing life as he rhythmically pumps with a foot pedal. Quickly, a book pops off the shelf, slides down the nearest track, rolls over their heads at breakneck speed, and finally plops into a steel basket atop of the mighty machine. As a last gesture, the machine spits out the card. "Don't lose the card or the book will never find her way back home."

Cat grins as she studies the tiny wheels along the book's binding.

"Libraries are important places. Grouard needs a library, a proper one. We shall prattle away, making machines. The world shall buy our machines. We shall give the machines to Grouard. And then, we shall be able to afford to build the town a library."

"Why Grouard?"

"Why not? Soon it shall become the capital of Alberta. All of the rivers and boats and barges connect to this town. Soon, the railway shall come. They already have an airship strip. All of the vessels and arteries of Alberta run through Grouard. Plus, there's a principle at work greater than all of these advantages."

"Which is?"

"What's that parable Jesus tells us? The Good Samaritan? What's the point of that story?"

"It was a way our Lord showed the folly of Jewish law, thus revealing a great theology than just rules and tradition. He uses metaphor to –"

"Wrong," Allbrung says. "The point is that we are supposed to help the person right in front of us. Don't think that preaching a sermon at a distant cathedral will do any good if you step over a bleeding body along the way. Help those right in front of your face; that is what 'Your Lord' was trying to tell you. We help Grouard because they are … closest." He pointed up to the library. "Five years ago, a student spent his time building this for me. He has since gone to Boston. The State[28] loves this kind of

---

[28] what the US has become

26

stuff. Mexicania[29], the Confederacy, and the Union all eat this up with a side of parsley."

He shows them more. They see the bird sanctuary, the boiler rooms, the gymnasium, the kitchens, and the lecture centers. Up and down, twirling and climbing, descending and traversing: as far as Brambley can tell, there seems to be no rooms off limits.

It is late in the evening when he takes them to their final rooms. It is a perfectly rounded room, made of timber panels and crisscross beams overhead. In the center is a spiral of bunk beds. In the rounded corners of the room rests an iron vanity for privacy.

"Here it is, home sweet home," Allbrung says. "This is where you shall be sleeping."

"Here?" Brambely asks. "But where are the men sleeping?"

"Men and women, boys and girls. There is a kennel for pets. The bath and toilet are down the hall. Each student shall be given a collapsible wardrobe with built in mirror and sink. Everything is here, as you need it."

"Except privacy and propriety," Brambley says. "What will the town say when they learn that you encourage cohabitation between the sexes?"

"How will they know? The town is not sleeping here. Plus, I find impropriety blossoms in privacy. If I give you your own studio, your own parlor to be alone: who is to say what could happen? Just try to play Don Juan as you are sleeping in a room with five, possible nine other people who are tired and wanting just to go to sleep. Just try."

Brambley stands stiff, hoping his indignation is felt and known by all.

It seems it isn't.

Allbrung wishes the two a good night and Cat is left grinning.

"Are you enjoying this?" Brambley asks with a holler.

"Maybe too much," Cat coos. "Listen, I intend to be your friend during this whole bit. Mates, okay?"

"I appreciate your kindness, truly –"

---

[29] n. – Mexico that owns California, adj. – lots of religion

Exhaust from the Tin Woods

"I'm not a kind woman. I am former Pony, a dancer, and a sometime escort. I am trained to be enticing, not lovely or fair. Bear this in mind because it might save your soul to be friends with an enticing Jezebel like myself."

"I am truly sorry for what I said in the shop. I –"

"It was the sweetest thing I've heard in months. And now we begin this thing, as friends. Do we understand each other?"

"Completely."

"Now, help me out of this corset. Time to sleep. I'm on the top bunk next to the window. All of the bottom bunks are free. Now, get me out so I can get into my sleeping costume. The latches are in the back ..."

.....

The next morning, Patrick and Cat leads Brambley down the stairs for breakfast. Sitting around the table upon their arrival are three new faces: all of them women.

"Look out," Patrick says to Brambley. "We're surrounded."

Brambley compared Cat to the others. Cat wears her silver jumpsuit, tall boots latched up to her knees, her flying cap, and favorite pair of goggles. The first girl is clearly French in every way: blonde hair in a thousand curls, lace upon lace, every pattern is a flower, lips painted cherry red to perfection, black leather corset with matching gloves, a miniature top hat, and a face in near white. Bellased to a hilt. The second girl is proper, without leather or a corset or her face painted. She is pretty, slender and pure in a zeitgeisted, old standard. Deep, deep green eyes. Rounded and curved gown, full of springs and ribbing and bone. The third girl reminds Brambley of an exotic princess matching an illustration from "2001 Arabian Nights". Chestnut skin with a shawl of a thousand colors. Her eyes wide, deeply taking in everything. Her arms toned as if she had worked her whole life with them.

A ballased[30] pony, a proper lady, and a princess next to a metalmanced[31] prattler.

Patrick extends his hand to the French girl first. "Pleasure

---

[30] stunning in every French way
[31] adding style and flare to machines

to meet you. I am Patrick Leighton from Kent. And you are?"

"Please, call me Joane," she says in a thick, Parisian accent. "I arrived just a moment ago. The Woods, it is cold, no?"

"Everywhere but here," Patrick says. "And this is Brambley, and this is Cat."

"My dear, can I see your goggles?" Cat pulls them off and hands them down to the seated Joane. Joane studies them, lost in the design and manufacturing. After a painfully long silence, she says, "This is a thing of beauty. Very posh, posh. I must admit, this is the first real pair I have seen. They are realm, not just a costume."

"They be my vorpal[32] goggles."

"I am sorry and thank you for indulging me." She laughs, and the men in the room cannot help themselves; they laugh too.

The other two girls remain fiercely still. "I am like a small child, here in Canada."

"Where are you from, if I may ask?" Brambley asks.

"Oh, Versailles. I have lived for four years as a Held Companion. You have heard of such things, no?" Joane asks.

"Are they not what noble ladies have with them when they are young. A girl from noble birth is given a Held Companion[33] until she marries. Not really a servant, but –"

"Oh, yes. Servant is good. It is a lot of hard work being a Held Companion, but without the stigma of the service industry. Like a butler, but without living downstairs." She says this, pointing to Suk.

Suk, looking down at his leather duds, glares back at her. "I'm not a butler. I'm not even staff. All I am is helpful. That's it." He marches over to the buffet and piles fruit upon his plate.

"And you are?" Patrick says, by-passing the other young, blonde woman.

She opens her mouth, as if ready to label the offense.

Brambley tries to read what Patrick did wrong. Did he go out of order? And if so, how is that important? Did he say a word wrong? Or did he address the foreign girl before seeking the British

---

[32] favorite thing

[33] a girl assigned to aristocracy to help in courtly behavior, usually of slightly lower birth who has little chance of prospects.

Exhaust from the Tin Woods

one first?

"Shweta. I would give you my full name, but we would spend half the day trying to pronounce it. Please, you honor me and my family best by just 'Shweta'," the dark beauty spoke.

As soon as Brambley laid eyes upon her dark green pupils, he could not breathe. Her beauty is sharp, dark, and fierce. A slender, elegant nose and full lips. But those eyes, with that sapphire glow which seems impossible. Like Cat and Joane, she is light and lean and moves like a dancer. But from where did she come?

"Shweta, how long was your travel?" Cat asks and relieves Brambley. Now everyone is participating in the introductions.

"It was a gentle three-day ride from my home in Vancouver."

"Is Vancouver a name of a British settlement in your land?"

"No," she says with a grin, baring her bright white teeth. "Vancouver, British Columbia[34]. I was born on the boat of the first settlement in Vancouver. My community is from India, but our culture is Sikh."

Patrick looks to the last girl, and she sharply replies, "I am Maillory, and I am, as well, from England."

That is all they received from Maillory, as Dr. Allbrung marches into the iron breakfast nook carrying a pillow for his back and a great Siberian husky on a leash. "Ah, good. You are meeting. We have a member of our staff and one more student to meet. Then we can begin."

Allbrung releases his dog. The dog looks around, studying the faces and ankles and shoulders of everyone in the room.

Maillory stiffens when the dog looks at her. Shweta leans over with her flowing red, embroidered robe, with her head covering. Shweta offers her dark brown hand to the dog.

"While studying here, you should think about getting a pet.

---

[34] this would throw off many of those who know the history of the Sikhs in British Columbia because they are a very old community, but their arrival would be the same time as this story took place. In this world, it seems, the Sikhs came a generation earlier.

Exhaust from the Tin Woods

Something small, something big, it does not matter," Allbrung says. "Animals are the best teachers about harmony. Watch Archimedes, my husky, and see who he goes to. He is pulled towards the most harmonious people or things in a room."

On cue, the Siberian Husky walks over to Brambley. He looks at Brambley, then at Cat and then back at Brambley. Quickly, he sits with all of his weight upon Cat's right foot and Brambley's left. He exhales in deep, peaceful satisfaction.

"There we go," Allbrung says. "Our last student shall arrive today, and we can begin studying how to use our machines to redeem the world."

Chapter Two
January 1895

"And you're not a princess?" Brambley asks Shweta.

She laughs, showing her teeth and dimples. She is Brambley's age and that of Joane, Patrick, and Cat. She looks across to Brambley, as they share the same height, but she towers over the rest of the girls.

"No," she says. "My parents are hardworking farmers for our community."

"But you wear that royal fabric over your head, and you have … face jewels."

This earns a deep, throaty laugh from Shweta. She points to her diamond encrusted nose ring. "Red is not royal amongst the Sikh. My jewelry and look are my own design, along with my gown. I am tremendously vain, that is all."

"And the head covering?" Brambley asks while pointing to the brim of his hat, as they walk along the steaming sidewalk. Surrounded by snow, he feels warm under his long coat and stovepipe hat.

"That," she says slowly. "That has more of a reason to it. It is a sign of Holiness, that God and the infinity of my deity rests upon me. My brother wears a turban as a similar expression of the Divine."

Brambley nods respectfully.

Cat smiles, almost blushing.

He tries to read the look which seems almost impressed. Why would she be impressed, he wonders.

Back at the Foundation, he would have been corrected. A good Christian, he was instructed, encounters and disagrees with anything outside of "correct religion". To say that the infinity of God rests in hat wear – according to the rigors of his Protestant upbringing – is blasphemy. His teachers and community, back at the Foundation, would surely have encouraged him to speak up and correct Shweta as means of proper theology.

But he didn't. He simply grinned and changed the subject, earning a smile from Cat. Why?

Exhaust from the Tin Woods

"So," he asks Shweta. "You're not given to these crushed pursuits of other disciplines? What is your specialty?"

"It used to be fashion. But I've become crushed too. It's a wonderful thing, integration. Everything connects. I'm afraid I'm a disciple of Allbrung."

"But competition in industry is based upon expertise and excellence. Can one truly be excellent in everything? No, one must choose and focus in order to have an edge in competition." Brambley says this as if it is a given. Certainly, it would be a given back in London.

"Then don't compete," Shweta says with a wry grin.

They talk about other things.

Patrick speaks of the news in London. Food riots take place in the east end. A robot went insane and killed several shoppers in a food market, Patrick reports. "Seeing gray, the machine did," Patrick says. "It had a human brain inside, controlling everything."

Brambely winces. He feels, within his new Canadian home, that those dramas are now on another planet. That is until he remembers the bear in the woods.

They enter the workshop. "During breakfast, Allbrung sounded like you know him."

"I began in September, taking a break in December like the one we shall take in July and August. I am the only one who has returned," she said in a clear, almost singing voice. She could easily be a baritone, with her Cambridge British accent. "I am the only one who survived ... metaphorically."

Brambely stops and twirls around, feeling the colour draining from his face. All he can think of is the bear that wanders the woods.

"Oh my dear man, he isn't that evil of a teacher. No, they couldn't keep up with their studies, and they left. They figured they could find an easier way of being prattlers and inventors than learning under the rigors of Allbrung's lessons."

"And you remained?"

"Of course. They are wrong," she says without emotion. She leans in, as to whisper in his ear. "Here is a hint, if only a small one. Allbrung appears relaxed, crazy, and gentle; his teaching is salt rock[35]. He's tough and relentless. Everything he says to you, whether in the garden or over tea or on the way to Grouard, it will be on the exam. And he remembers everything and every detail matters. Oh, he will quiz you on everything, not just making machines."

"But -"

"You shall be worked, my good man. You shall indeed."

Brambley looks over to the group ahead of him. Patrick is speaking and laughing and holding court, with Joane and Maillory hanging onto his every word. He is the clear favorite, with the Sikh willing to take a turn with him to their shops. He looks around further: Cat is nowhere to be seen.

Suk stands in the center of the large box of their workshop. The group meets him, forming an unconscious half-circle audience.

"Welcome," Suk says. "Each of you shall be given a platform that is suspended by titanium chains. The platform has its own kiln, table, and a small box of basic tools. Basic lubricants and a cache of different metals are under the table. To get to each platform, you are to use the girding hoist system provided. For the big tools and the rock salt kiln, we share.

"Today, while we wait for the last member of our little community, the doctor has given you a task. Within a day, you must make something. Anything. It is to be representative of what you want to learn. And now, pick your stations."

Patrick goes to his station, the only one on ground level, and Cat is nowhere to be seen.

Brambley looks to a hoist rigging and can't figure it out, until Shweta comes, places her sandaled foot in a loop, and the rigging swoops her upward. She flies to the tallest platform with the ease and grace of a ballerina.

Brambley looks and finds the only free loop left. He copies Shweta's movements which sends a message to the hemp ropes to lift him in flight towards his hanging station. Once he arrives, he looks around. Everything is neat, clean, and as promised. He looks over on the only other platform at his height to find Cat, hard at work at her station.

---

[35] extreme, over the top, difficult

Exhaust from the Tin Woods

Their eyes meet, and she grins. "Glad to have you as my neighbor," she says.

"Yes," he says, and he smiles without thinking. "A friendly face." He finds himself genuinely meaning this statement.

'*Have I blended, more and more, into this new world of the Tin Woods?*' He laughs, surveying the table to find a standard set of tools along with a long row of needle-beetles and about ten different sizes of wiring. The last student to use the station must have genuinely loved wiring.

Brambley removes his gloves. He stares at the open space of his table.

"Any ideas?" Cat asks. "Either your mind is blank, or it's racing in a million directions at once, trying to land."

"It's a blank," he says with a nod. "Would you believe mechanics was a hobby of mine, not a pursuit? I studied … theology for hours and spent only minutes prattling."

"And now you can do your hobby all day. It should be a relief," Cat says. "Or is it?"

"If it's a relief, I haven't felt it yet." Suddenly, he finds a black, metal box that was left behind. The box is simple, made with thin sheets of metal, with only the corners forged together.

"Find something?"

"Maybe," he says.

"I knew it. You have the eyes of a joywigger[36]."

The sun sets early in Grouard. So, just before dinner, Allbrung comes with his dog into the workshop. "Come down, my students. Come down. Show me your creations."

Zipping sounds erupts when the students descend with their creations in hand.

They line up, and the first in the line is Patrick. He steps forward and offers a small, silver chain. "I came here to understand clock making. Having said that, I haven't a clue about such devices. I believe the clock can order such things as hospitals, offices, and filing. Clocks, not time. So, I made this." He gives him the chain.

Allbrung immediately smiles. "On the surface, it looks like you just made a fob chain. On the surface." Quickly, he snaps the

---

[36] a joyful inventor

chain as it grapples the top of the nearest platform. "Interesting." He pressed a small button and the chain recoils.

"Say a bobby is chasing a lurkjerker[37]. He can fire this at a nearby outer stairwell. The chain can lift him up and swing him to the perpetrator. It's sturdy, handy, and, well, it can support my weight."

"Excellent. Next?" Allbrung asks.

"I want to understand metalmancy," Shweta says. "So I have made a knife that can be used as a corkscrew for a wine bottle, a letter opener, and turn to scissors. It is bejeweled so it can fit in a lady's handbag."

"Again, excellent. Next?"

Joane presents an extra-long set of iron tongs. She presses a button, and they shoot out, extending, becoming twice as long.

Allbrung grins.

For Maillory, she presents mood glass: posh goggles that change based on the wearer's body temperature.

Cat presents black painted nails that can cut through metal, creating shavings and sharpening of steel.

The last one is Brambley. He clears his throat and pulls out a black box. It looks like the darkness box used for photography. A pin-hole catches light from the gas lanterns. A few seconds later, a slender light shoots from the other end of the box and bends and wraps around a pen in the pocket of Allbrung and lifts it for a second. Then the pen bursts and explodes.

"What are you trying to do, Brambley?" Allbrung asks.

"Bending light and using air particulars to weight the laser. It's been some scientific principles that I've been working on, but can never get right. I want to pick things up with light."

"You've created a laseri[38]! A laseri beam!"

"I blew up a pen. Sorry," Brambley says with a bow. "It's a bit of a mistake. I wanted to pick things up, not destroy them."

"You're going to have to embrace mistakes. Own them.

---

[37] thugs, pickpockets, kidnappers who hide in shadows and have cybernetics

[38] a crude laser

Exhaust from the Tin Woods

You have invented a pen destroyer. Excellent." He laughed. "A laseri had already been created by some Italian scientists about ten years ago. Still, it's a bold experiment. And wonderful!"

"Any practical use?"

"If we declare war on Revenue Canada, we have a weapon." Allbrung grins slightly at his joke.

The group leaves for dinner, heading to the dining room. This one is next to the parlor, but Brambley cannot remember ever seeing it before. The room's location is handy for the students can dress for dinner. The ladies withdraw behind their vanities, and the men take a sponge bath before getting into their coats and ties.

Once dressed, they each enter the dining hall. Sitting at the edge of the table opposite to the entrance awaits the new student.

She sits with her long arms and slender hands, wrapped in black lace gloves, under her chin. Everything about her is poshed: her black top hat, the sharp and narrow design of her eye liner, the chain mail/black leather of her corset, her long boots ribbed with broken metal, her brown hair in sheer bangs and rigid curls, the white dusting around her shoulders and arms, and her frayed gown attacked by designers with hand razors.

She looks up without expression. She snorts in a nod as Patrick makes the introduction. "I'm Beattrixx," she says and looks around with her hazel eyes. She looks up and down Brambley.

Brambley studies her: hard lines around her mouth, a scar on her neck, and her broad shoulders suggest a lot of use in hard labor. She appears older than the other students, but it's something Brambley can't prove. There's a hardness to her, something that's elusive to him and from his instincts.

"Where are you from?" Maillory says with an extra sweet voice.

"Everywhere, but mostly from the State."

"Union or Confederacy or Mexicia[39]?"

---

[39] now this is a very clear division of how the United States, in this world, had been split into thirds. There was Union, which I guess would be the Northern States; the Confederacy, who seceded from the Union and owned slaves; and Mexicia, which would have included the West and all of the territories that had not become states. From what I can gather, the Union was in a chaos along with the rest of the country. This affected Canada's

Exhaust from the Tin Woods

"I was born in the Nation of Texas[40], but I've been all around. Even to Paris," Beattrixx says with her hazel eyes pointing to Joane. "I've been everywhere. That's not a boast or a complaint. It's neither exciting or hard. Just is."

"We're glad to have you," Joane says, and the group sits down. In proper fashion, girls sit to the right, and the boys sit to the left. Suk comes out with large bowls of soup, bread, and salad. The dinner begins, quietly at first.

No one talks until Cat looks over to Joane. "I've never been to Paris or Versailles, to be precise. How is it?"

"To the rich, it is magical," Joane says without emotion. Brambley wonders if this is a joke or if she is setting up for a punch line.

Nothing follows.

"It's the center of all fashion," Maillory says.

"Everything and anything that is important comes from Paris." Joane nods. ' When I create my own empire, I plan to have my home and office in Paris."

"Your empire? Your ambition is intriguing," Patrick says. He is without guile for there is nothing ironic in his statement.

"That's why I'm here. I need to learn how to design machines, how to create working, functional, Hollerithed[41] toggles and machine wear. I believe cybernetics shall become the pinnacle of fashion, as more and more chose to have a metal arm or a robotic foot. If they don't need it, they'll want it. The want is fashion. And that shall be my empire."

"Dream big." Patrick says, raising his water glass as a toast.

"And that shall be my witness," Maillory says, and the room is silent, waiting for another punch line. She soon reads the lost looks around the table. "Oh, I am a Christian woman from a good, Christian home. My father is a minster. My ambition is not for myself, but for my Lord Jesus. My plans are simple: make a

---

time line little, other than making the northern neighbor to the US seemingly more stable.

[40] is there a fourth part of the US? The Nation of Texas? Or is this just an expression?

[41] a machine that makes something simple

large empire and then credit the sovereignty of Christ. The empire shall be a monument to what one can achieve through faith and hard work. All glory to God."

"Indeed," Patrick says with a bit of guile. He turns uneasily to Brambley. "You're a bit of the religious, aren't you? Not in a Mexician way but in a real, honest, help others sort."

"I wish to be the real deal, sure. And yes, I am religious. I hope not to the level of enthuzimuzzy[42], but with vigor. I just don't know how it all fits, I guess. The problem with having a specialty in something: it's like being marooned on only one island."

"As opposed to being marooned on many islands?" Beattrixx asks.

Those in the room politely chuckle.

"I'm not sure what I'm really doing here, I guess. All of you have your own ideas and concepts and designs. I don't. You know, today, I just recreated a mistake I made. That's all. I ruined something, and it did something else. I then repeated that today, trying to make it do that wrong thing again. I don't know. I guess if religion can lead to a specialty of repeating mistakes, I've got my vocation in life."

"To greater mistakes," Patrick toasts with his water goblet.

"How about to no mistakes?"

"Can't toast to the impossible, old boy. So how about making your mistakes count?"

Dinner continues, and it is revealed that Cat can sing.

After the meat is served and finished, Suk takes the ladies to the parlor to prepare the forte for her concert. The boys are served coffee, away from the girls.

Patrick looks at Brambley.

Brambley looks are Patrick.

Silence follows.

Then Patrick makes an observation: "There's nothing to say when we're not surrounded by pretty girls."

"No, we're quite dull," Brambley says and they both laugh. "All of them are pretty. Every single one. Why did he enroll only pretty girls?"

---

[42] annoying or loud enthusiasm

Exhaust from the Tin Woods

Patrick laughs even louder. "He sherlucked[43] that one, I think." He stops to ponder. "He said to me that there's no more equality left in the world, except by creating and inventing things. Perhaps he's trying to right a wrong that us boys have made of things by giving the girls a crack at besting us with their brains and might. As to why they're pretty, they are quite beautiful." He laughs. "And there's you and me. Split down the middle, we both shall have a harem."

"I think one partner would be enough, I should say," Brambley says in a reasonable whisper. "It is moral, befitting of God's character, and most gentle on one's bank drafts."

"Quite, but I don't want a partner. I want a passionate, half-mad, demon lover. Bryon in a girl's body. And you?"

"Again, like my vocation and in love, I don't know what I want."

"Then the sky is the limit."

The boys wait a little bit longer until Maillory fetches them and brings them to the parlor. Cat is already singing a song, one that she had performed in the dance hall before coming to Mercyminster. The song is a melancholy ballad about a man who falls down a well and is trapped for a month. Tragedy, death, sorrow, and depression: they are the flavor of the dance hall.

Maillory, during the song, stiffens and keeps studying the multiple clocks in the room.

Brambley hears the song and feels a pang of homesickness. This, he feels, is the first time he can sit and rest. He remembers the Foundation, surrounded by children and games and laughter. After dinner, he would lead games or read out of a book or, sometimes, he would tell them fantasies. There, he fit and had a role. He could be a theologian and an old brother, all at once. He thinks of London and the fog and the twisted streets and the babbaged streets filled with metal machines and the factories.

The song ends, and Cat's bright eyes look to his. "You look like you went somewhere else," she says.

"Home." He smiles. "Isn't that proof of great music? It transplants you someplace else?"

---

[43] when someone makes a deduction not based on reason or science

Exhaust from the Tin Woods

"Where did you go?" Joane asks.

"Someplace happy."

Beattrixx walks over to the forte. "I'm not used to these without engines. The music of the player forte is more … clean. All of the notes are exact, weighted, and equal." The dark archon[44] looks over to Cat. "You played beautifully. Thank you."

…..

Allbrung's lessons are as Shweta had promised.

The typical schedule is the same, with little break: breakfast, chores, classes, lunch, lab, dinner, and then break. Every lesson is tied to the lab, every equation applied to their project. On the first day, Brambely didn't pay attention to the lecture. This is too much theory, he thinks. I'll never use this. Then he is proven wrong by the project: make a small, handheld steam engine using all of his equations.

For the first two weeks, most of Brambley's projects are incomplete. He asks to stay behind and skip dinner to finish his projects.

"No," Allbrung says. "You must leave it incomplete for today. Time for work, time for dinner, time for sleep."

Allbrung is alone with Brambley as he says this. They stand outside of the shop, with the warming steam of Mercyminster wafting over them. "But I can't keep up with these assignments."

"No, you can't. Perhaps that is the first step in living in harmony with the lesson. Soon you will. Or won't. But changing the schedule and losing something important is not a solution. The day is given to you, and you must walk away with an incomplete desk." Allbrung stresses the word "you" in this sentence. He is without emotion in this exchange.

Brambley is silent after this discussion. He eats quietly and only listens to the chat around the dining table.

After dinner, he withdraws to the library. Alone, he sits in a leather and steel chair. He stares at the books and iron statues and paintings of machines and the steel-wool rug and the brass ceiling and the gears slowly turning and the frost on the window. He cannot take it all in. The machines are too much, he thinks. He finds

---

[44] a street urchin, a punk

Exhaust from the Tin Woods

everything a challenge. Daily listening to lectures about ideas he has never thought of before, making machines, living with machines, the steam, and always being around people who are in absolute passion towards machines … too much.

Shweta enters the library with a plate of cookies. "Are you praying to your God?" she asks.

"I should, but no. Just in a dark humor," he says.

"To live in harmony, one must change to play a part. Change, learning, adaptation: that is all a part of what Allbrung expects in the virtue of harmony. Not to give, not to participate is against harmony; to take and to refuse is exploitation."

"This sounds like one of his lessons," Brambley says, and he hears how sharp he sounds. "Sorry, I feel defeated."

"What I am trying to say is that you will learn how to finish. It is inevitable. Harmony commands that you finish your table and you will. Look around you when you work. Are you the only one?"

"I –"

"No one has finished Allbrung's projects. Except me and that is because I have been a student for four months. You are in harmony with others. When you complete, they may complete. And when you complete, you will start making amazing machines."

Brambley takes this advice, and at the end of the week, he finishes his first project. His assignment is to make a clock in a different shape. He designs a clock to fit into a cane. He applies Allbrung's principles of bending gears, and he adapts the gears into chains. His project finishes ten minutes before dinner. At dinner, he presents it to Allbrung.

The old man studies the cane. "And now a man cannot be late on his evening constitutional, even if he wants to be," he says with a grin. "This is good. This is made well. And now, here is the tough question: who would you give this to in town?"

"I don't know anyone in town."

"That is what is missing. But you have done good work. And watch. A magic thing shall happen the moment you show this to your fellow students."

The next day, everyone completed the tasks given. They were thrilled and Allbrung points to Brambley. "We have a leader.

Exhaust from the Tin Woods

A clear, strong leader," he says.

Brambley looks away, blushing.

Cat kicks him on his side.

"Good. Now for the next question: who would you give this to?" is what Allbrung says concerning all of the projects. "I mean, these are great gadgets and designs. But who are they for? Who do you know personally whose life will be better because of your invention?"

Three days later, they are assigned to build a clock out of non-metal materials. Cat and Maillory make theirs out of wood; Brambley sews his together using starched linen; and Shweta out of crystal. Patrick was sick that day.

When all of the clocks were presented, Allbrung nods. "Good, good. Now, who would you know, personally, who would benefit from a clock without metal? The clock construction is the basis for all of our technologies. But it doesn't mean a thing if you can't give away your invention as a gift to someone whose life is now better because of it."

A day later, the challenge comes out again. Brambley sees Cat turn bright red, which is stark against her bright, almost yellow hair.

Later, Cat sits with Brambley to drink tea. "Who are we supposed to give our projects to? I made a cybernetic attachment that can turn fingers into screwdrivers, chisels, corkscrews, and a paint brush. No one in our class has a metal hand, let alone would want a paintbrush thumb."

"We then need to go to town," Brambley says. He had thought about it, hours before the class, but didn't feel it was a good idea until that moment. Mainly his doubt came from the fact that he didn't think anyone else would do it. "If this is the question that will always come after our projects, we need to learn a bit more about Grouard."

Cat likes this idea and shares with the rest of the girls that night.

Beattrixx nods and doesn't speak.

Joane says, "A trip to town would do me good. I would like a bit more sparklization to my projects." Lost looks surround her. "Something to make it look posh, to make it look pretty. Sorry, it's my own word."

Maillory shakes her head. "I have too much to do. I'm not going to waste my free day hanging around a bunch of dirty trappers. There is no shopping in Grouard and nothing of worth. Sorry."

So they decide to leave her behind. The rest of the students dress their best, including Beattrixx who wears an all-black gown and corset made of leather and metal teeth.

All the girls wear bonnets and men don top hats.

Suk brings around the carriage.

The girls ride inside; the boys ride shotgun.

After fifteen minutes of travel, they arrive in town.

The town is cut in half by a long, expansive sawdust road. The sawdust is mixed with sand, fresh and the only color shooting out from the expanse of snow.

Ice forms clumps and points atop the buildings, with steam wafting through the log cabins and A-frames of constructions that would be a shanty town anywhere else in the world.

Shops display signs with misspellings like "Blaksmith" or "Tafern".

Coughing and horses trotting are the main noises of the afternoon.

The ladies emerge from the carriage once it comes to a stop.

Joane, with her oval face and wide eyes, drinks in the smoke and steam and pine smells of Grouard. She turns to Shweta. "Is this like Vancouver?" Joane asks her.

"This is very, very small compared to Vancouver. Besides, I haven't spent much time in Vancouver. We don't really go into the city. We have our own community. Many of the citizens do not like us or allow us into their places of business."

"Sod off rotten," Beattrixx says. "That's what they are. And it's everywhere. In Texas, it's Mexicans; in the Confederacy, they have slaves; and in the Union, it's immigrants. Every civilization that thinks it's God's gift to the world needs a whipping boy. Or girl."

Patrick twirls off the platform and lands near Joane, all in one movement.

Exhaust from the Tin Woods

Brambley climbs down along with Suk.

The three men form a barrier around the ladies as they walk down the frozen sawdust.

They approach the trading post; a large building made of spruce logs, wallpapered by old copies of the Edmonton Bulletin, and powered by a steam engine and warmed by a mammoth wood burning stove.

As they enter, Brambley overhears three older gentlemen chatting on deck chairs, pointed towards the furnace.

"That's the third citing this week of the Bearman," the one with the beard down to his chest croaks. "The Bearman, they say, drinks the blood of his victims."

"He's more with it than most of the stories say," the one to his left says. "There's a Cree trapper, looking for minx, that was pinned down by him and had an eleven-minute conversation. The Bearman let him go after it. The trapper told me he was a nice man."

"Nice man? He's got bear and robot in him! How can he be a nice guy?"

"It's what I hear."

Brambley leaves the hearing radius of the elder's circle. He wanders deeper into the trading post. Looking for his pack, he finds the girls looking over a box of dresses.

Patrick is studying a table full of tools.

Suk is missing, as Brambley scans the entire room.

Suddenly, Suk clears his throat as it is evident he had been trailing him. "You dropped in to hear about the locals talk about the Bearman?" he asked.

"How did you –"

"Because that's what I was doing and you joined me. Have you seen the thing?" Suk asks. He straightens his stove top hat against the tangle of dreadlocks. "What do you know?"

"The first day I was here, and I walked through the woods, we saw the bear. It looked like the work of a skin seamstress[45], mixed with babbaged[46] metal and the kitchen sink. It was a mix of

---

[45] through genetics and splicing and surgery, scientists that fuse animals with humans. It was mostly unsuccessful

Exhaust from the Tin Woods

metal and fur and skin. I didn't think that making something like that was even possible."

"It hasn't been yet," Suk says. "Back in the Kong, I ran with some skin seam stresses. The science is flawed and has made more corpses than any man-beasts. A sew that perfect is light-years beyond any of their science. And yet, we've got a bear-man-bot." He laughs at this last title. "Sounds like a pulp? I blame the castle."

"Castle?"

"I should let Allbrung tell you, although he won't, and if he does, it will be with great hesitation. Simply put, we're not the only scientists in these Tin Woods." He smiles in the direction of the girls. "Keep an eye on the girls." His eyes then flash to a group of men, still wearing furs, caps, and scarves around their faces.

The group of men, about five in count, stand against a corner, their eyes and bodies pointed at Cat, Shweta, and Joane. Their eyes are hungry as if the girls are the only plate of food in the entire town.

"I'll keep watch, tell Patrick. I think we should go." Suk turns to find Patrick.

Brambley walks up behind Cat, tapping her on the shoulder.

She turns to see him only to meet his eyes pointing to the five men wrapped in furs.

"Who are they?" she whispers. Brambley shrugs. She nods. Her eyes narrow, her mouth tightens, and she stands tall. Quickly, she whispers to the rest of the girls.

They drop everything and head to the door.

The group of men follows.

Once outside on the streets, Brambley asks Suk to fetch the carriage.

Suk runs off.

The group marches down the street, with the men in pursuit. They no longer are trying to look casual, but keep the same pace as the students. The girls lift their skirts to aid their jog. People in the street now notice, and are staring.

---

[46] based on Charles Babbage's first computer, it's when something human has been replaced by a machine

Exhaust from the Tin Woods

Suk is ahead, but just barely.

Suddenly, a man from the fur pack breaks free as his sprint is five times the speed of a normal human. Within a flash of light, he grabs Beattrixx and drags her into a back alley. Beattrixx is gone, the group charges to follow her.

The man is far away, behind a large metal box holding wood. He throws Beattrixx down in the snow and stands over her. "So hungry," he says in a growl.

Beattrixx lands on her back spread eagle, and arms flung over her head. For a second, she is dazed; lost in the racing, screaming moment.

He lowers slowly, exposing his large metal hands. He pulls aside his coat to reveal his metal legs. His hands shake as they open around Beattrixx's throat.

Beattrixx screams as she kicks at his lower abdomen. Her boot hits something solid, almost rock solid.

He laughs as his hands clamp around her neck, squeezing the life out of her body.

The group meets up with them. Shweta whirls around to greet the fur-clad lurkjerkers running at their heels. She grins. A second later, she is in the air with her right foot guiding her body's flight. The booted, sheer heel sinks into the chest of the man in front. He screams as steam erupts from within his heavy coat. Sudden, sharp, white air burns his neck and face as he collapses.

The three other men stop to face Shweta.

She lands softly on all fours, ready to spring like a cat to attack.

Brambley throws his hands in the air and runs at the back of Beattrixx's attacker. He screams as he tackles the top of the man; Brambley finds tackling a brick wall would have been softer.

Patrick follows Brambley's example and also runs, screaming at Shweta's attackers. One of the men raises his hand in Patrick's direction, fires a dart, and Patrick goes to sleep.

Brambley cannot make Beattrixx's attacker desist. He lunges, shifts, and shoves with the mostly robotic man hunched over Beattrixx.

Cat runs to his side, picks up a pipe and hands it to Brambley.

Exhaust from the Tin Woods

Brambley swings at the back of the man's neck, hearing a metal on metal thump. He strikes again, near the back of the man's head with similar effect. Out of desperation, he begins hammering at the neck in successive sounds. If a symphony would be nearby, they'd be tempted to play the "Anvil Chorus".

Meanwhile, Shweta rolls to the ground, springs up to one of the men and pulls out a hose on his chest.

"Blast it," Joane shouts. "They're cheap Steamies!" Joane goes to the last man, pulls out a vial, and dowses the man. Steam erupts over his whole body, as he screams and runs to get himself to the nearest horse trough.

Following this discovery, Beattrixx goes to work on her attacker's chest. Within a few seconds, she's removed a pipe and a valve. The man, now with a crooked neck and leaking oil, collapses beside her.

A strange stillness follows. The students all look at each other. Only when each of them nods, do they begin to breathe normally again.

The stillness is broken by the sound of a dozen stomping feet.

Shweta sees them first.

"Are you okay?" A man's voice asks.

It takes a second for Brambley to realize who these people are: two Cree trappers, some women, a Royal Canadian Mounted Police officer, and two shopkeepers from the trading post. The townspeople are there as a rescue.

"I am fine. These steamies[47] … they attacked my friends," Shweta says.

"And you attacked most of them," the RCMP[48] officer says. "Good show! Do you need a job? I'd love to hire you at the detachment."

"I am a student of Dr. Allbrung," Shweta says as two of the women wrap her up in a blanket as if she fell into the lake.

The officer approaches Joane. He stops, freezes in fear.

---

[47] people with really shoddy cybernetics

[48] this is out of time, really The RCMP weren't serving, in this capacity, in this time period unless some events sped up their arrival and formation.

Exhaust from the Tin Woods

Joane quickly grabs her face as if she would be bleeding. He shakes his hands and tells her she's fine. He runs away to help Beattrixx. She sits up and rubs her sore neck.

"Are you okay?" the officer asks.

"I am fine," Beattrixx says with a wry, mischievous grin. "What did you put on that guy?" she asks Joane.

"Oh, I purchased some Palmer's Oil. It wreaks havoc on cheap gears."

Beattrixx rises to her feet, dusts the snow off, and sneers. "Weren't we shopping?"

"Not now," the officer says. "Please, let's get some food in you kids and try to see if we can identify –"

"We know who they are and where they come from! They're from the castle and probably drinking buddies with the Man-Bear."

"Still, I insist. There's a saloon down the road that can get you kids some sandwiches. It's the least we can do. You're guests, and we want you to think well of our little town."

"I already do," Brambley says as he lifts up the awakening Patrick. "You didn't know us, but you came to stand up to those dangerous steamies."

"Consider it a debt to Dr. Allbrung. His inventions have saved our town."

.....

With a warm cup of soup in her hand, Beattrixx looks as though nothing has happened; this unsettles Brambley.

Joane and Cat are wrapped up in blankets, drinking some really strong tea.

Patrick is finishing his sketch of what one of the men looks like.

Shweta studies the bar. She whispers to Brambley, "I think we've found the next application of our inventions. Look, the bar is about to fall apart."

"But it's a bar," Brambley says. "A den of iniquity."

"A den of sandwiches, Rev. Brambley. And they did not have to be so kind. They are compassionate, and my thinking is they have done this before. This town has no hospital, but they do have a bar."

Exhaust from the Tin Woods

Brambley looks down, feeling his head turn very heavy. "I am sorry. That was wrong and arrogant of me to speak that way. I am sorry. How can we help these people?"

"Good," Shweta says. "Now you are thinking in terms of harmony. What do these people need?"

Brambley looks across the bar. "Their draft system for beer is messy. A lot of waste, a lot of spillage. They could save so much money not spilled, not wasting through drips and sloshes and such. Is that what you see?" Brambley asks.

"No," she says. "I see something else entirely. But you are right. You are very right."

.....

The next day, after Allbrung heard the whole story, Brambley asks him if he could take a detour. "Go on," Allbrung says.

"Could we look into valve technology? You know, how you regulate the pouring of liquids?" he asks.

Allbrung smiles and nods. For the next week, he commits most of his lectures to the science of valves.

After their chat over breakfast, Brambley walks Cat to the kitchen for it is their turn to do the dishes. As they begin to scrub, Brambley says to her, "Beattrixx was odd after her attack."

"She was her perfect, normal, cold self. How did she behave oddly?"

"Because she was her perfect, normal, cold self. Patrick turned silent, Shweta spent some extra hours in meditation, I couldn't sleep, and Joane chatted Maillory's ear off. Were you different?"

"Yes," she says. "I had to chop wood. Call it crazy, but I had to do something physical."

"But Beattrixx, seconds after her attack, she wanted to go shopping. In the bar, she was amazed by all of the fuss made over the attack. For her, it was almost expected that she would be attacked."

"Do you expect a conspiracy then? Was she part of some spy set-up?" Cat asks with a delicious, evil smile.

"No, heavens no. I truly believe she was surprised, and a victim of their attack, but the fact that she wasn't too surprised to be

Exhaust from the Tin Woods

a victim is suspicious. Not in any Robert Louis Stevenson intrigue, but it does cast this question: what kind of life did she lead before coming to Mercyminster?"

"I don't know. Does it matter?"

"Hardly. We're here, and the past is, well, passed." He grabs his face. "Still, my brain can't keep asking questions: why did they single us out? Hundreds of people in Grouard, why us? Why such a desperate attack? Plain daylight, surrounded by the town, and in among public buildings. What drove them to be so insane, so full of bedlam to stand over Beattrixx with an aching hunger? Was it planned or as impulsive as it looked?"

"I don't know, but it makes me want to look more into this castle the townspeople speak, don't you?"

…..

The day after the attack is Sunday, the day of church.

The people of Mercyminster ride the coach into town, unharnessing the horses and tethering them to a post of the only white building in town. The girls are dressed in their best, but modest clothes: all oblige except Beattrixx. With knee high boots, a tight jumpsuit, and her leather cap, her clothing looks more like something she'd wear in a shop than church.

Maillory asks Allbrung if this is allowed. He responds: "For some, the burden of church is greater than others. Church, by no means, is on her terms and representative of her world. So if she wishes to bring her world into church, so be it. She is still going along with the wishes of Mercyminster."

"But people will stare. They shall be bothered. They shall talk."

"And they do not have to. And if they can't stop, then it is their burden of church and not Beattrixx's."

This conversation takes place just outside of the church, besides the coach. Brambley hears it all, and he believes, and so does Beattrixx for she smiles.

The church is an A-frame of withered, white wood. Three crooked steps lead up into the church. Once inside, the students drink in the woodwork, the ornate hanging chandeliers made of crystal, and the elaborate rugs along the floor.

"Oh my," Patrick whispers.

Exhaust from the Tin Woods

They pass by a mammoth furnace in the center of the church to sit in the front pew. They wait silently for the service to begin.

Brambley scans the congregation and finds only one familiar face, the Mountie. He gets a better look at the man. He's middle-aged, wears thicker glasses, and is moon-faced. He waves at Brambley: a gesture, he figures, would get him into trouble if he came with a lady. The man seems to be a bachelor, demonstrated by his mismatched suit and trousers.

A man approaches the lectern and announces, "Good morning. Welcome to Grouard Baptist Church of the Savior. We welcome back Dr. Allbrung's students and mention this to any visitors. In the last ten years, we've been unable to attract a pastor. We, by circumstance, are lay-led."

The service is simple. Three hymns. A prayer. Then the man who made the announcements reads from a book of John Calvin's writings. The church closes with everyone filing out, silently, and without making any eye contact with each other.

Once outside, a large woman charges to Allbrung. "My dear man," she says, and the rest of their conversation is in Flemish. The students watch without any of the Christians speaking to them.

Beattrixx says to Cat, "I liked it. I like the singing. And the reading."

"I didn't understand any of it," Cat says with a shrug.

"I prefer not to understand any of it, so I'm happy. The moment I start understanding Christians is when they start offending me."

Patrick grins, overhearing their conversation. "There's money to be made with long sermons, confusing lyrics, and cold services. There still is a market for Christians who would like to reduce their worship to a meager, weekly duty," Patrick says.

"Would you prefer something different?" Brambley asks.

"Are you kidding?" Patrick asks, and he drops his grin. "I'm starving for anything different. Please, I would love to see a Monday askew because of the church service on Sunday." He pulls out his handkerchief and buffs one of his brass, coat buttons.

Allbrung comes to the little group. "Today, we shall have a full, Sunday lunch. I insist on one important rule: you eat

Exhaust from the Tin Woods

everything that is on the plate. Everything."

They follow him back to the carriage, where Suk takes them through the town. On the far side of the town, facing a big and bold stretch of white stands a wide A-frame. It actually looks more like an "A" half smashed, with its base stretched impossibly by the wrap-around deck. Smoke and steam and mist plume from all of the windows and chimneys of the house with several waist-high metal cylinders vomiting smoke to the heavens around the yard.

The old, round woman gets out of her buggy and runs over to Joane. She smiles at the group; she likes Joane the best. She says something urgent and joyful in Polish, grabs Joane's right cheek for a moment, exclaims something further, and then runs into the house. Allbrung gets off of the carriage's steering platform and laughs.

"Is she seeing gray[49]?" Joane asks.

"Apt question, for you should consider her right arm," Allbrung says and Brambley spies through the living room window, revealing her kitchen. Quickly, the woman screws off her right hand and attaches a wire whisk. She mixes a bowl of steaming potatoes with cream from their cow. "No, she isn't crazy. Just very happy. She lost her daughter, five years ago, from wolves in the woods. Joane, she declared, is as pretty as her daughter and she now can have a family feast again."

The old woman charges through her house, stirring pots and loading wood into her stove. The students wait outside, sitting on the porch. Her husband, a small man who perpetually smiles like a gnome, marches around the porch, refilling steins of beer.

Brambley, after his second beer, stops; he is an extreme lightweight, having only drunk alcohol once before.

Cat slugs the beer down, enjoying every drop with rapid passion.

Maillory just declines.

In ten minutes, the old woman bursts out of her house with pots and plates full of borsch, pirogues, buns, heavy cream sauce, candied carrots, mashed potatoes, herring, cabbage rolls, and headcheese. She speaks once every few minutes, silently piling on

[49] a psychosis brought about my too much cybernetics

each of the student's plates until their food is at multiple levels.

"But I don't want this much food," Maillory protests. The old woman smiles at her and pinches her chin. "What did she say?"

"You're welcome," Allbrung translates. When the old woman is finished loading up Maillory's plate, hers is twice as big as the rest.

The old woman surveys the young people's feast, leaps in the air in triumph, and runs inside.

"No," Maillory says. "This is too much. I can't."

"You can and you will," Cat says. "This is more food than she sees in a month. You will eat and possibly get seconds."

"But why did she cook so much food for us?"

"It makes her happy," Allbrung says as he nibbles on his headcheese.

Patrick gulps down a pirogue and grins. "I say, if she ever wants to be the head cook in one of England's great houses, I'd write a personal recommendation. She's a genius with an oven."

"Patrick," Cat asks with a start. "What are you doing here?"

"I'm eating pirogues. Next, I'll get to the herring," Patrick says.

"No," Cat says. "I mean at Mercyminster. Alberta. Being a prattler?"

"There's no easy answer to that question."

"Then be difficult," Allbrung says. He grins.

Patrick exhales to think. "Okay. Three months ago, my mother gained a robotic hand. She didn't need it but wanted one because all of the great ladies near us were getting cybernetics. My youngest sister walks around with welding goggles. She doesn't work with metal but finds the goggles both fashionable and comfortable. I have a cousin who dresses in sheer black, complete with a copper top hat and a tool belt around his waistcoat. He cannot fix his way out of a paper bag and lives in the south of France, but wants to be considered a poshed prattler."

Beattrixx overhears this and laughs. This is invitation enough for Patrick to look to her and include her in their conversation.

"Insanity, isn't it? Well, there is a method that has led to

Exhaust from the Tin Woods

this madness. Right now, you pick up any of the daily rags, and they are all about steam and prattlers and posh and all things babbaged. Gizmos, glitz, and gadgets are the latest thing, and they are from the streets, burrows, and by-ways of London. This is a given to us, but a shock to the ruling class which is no longer ruling. They're on page 8 or not at all of the newspaper. Once, England wore what they wore; now, they are obsolete like a gas powered engine."

"So, you've come here to become vogue?" Beattrixx asks with a smile.

"No," Patrick says, leaning into his dark-haired companion. "My friends with all of their servants and comforts and pillows and staff and insulation miss the point of the fingerless gloves and iron wired corsets and robotic arms. Their mansions and parks and high places have left them out of the heart behind what Dr. Allbrung seems to be doing."

Allbrung eyes perk up, widening with Patrick's words.

"So, what's behind all of the fashion?"

"To get steam, you need sweat; the rich fear sweat, the poor are forced to embrace it." He is done. He shows everyone his fork and pierces his herring with a bright flourish. Taking a bite, he grins in delight of telling half of his story.

"Is that it?" Cat asks.

"Afraid so. Looking for hard work. That's my quest, my grail," Patrick says.

"But why?"

He does not answer. Instead, he eats and smiles.

Allbrung is the only one who returns his smile.

Brambley, seeing a break in the conversation asks Allbrung, "Are you from Canada, originally?"

The old man chuckles. "I am Dutch, the land of the windmills and farms," he says. "Although I have been around, I guess. London and Russia, mostly."

"Russia?" asks Cat.

"For a good spell, I lived with a commune led by the writer Leo Tolstoy. He had some wonderful ideas about community, civilization, and … most everything." The old man pointed at Brambley. "You would like his thoughts on the Kingdom of God.

Exhaust from the Tin Woods

He believed the Kingdom of God is not out in space, surrounded by ether and other gasses, but within the human heart. This Russian would say there are no metaphysic, no mystics to the Kingdom of God: it is alive when it is lived."

"I would say, this is nothing new: most Englishmen would agree."

"Then why, " the old man asks, his blue eyes looking up at the clouds. "Do they fight so many wars?"

The group is silent. Beattrixx, because she cannot contain the smug power of her grin. Maillory and Patrick because their Empire seems to be bested. Shweta and Cat because they want to see the defense. Brambley because he is in the presence of a pacifist.

Brambley grew up in the church and was warned to never get too close to a pacifist. The church where he worshipped at had reams of sermons warning young men not to forsake their duty to God and country because of the seductive lull of pacifism. A pacifist, Brambley believes and was taught, looks like God-fearing Christians and may even agree with many things of civilization; but something dark, he believes, lurks askew in the bent machinery of his mind.

Brambley sees Allbrung as the first pacifist he has ever met. Always the dark phantasmagoric specter in sermons about patriotism and civilization, Brambley knows not to trust pacifists.

"You seem to be against one defending oneself," Brambley states.

"Tolstoy believed in such things as peaceful resolutions to conflicts, the imaginative powers to end quarrels, and the banality of the military. That was Tolstoy."

"I hope you disagreed with him, especially when it comes to taking up your arms to defend your own country?"

Allbrung laughs and shrugs his shoulders. "My young theologian, where is my country? I am Dutch but have lived in Russia, Prussia, Germany, England, and now in Canada. Everywhere I go, I am greeted as a guest even when I return to Amsterdam. Who would claim me as their own? I am a National Orphan."

"And what if I am called to take up arms and defend

Exhaust from the Tin Woods

England's honor through battle? Would I be wrong?"

"I doubt England will wire you the command to shoot enemies here. In Canada. So, for all of our talk, you stand here as a circumstantial pacifist. Now finish your plate; I promise you every morsel shall be weighed and measured."

A silence grows and brews over the group, punctured only moments later by Patrick. "You say this woman experienced joy today by feeding us?" he asks Allbrung.

"Her kitchen is now a piece of newfound heaven."

"Would it be greedy; would it be selfish for me to return for another meal at a later time?"

"You would be bringing heaven to her."

"Then, if it fits your good counsel, could you make the request that when we return to the town, this is where I may have my lunch. I shall seek to always bring Joane, for she appears to be her favorite."

"Please, don't be greedy," Joane starts.

"I'm trying to be the opposite. It is either this or the pub or stale leftovers from our kitchen. And if heaven can be given away by a mere meal, I'd be willing to cook that meal or, at the very least, eat that meal. Would it be wrong?"

"Tolstoy would say you, at this moment, have the Kingdom of God within you. I shall make the enquiry on your behalf. More importantly, Patrick: you have mastered today's lesson."

Chapter Three
February 1895

Brambley stares at his desk, unable to move his eyes.

"Brambley," Cat asks. "I need a pair of needle beetles[50], you know, the pliers. Can you spare yours?"

He cannot move. He sits in the center of his raised platform, hugging his knees and closing his eyes. "Sure," he says. "Just a second."

"Are you okay? You look like you're going to get sick."

"Far from it,' he mumbles. He looks over at Cat who is wearing only a bra and pantaloons, her naked ankles fully exposed in the light of the room. This is all she wears today, for the project required lots and lots of kiln work. The entire shop is a hot, sweaty place and Cat, in order not to pass out, is disrobed.

Every time Brambley thinks about Cat, he shakes and trembles and gets tired. This, he reasons, is not love, but lust at its sickest form.

He gets up and reaches for his pliers. "Is it too vorpal to loan?" Cat asks.

"No, it's fine. I have another pair. I'm done with it today. I'm not doing any wire work."

His eyes meet hers. Her bright, electric blue eyes are narrowing. She is nothing but angry. "What have I done? Please, tell me. You and I: we're mates in steam. Tell me. I've thrown out several chatter starts, and they've fallen dead on the floor. Out with it. What's wrong?"

"You are hot and full of sweat and almost naked. There. I can't think straight because I see all of your curves and bits and bumps. There."

"And that morally offends you?"

"It excites me because you're the most perfect girl I've ever looked at. There." His voice now trembles and shakes. He looks down, feeling even redder than when he had bent metal in his

---

[50] needle nose pliers

kiln. "I have said too much."

"No," Cat says, the anger in her voice dropping. "You haven't said enough." Her voice is now warm.

"A gentleman does not admit excitement over the naked ankle of a young girl. It's just not done."

"And it should be done more. Tell me," Cat asks with a grin growing wider and wider by the second. "Should a gentleman not have excitements for a young woman's ankle or should a gentleman not express such inclinations?"

"Polite societies demand that one is quiet, resolute, and stoic on such infirmities."

"Mine or yours?"

"The infirmities are all mine, and I should, in no way, burden you. I know it is blistering, sweltering hot. To demand you to labor in boots, a corset, and a proper gown would be cruel. And yet, I cannot help myself and have failed in defending your honor."

"My honor? By breaking this weird, twisted, substantially flawed gentleman's code by telling me what beats in your heart is a far greater honor than any cheap, Mexician rule."

She runs across her platform, jumps over their rift, and wraps her arms around his waist. Brambley gurgles in horror as she hugs him tight. "Someday, I'd love to be the type of girl you think I am. You have, in no way, discredited me." She lets go and steps away. "What shall we do? Should I get dressed?"

"No, you'll get sick. We are working in Hades right now."

"Should I leave?"

"The projects are due."

"And you shouldn't leave either."

"I have never felt that you would dress the way you do for the solitary purpose of exhibition."

"Thank you." She bowed. "How about this? You just talk to me about what you're feeling. It'll be like you're telegraphing me your thoughts. Speak 'em, they won't have as much power."

"Okay," he says as he hands her his needle beetle. She bows again and turns around.

"Now I am looking at your backside ... now I'm not ... I see you jumping in the air ... and landing ... I feel nervous every time you do that ... I'm going to my work ... I'm thinking about

Exhaust from the Tin Woods

your ankles ... now I'm not ... now it's your breasts ... I've stopped ... I'm working ... I'm okay ... I need to finish my box ... I'm relaxed ... this feels good ... I'm turning to look at you ... I'm staring at your breasts ... your cleavage ... now your ankles ... I feel shame ... deep, cutting shame ... I'm thinking of my pastor's message, back in England, about Hell ... Hell ... it's as hot as it is here ... Hell ... your cleavage ... your perfectly round breasts that defy gravity as you jump from platform to platform ... Hell ... shame ... I'm so horrible ... so ... horrible."

Cat crosses her arms, and her eyes are filled with pity.

Brambley stops and looks up at her, sweat streaking his face. He shakes and gurgles.

Silence proceeds and Cat shakes her head. "Wow," she says. "Queen Victoria's England has really made your brain a heaping wreck."

.....

Brambley wakes up, seeing the morning light flood their circular room. The iron bars above him creak and shift, as Cat looks down at from the upper bunk. "Awake long?" she asks.

He smiles. "Not long. No. You?"

"I woke up with theorems and formulas and equations racing through my head. Is it me or is Allbrung becoming more theoretical?" she asks.

"You say that as if he's coming down with a virus. 'Theory' is akin to the measles or the flu." Cat smiles. Her eyes scan his bed, his little shelf by his head.

"You just have a Bible. You're really salt rocked about such zeitgeisted notions."

He shrugs and then clasps his hands behind his head. "It's my former world, I guess. The Foundation provided loving caretakers and loving teachers and had a reason for everything. You can't run a program like that with just people who've been talked into being nice. I think you need some sort of religion."

"So you believe in God and Heaven and England?"

"2 out of 3. You?"

"Raised on the streets, felt lucky to be a dance hall girl and a pony. Spent most of my life under the pink lights of the Pantomime. Crooked men with silver fingers, wandering and roving

Exhaust from the Tin Woods

over anything unprotected. I didn't have the luxury to be around nice people," she says without emotion. Her blue eyes stare straight into his.

"You didn't answer my question. Do you believe in God and Heaven and England?"

"I believe in Heaven. I'll start there. Heaven's easy, for I keep bumping into it every now and again." She looks to her left. "Do you want to see something? I've made an important discovery about this place."

She leaps off her bunk, wearing a long bed shirt made of a thick, patchwork quilt. She resembles a ball of red and black and green. Brambley wears his pajamas with the Foundations crest embroidered on his right chest.

"This is a bit of granding[51] I wasn't expecting," she says as she pulls out her pocket watch. "Ever wonder why we are only to use the study during certain hours? Why we can't have breakfast in the dining room? Why we're forbidden to using the water closets at the wrong time of the day? And why we can only play the forte at night?"

"These are all good questions. Why?"

"The list of good questions continues. Ever get lost? I mean, we've been here for over a month. And all of us are still getting lost. Suk, who's been here for over a year, gets lost all of the time. We get lost, I think, not because things are still new but because of something else."

She takes his hand and leads him out of the bedroom. She looks at her watch, carefully studying the second hand.

The hallway is dark, full of shadows in the shape of snakes and coffins.

Cat can barely see Brambley at times. At times, he only appears to be a tall tree against the darkened forest of the halls.

"So, why?" she asks. She takes him across the hall and points him to the auxiliary parlor, full of tubes and pipes and shafts. In the center of the room is Allbrung's Difference Machine, untouched and unused and powered by gaslight and ether.

The rule, Brambley remembers, is that students can only

[51] something made amazing by technology

61

Exhaust from the Tin Woods

use the Difference Machine at night.

"You are good at sherlucking, I'll let you figure it out. But the clock is ticking. Five seconds to figure it out."

Brambley bites his lips. He feels his stomach tighten with anticipation. He closes his eyes, replaying all of Cat's questions. Suddenly, he hears a clicking sound of the house' clockwork. Something snaps from below his feet, providing enough catalyst for a deduction.

"The house," Brambley states slowly. "Changes."

As soon he says this, the room moves. The desk collapses, sealing the engine within the floor. The right wall folds down, forming the new floor. Lanterns are hoisted up, plugging up holes in the tin ceiling. A new couch stretches from under the window. A new light, a chandelier, drops down and bursts with gaslight. A Persian rug rolls out, ending with a newly emerging bookcase. A click sounds, followed by a snap, revealing the new morning sun room. A sound of percolation erupts, as the built-in tea and coffee machines work on the morning brew.

"Rooms collapse and shift and fold up, depending on the time of day. It's like living in one, big glockenspiel. Like dolls, we rotate from scene to scene."

"What happens if we're in a room when it changes?" Brambley says as he looks up, discovering for the first time the hinges and pumps and shocks that allow the room to change the moment a weight runs out.

"For some rooms, you may just lose your chair; other rooms, a two-ton wall might collapse on you. I would hate to imagine someone trapped in one of these rooms collapsing, batty-fanging[52] to get out."

"I now feel very, very nervous." He takes a deep breath. "I guess we need to be extra strict on the day's schedule. I wonder how many former students broke loose from the schedule only to fall victim to a changing room?"

"I'm not sure. Since I discovered this about the house, I've been looking for funny stains on the rugs."

The two walk down the hallway back to their rooms to

---

[52] to thrash thoroughly

Exhaust from the Tin Woods

dress for breakfast. When they arrive, the other students are awake.

Joane and Shweta are tying their hair in elaborate weaves.

Patrick emerges from behind the vanity wearing his charcoal suit, and Maillory is still in bed.

"Corset?" Brambley offers Cat.

"No," she says. "I'll be dressed in pants and a shirt. Somehow, I foresee a burning kiln in our future, and I'd like to be comfortable. If I dress against my sex, it should be easier. But thank you." She smiles and hides behind her vanity.

Brambley does the same, dresses into a suit, and emerges to join Patrick to stroll down to the breakfast nook.

.....

Dr. Allbrung runs across the hall of Mercyminster, his eyes darting over his shoulder with a worried look.

Brambley sees this as he takes a tea break in the sunroom. "Dr. Allbrung?" he asks.

The old man runs into the breakfast room and closes the door behind him. "I am a victim of my inventions, I fear. I am being chased ... by time," he says in a whisper.

"I'm not following you," Brambley says.

"Nor should you. Nor should anything." He smiles and exhales, as his breadth returns. "So, how is your stay here in Mercyminster?"

"Good. I seem to be getting into the rhythm of this community."

"Good," he says and bows. "Every community has a rhythm, full of rituals and rites and procedures. We do not have to eat breakfast in the breakfast nook, but we do so out of ritual. You are on dish duty tonight and could very well invent a device to get you out of such a task, but it is a good rite to do, and we could have made separate quarters for male and female, but I believe it is a blessed procedure."

"That," Brambley says. "Has been an impediment to my education."

"Oh, I would have thought a co-ed living arrangement would enhance one's science. Please, inform me on all of the problems."

"Simply put, I feel it corrupts the mind when I must sleep

in the same room as that of the fairer sex."

"It depends, I guess, on how fair the sex may be." The old man chuckles. "I jest with a soldier's salt. I do apologize." He looks up in the air, studying the light. "It is Cat, is it not? She impresses you and makes you think of lustful fantasies?"

"It has nothing and everything to do with Cat. She is a female, and I speak on principle. It is not right for a man to bed near a woman. It is scandalous and leads to sin."

"Then do not sin. Simple." Allbrung opens up his large hands as a shrug and as some form of prayer.

"But it is an enticement to sin," Brambley says with a firm thud in his voice.

"Then heed not the lure."

"It looks wrong."

"Then be right, overcompensating in appearance. That is quite a noble virtue to perfect."

"Men should not sleep near or with women."

"But husband and wife –"

"Only bed together if they are poor, which I have always felt being a means of oppression for the rich can only live according to Queen Victoria's virtues."

"Or the rich invent virtues to match their own peculiar lifestyles," Allbrung says. He clears his throat. "Here is the thinking behind your sleeping arrangements. Lust, rape, and the addictions therein exist when sex is a mystery, hidden away in the dark and spoken of only with great, moral reluctance. When the woman's body is hidden and men pride themselves of never wanting to look is when it becomes enticing, the nude becomes a lure. But if you must see Cat when she wakes up, without powder or glitz, you see her as a person, as a human girl. No mystery, no romance. Just Cat, nothing more. This, I have found, creates the best workplace. A student learns with the opposite sex, not in competition or against or over.

"Cat should become a body, nothing more. Not to be worshipped or despised or both. She is a girl and must be loved as someone you live with."

"And what if sexual desire is aroused?"

"Then marry the girl." Allbrung snorts with a small laugh.

Exhaust from the Tin Woods

"And don't you dare sleep in separate rooms when married!"

"You are quite mad," Brambley says with a respectful bow.

Allbrung bows back.

"I might be. Now I must be off to continue to hide from a motorized clock that's looking for me. Long story, my dear Brambley." The old man rises and runs out the door, his eyes over his shoulder.

Brambley sees Allbrung run off and does not see anything following him.

.....

Cat sees Patrick as she sits on the wooden deck of the main street of Grouard.

Brambley sits with her under the rare, warm sun.

Under Patrick's arm, he carries a basket of fruit and biscuits and sausages.

She marches straight to him. "She's making you baskets now?" Brambley asks and Patrick only laughs.

"Hers is the simplest of relationships. The poor woman misses her children, so she has attached herself to me and feeds me like a son. She speaks not a word of English, and my Polish is only academic. According to Allbrung, by cooking for me, her health has been improving, and she is incredibly happy. Now, where else but here can one eat and lift the spirits of someone else?" Patrick asks with a grin.

"We're on a fact-finding mission," Cat says. "Joane and Shweta have been focusing on improving the public house, so we now need to find something else that needs to be glitzed."

"Any more steamies?" Patrick asks Brambley.

"They all disappeared on the day they attacked Beattrixx. And the Man-bear has gone missing. Good riddance. It's nice to have a nice, calm woods to look at in the morning through our window."

The three walk down the planked sidewalk towards the trading post. "Where is Joane?" Cat asks.

"And why do you ask me?" Patrick asked.

"If I could see anyone cozy up to you it would be her. You two seem a pair."

Exhaust from the Tin Woods

Patrick laughs as he places his brown, stovetop hat on his long, curly hair. "She is the most pleasant and easy to talk to girl that I've ever encountered. It could be because she's from service and she's professionally trained as a Held Companion. Still, she's an angel," he says and looks around. "But there's no madness."

"Madness?" Brambley asks.

"In Germany, some toggled prattlers have made a device called the ontological lapsometer. It records, amongst other things, when the brain experiences religious epiphanies and other spiritual enthusiasms."

Brambley chuckles and raises his gloved finger in protest.

"No, hear me out. For whatever reason, it records different colors when pointed to the brains of people in thick, religious euphorias. There's a term called 'going red': it's the peak furor and the greatest of brain activity. It happens when sinners walk down the sawdust trail or the preaching of damnation. Now, this same lapsometer has been used to measure the activity of parents, without a nanny, raising their children. Parents – fathers in particular – 'go red' in the midst of disciplining their kids. And when a man falls in love with a girl, they're recorded 'going red'."

"So –"

"So, I've never gone red with Joane. Not yet. And until then, we shall be just companions."

They reach the teahouse and Cat excuses herself to freshen up. Patrick points to Cat.

"What about you two?" Patrick asks soon after he leans in.

"My good man, all I have is 'red' with Cat. I am quite desperate for any other color, I fear, otherwise, I shall be quite mad. Her legs, her bosom, her face: it is all in my mind, every day. She tried to be modest, to have some propriety but it only adds to the seduction. Did you know she bought a full-length dress the other day and tried it on for me? The night after, I couldn't sleep! She's wearing perfume and powder and … it's entirely unfair. And her chest! What kind of diet and calisthenics does a young girl need to do to have a chest like the one possessed by Cat! She's is driving me mad and this madness, in no way, can ever lead to any sort of love whatsoever."

"So, you are physically attracted to her, and that is a

Exhaust from the Tin Woods

liability to your romance?"

"Quite," Brambley says.

"In love with a beautiful woman who might fancy you back … well, I guess we all have our crosses to bear." Patrick says this in a chiding tone.

Cat comes out of the teahouse and gives Brambley a cookie. "I thought of you when I saw this," she says with a smile.

He takes the gingersnap and bows in thanks.

She walks out, and the boys follow.

"So," Patrick says as he surveys the frozen streets, the frosted windows, and the yellowed tin roofs of the town. "Find anything?"

"I think I would like to build more musical instruments. The town … has no song," Cat says. "Some player pianos. Something to brighten this place up." She turns to Brambely. "Could you help me? I mean, if Allbrung agrees and he gears our lessons around Difference Engines driving music and the like, it's too much for me to take on. Could you be a real steamboat[53] and help me?"

"Well, I have no real inspiration now –"

"Do you? Do you really?" Patrick inserts from over Brambley's shoulders.

Cat blushes but does her best to hide it from Brambley.

"– and so I shall be only too happy to have our contraptions to work in harmony with one another."

"Be still my beating heart," Patrick whispers to Brambley.

Brambley playfully strikes Patrick.

Cat does her best to pretend not to notice this. "I guess this is how one prattler seduces another: will your contraption be in harmony with mine? And to think, I would have pegged you two as good, Christians."

The trio leaves the town, and they hike back through the woods. It is a warm day – comparatively, since it is still well below freezing – but the snow is gentle, and there is now a clear path through the woods to get back to Mercyminster. After a good half hour hike, they come to the iron gates and stone walls of the manor.

---

[53] a kind man who helps out a damsel in distress

Exhaust from the Tin Woods

Allbrung is outside, beating a rug with a device that burgles and burps and powers a swatter to strike the hung rugs.

"Allo," he says and grins at Cat. "And what new discoveries did you find in Grouard?" If these words had come from any other gentlemen, Brambley would think Dr. Allbrung was condescending. On the surface, here is a kindly old man addressing a young, pretty girl. In England, this scene would be ripe with condescension. However, from Allbrung it is a true question demanding an equally true response.

"I have the ambition to bring music to the town. I think if I could build some instruments, there would be many establishments only too happy to take them and apply them. I think it could really posh up the town."

"What would be your ideas?"

"There is the player piano," Brambley says. "What about the player flute? The player hurdy-gurdy? The player xylophone? All based on Difference Engine principles."

Allbrung stares down Brambley. He seems almost angry. "The Difference Engine and inspirations sprung forth are dead ends. The Difference Engine should never have been invented." He continues to stare him down.

Brambley feels hot under his collar. What? Brambley muses, is this Luddmunster type rambling coming from one of the world's leading scientists?

"Would you like to see why?"

"He has a machine that is to replace Babbage's Difference Engine?" Cat wryly states.

The old man cracks a smile and puts down his motorized rug beater. He motions with a head tilt for them to follow him into the manor.

They enter the warmth of Mercyminster, marching across the brass atrium and to a small, lean doorway underneath the stairs. "Babbage's Difference Machine[54], which is all of the rage now in London and Toronto and anywhere else that believes itself to be

---

[54] within our history, this device never "caught on". However, this might be one of the major changes from the book's history and ours. Simply put, the home computer became a Victorian mainstay in this time line.

Exhaust from the Tin Woods

important, is just a steam powered abacus or abax. A counting machine, nothing more. A gas lantern lights it, the clock parts in the box make patterns and designs for the shadows in glass. Someday, very soon, the photograph will be able to make pictures for people to interface with counting. Neat, tidy machine. Wonderful, really. But it's just a counting machine, nothing more. It does your math for you."

The old man ducks his head and walks down a spiral staircase worthy of a Mary Shelley novel, hugging the abject darkness of the cellar. The students follow him down. He flips his belt buckle around to shine a wide light, showing his feet where next to step.

"But there is more to information than counting, right? Soon, Babbage's machine will be able to play small parlor games on the thing based on numbers and simple equations. Sad for the Funfairs, as people will never have to leave their parlor to play a game, but that's only just biding time until ultimate obsolescence."

"Every home, every house of importance has his Difference Machine," Patrick says. "With the promise that our children will be smarter, our lives will be richer, and we will have more free time." Patrick is almost singing. Brambley figures he's wearing a bright smirk.

"If a machine replaces your brain's activities by simplifying a task, you don't become smarter. You simply don't." Allbrung shrugged and looked around. "This is my rule of invention: a machine must do what a human can't – not what a human is unwilling to do. A 'labor saving' tool is a myth; it really should be a 'labor robbing' tool. We're designed for work, for labor: that's how we have harmony with things and people. But to do something new, something never done before ... that's what I want. Sure, we have some machines that can do what our hands are unwilling: but that isn't our goal. And that's not what the AA is all about."

"The AA?" Patrick asks.

"I'll explain what the two 'A's' stand for in a bit. For now, hear me loud and clear: the path to thought life is not found in counting and probability. Thoughts are connected to memory; thinking is akin to remembering. Babbage is all about counting and

Exhaust from the Tin Woods

counting only one thing at a time. Very quickly, but it's all about counting. It will never think or never aid the human brain in thinking. What the AA does is something humans cannot do and will help us do the things humanly better."

The final step takes them to the cold, hard stone of the basement's floor. Allbrung shines his light on a curved, bubble looking machine that resembles more of a submarine than an engine. Round tubes stick out the side, fat coils on the top, a large crystal at the bottom, and pumps and gauges all around the desk part. In the center is the all-too-familiar gas lantern glass displaying shadowed images of the computations.

"This," Allbrung says. "Is the Analytic Apparatus."

"How is this not a Difference Engine?"

"A 'DE' counts; this remembers, recalls. It learns, it watches, and it records. Later, it will be able to decide based upon all of the facts, figures, and memories." He walks over to the machine, grins as if it is his newborn son. "This Apparatus was made by one glorious mistake. Years ago, while I was in London, I was asked to investigate haunted houses. Now, at first, we found nothing except near to collapse, dusty and creaky buildings. Then we found, in certain scattered places, rooms that felt more frightened than others. It was purely intuitive, which means to me that there isn't a science yet to explain what we were experiencing. So … I began to study."

"Through lots of tests, I found that the previous owners had suffered from some horrible tragedy. A death. A murder. Sickness. Something. And I, as a stranger, decades later, felt sensations of that tragedy. A ghost? No, but an emotional resonance. And since I was not in the throes of that particular tragedy, the residue felt illogical and out of place. No harmony."

"Further investigation found that there was metal, unique to only those places, that was embedded in the construction of the house. From a certain quarry, made around the same time: there was a metal that could retain emotion and then transmit it. That was the haunting."

"So, this is made from that metal? An AA can remember feelings?" Brambley asks.

"No, certainly not. Once I researched and figured out the

Exhaust from the Tin Woods

metal that remembers feeling – emurlogy, this new science I had just made – I quickly discarded it. What use could it be to experience the past's feeling? Why make a machine that does that? What's the point? We already have our brains that can perceive present feelings and isn't that more valuable, more human? But what emurlogy taught me was the data transfer: how can metal be imprinted upon and store date, ideas, and facts. As well, how can the machine later pour over this data and pick our similarities, trends, and then package them for retrieval? This is what I seek to design the AA to do."

"So how does this have anything to do with a player piano?" Cat asks.

"I'm so glad there's some intellectual impatience to you. If we were stuck with my timing, we'd never have a transition from the whole point I was making," Allbrung says with a grin. "Why talk about the AA? Simple, I detest player pianos. Why turn on a piano if you can already learn to play the piano? It is a machine replacing the work of the human mind. But what if the piano remembers what you played, learns from your playing, and can pick out all of your mistakes? Your strengths? Or, what if the piano can learn from your playing as to when the best kind of flourishes or improvisations would best suit your playing? Or what if the AA can read into your playing and find common mistakes, like songs, and then can review the world's catalog of music? All of a sudden: the thinking of the machine is now enhancing the player."

"What about a tutor? Wouldn't a teacher or tutor do the same?"

"The AA will always aid the human tutor because, no matter what, a machine can never tell you what you're playing seems like. Harmony with the tutor and the machine, not exploitation or dominance."

"So, what? You want us to make a bunch of musical instruments that can teach or aid in the teaching of people in Grouard on how to play music?"

"That is another application. And what happens then? Music will be on the streets of the town. Not played by machines, but through people." He steps back. "Now you understand me. Hopefully, this soon will be making sense."

Exhaust from the Tin Woods

"But we don't know how to do that," Cat replies.

"Neither do I. That's why we prattle around. Let mistakes be your best teacher. Make a bunch of errors, sherluck, and do a bunch of different things. Failure is something a well-run machine can never replace, and it is often the best of teachers."

Brambley smiles and steps back.

Cat, almost reading his thoughts, grins as well and asks, "Dr. Allbrung, we saw you using a machine to do a simple, domestic chore. You were using a steam powered device to beat the dust out of the rug. Isn't that … isn't that going against everything you said about machines working with man and not replacing them?"

Allbrung shakes his head and clasps his hands behind his back. "Good. Yes. Good. You are correct. I was using the machine for what it was intended to do. A gift from a former student who could not complete the program. Yes. However, my intentions were not to replace my labor. No." Allbrung pats Cat on the head. "Far from it. I was hoping to use it and use it wrong, hopefully making a mistake and by that mistake, I might find a far greater purpose for it. I was … playing with the machine. Alas, I think the thing only has one purpose, and that is to perform a task I can do better myself."

…..

"Are you awake?" Cat asks Brambley from her upper bunk.

"Yes," Brambley whispers, not to wake the rest of the students. "Just thinking about London. The toggles and the steamies and the streets all shiny and everything posh. Do you miss London?"

Cat sighs. "Never. The moment I got on the airship to come here, I never looked back. I don't miss a thing about London."

"Why not? It's where all technology comes from."

"Technology is about things, and London is where I was treated like a thing," she says in a husky, sad whisper. "Dr. Allbrung doesn't treat me like a thing. The rest of the students, they don't treat me like a thing." There is a long pause. Brambley cannot imagine what is causing the pause. Cat's voice turns really, really quiet. "You don't treat me like a thing."

Exhaust from the Tin Woods

"I do my best." Brambley does not sleep for the rest of the night, for he thinks about Cat. Cat is his Canada. She was one of the first people he met. They paired off with each other upon his arrival, and now all of their work is coming together. He can't think of Mercyminster without Cat, without her voice or ideas or anything else. Her small body, coming just to his chest, and rounded, bright yellow hair, and long slender nose: this is what he trails around him.

And most would call this love, lying in bed and thinking of a woman. For Brambley, it adds to his torment. For if Cat sees acceptance and love from Brambley, then now he is entrusted with a great amount of responsibility. For she needs his approval and he cannot help but see all of the sensuous lines, curves, and circles of her body. She excites him, and she wants nothing more than to be loved. Even when she is modestly dressed, he cannot escape the excitement.

"Where have you been? I mean, besides London?" Brambley asks her.

"The State, mostly. You know, it's crazy there. Wars and religion and every fighting. They're still fighting, you know," she says. "The North and the South and the Protestants and the Catholics and everyone. It's a place of tribes. No one likes or gets to know anyone. I got with a bunch of dancers on a Riverboat. Fun times. It was a really good sisterhood. Tramped around. The boat got bought out by Mexician money, and we lost our jobs. Got scattered. Came to Boston and picked up prattling. Worked in a cybernetic store, making hands and things for steamies and lurkjerkers. Got the invitation to come here."

"I don't think I'd like The State or Mexicia. Everyone seems so loud there," Brambley says with a shudder.

"They dress like me there. All of them. If you have a problem with me, you'd have a problem with them."

"I don't think I have a problem with you. I used to." He shudders in his bed because he feels like he's lying. The issue is that he doesn't want to have a problem with her. "You're … a precious person. I feel bad for how I spoke about you."

"Don't feel bad. If I'm precious, you're amazing."

"Why would you say that?" Brambley asks. "You hardly know me."

Exhaust from the Tin Woods

"I know enough. I know enough. I think I might try to go to sleep. Good night."

He grunted and continued to lay in his bed.

.....

The students stand in the cold snow, wrapped in blankets and furs and long coats. A snowball is thrown at Brambley's head. He whirls around, seeing Shweta and Patrick grinning behind him.

"Now think," Shweta says to him. "Who is the most likely to throw a snowball at you?"

"The one with snow on her mittens," Brambley says, pointing to Shweta's right hand.

He turns around and does what the rest do: face a large barn tucked away behind the workshop. Upon the chimney pluming with smoke, he deduces that there's a kiln inside. How big? He's not sure. Is it just an outside kiln?

For safety, it needs to be far away from the house; possibly, especially if it gets really, really hot. A big kiln, a big ...

The collapsible, rolling from door lifts up to reveal a dark, shadowed single room lit only by the orange, smoldering fire of a furnace. A tall giant comes out from beside the furnace. The figure walks and just when Brambley thinks the hulking mass can't get any bigger, the figure takes a few steps closer. Towering like a tree over the group, the figure steps into the light.

"Hello, there," a deep bass speaks, shaking the bones to the feet of all standing near. "I been away for a while. Good to be back," the man says.

He is Brambley's first African. He had grown up with pictures in the newspaper, heard dark stories about them, and once – when the Foundation was visited by a Lord – he had a servant with dark skin. He understood that the Confederacy succeeded from the Union to have the right, the privilege of owning these people as property ... an idea abhorrent to Brambley.

But there he was, an African.

"I am one of your teachers. Allbrung be your main teacher, I be ... his assistant. I get to teach you about the smithy and how to bend metal and how to make shapes. Before my time, you've a toy kiln to make gadgets and things. Same principle, but you need a lot more skill for something like this." He looks at the girls. "And

74

Exhaust from the Tin Woods

strength."

He is a middle-aged man without hair except for on his eyebrows and chin. He has broad shoulders, toned muscles around the neck and chest, stovepipe arms, and withered hands. He wears a leather apron and a fresh pair of those new denim jeans.

"I'll be slow; I'll be patient as a teacher. I just want hard work in return. For the next three days, all of your classes are going to be in the smithy." He grins. "The name is Noah. Now, I get to pick the one who gets to be worked."

He pointed to Patrick. "You. Dandy. I want to see your hammering skill."

Noah pulls out a shining, red shaft of metal from the fire. He lays it on the anvil. "Now," he says. "Turn this into a circle."

Patrick grins, takes off his waistcoat, and rolls up his sleeves. He hammers and hammers, unable to make even the slightest of bend. Again, and again. The red glow burns bright with every strike, filling the smithy with light if only for a scant second.

After two minutes, Noah says, "Had enough?"

"Just got started," Patrick replies. Sweat drenches the front of his crown. His cheeks burn bright red. His white shirt clings to his chest. However, he does not slow down.

Another three minutes. "Take a break?"

"Not at present," Patrick says, continuing to hammer. More times elapses.

Noah just laughs.

Maillory looks to Cat; Cat shrugs.

Brambley leans in, seeing if Patrick is hurting himself at all.

Patrick strikes and strikes, with all of his might. He staggers and sways, but returns to the rhythm of striking at the anvil.

"Now then," Noah says, and Patrick keeps working on bending the metal. "I think you've had enough."

"Am I tiring you out?" Patrick asks in a pant.

Joane grimaces, covering her mouth and flutters her eyes in an anxious roll.

Patrick sways and leans backwards. He lurches forward only to stumble over the anvil. The glowing metal burns the side of

Exhaust from the Tin Woods

his right arm, but he doesn't seem to mind. Instead, he topples to the ground. His breadth is wild and deep, heaving violently with a threat to break his ribs.

Joane swoops over him and surveys his face, his eyes. "Are you okay?" she asks.

Noah erupts into a loud, boisterous laugh. He places his grand fists on his hips, pointing his mouth to the heavens as he fills the entire kiln with the sound of his laugh.

Brambley darts a look at Shweta whose sharp confusion is obvious in her brow, her shoulders, and her gaping mouth.

"Well, you don't waste any time, do you?" Noah asks. "We understand a' nother, don we? You won't be called Dandy, and I won't be scared givin' ya' hard work. We understand each other: two cracked nuts."

For the rest of the day, Noah shows them the workings of the kiln. It is mammoth, four furnaces with an opening to one, containing a roaring fire. The kiln must always be stoked so that when one is not bending metal, then one is chopping wood. Noah shows them the tools: the tongs, the hammers, the molds, the picks, the slicers, the magnets, the rollers, the groovers, the shavers, and the anvils to bend great metals.

Noah is brief in his descriptions, although when asked he elaborates and seems willing to linger on a subject until everyone understands him. His pace in speech is slow, making his lean sentences and exact words have a greater weight.

Later, Joane expressed to the group she almost wanted to take notes, but whatever Noah said, he showed, and he had everyone duplicate afterwards.

At the end of their class, he announces, "When you come back tomorrow, the fun will begin." He laughs.

True to his word, the next morning at breakfast, Allbrung is having tea with Suk. When the students come in, it appears they're having a conversation centered around blueprints, numbers, and equations that cover their small, round table. Allbrung looks up, with his cup hovering in front of his chin. "Go back and change into work clothes. And not British work clothes, real work clothes. Dress for hot weather. Today, it's to the kiln."

Brambley's eyes widened, and his jaw drops.

Exhaust from the Tin Woods

Cat swirls around and slaps him: he's not sure if it's on his backside, for he is still in shock.

Having had their breakfast, the students dress in layered work clothes and meet back at the kiln

Noah stands outside, gulping in the frosty, ice air as he spent most of his strength in a round of chopping wood. He is shirtless, down just to his breeches and boots. Steam erupts from his pores, giving him the appearance of an out-of-control steamy.

"Hello," Noah says. "All eyes up here. I found the cuckoo of the group yesterday. I need to find a new one." He looks over each student, all bundled up in their coats as the steam from Mercyminster and the heat from the kiln has not reached them. Shivering, cold, and nervous: only one of them makes steady eye contact with him. "You," he says and points to Joane. "I think I'll go far with you. Here's da' plan: I train her in the morning, and the rest of you chop wood. Tomorrow, she'll teach a whole bunch o' ya while I take a few more to pick out rocks. More skills, scattered around the group. Ye will learn from each other as ye learn from me. When not getting coached, you do hard work. Some of you need muscle."

Joane looks over her shoulder and grimaces. The rest of the students leave to chop wood. "Know how?" Patrick asks Brambley.

Brambley nods and looks around: no one else knows how to chop wood. He raises his eyebrows at Shweta. "I have brothers." Then to Cat. "You'd be surprised how little real, from the tree wood, exists in London. There's firewood, but it's from the factory."

Brambley shrugs as he pulls off his coat. The chopping block is between the steaming shop and the heat of the kiln.

Brambley looks around the corner to a two-story shed to where all the chopped wood is stored. He grins, seeing a breathing shell around the frame to keep out all moisture.

"Do you mind if I set a plan to chop the wood?" Brambley asks as he returns to the group. "Shweta and I will chop, the rest will load the shed. When we get tired, two loaders will replace us. We always move, always work."

Brambley strips his top, remaining in his breeches. Shweta

77

Exhaust from the Tin Woods

ties her skirts around her knees, her waist, and her hips: her covering remains, her arms and legs are exposed.

"And you are letting a Lady do the rough work?" Maillory balks at Patrick.

"Watch," he says with a grin.

Shweta attacks the wood, her chiseled arms and defined leg muscles bulge and flex as a machine perfected for this work. The swing, the strike, and the pull away are a dance, a fluid singular motion. She is barefoot, crunching on the leaves as a swish of the blade and her footing braces each strike.

Brambley's swings are less precise and slower, but his strength carries him besides Shweta's economy of motion.

Forty minutes into their work, Beattrixx mentions to Cat, "Someone should invent a machine that chops wood, saving us this trouble."

"It's no trouble," Cat says. "How else would we see Brambley's bare chest?"

"It's indecent," Maillory says, overhearing their discussion.

"It's glorious."

"I can hear both of you," Brambley says in a croak.

"I am not whispering," Cat says with her steel, blue eyes locking onto his. She smiles quickly with a smug air of triumph before she returns to carry another load.

"The work is good," Shweta says. She stops and exhales deeply. Her black hair is matted with sweat, her sienna skin bursting red and flushed. "Seek to find a rhythm and work with gravity and the wood and the split. It shall become light work."

"The yoke will be easy, the burden free?" Brambley asks, quoting the Holy Bible.

"If you wish," she says with a shrug. "And it will build muscle, not strain it. It's a dance, a fluid. The moment you chop in parts, you tire. Use the weight of the axe as part of the swing, part of the movement." She says this while chopping, while smiling.

"How do you know so much about this? This is your first day in chopping wood, is it not?"

"I know nothing about chopping wood, but I listen. I listen to my body, I feel the weight of the axe, and I embrace the

Exhaust from the Tin Woods

resistance of the wood. In this, is an equation: $S + G / W$. Shweta plus gravity divides wood. Listen and feel everything, you'll find the right rhythm."

"Is this a Sikh consideration, shaped by your religion?"

"All labor is religious: replace labor, replace your faith. For example, consider Patrick. He works, he toils, and does so without relenting. He is searching for his religion, so he works harder than anyone else. And you, you genuinely believe and stepped in, as our leader."

Beattrixx turns and looks to Brambley as if she wishes to say something. She bites down on her tongue and turns around.

Shweta sees this look, and her grin widens.

"Don't think I don't see what is going on? Don't think I notice? I see, and I like it. You will make a fine leader. Natural fit."

"I don't think religion shapes how we chop wood," Brambley says in a different tone, to change the subject.

"Oh no?" Shweta asks and, almost cued to enter a stage like an actress ready to deliver her lines, Maillory enters.

"Can't we take a break? My feet are hurting! I didn't come here to do common work but to learn. How does this teach me about designing steam? My neck is sore." Maillory moans.

Brambley grins and puts down his axe. "Let's draw some water from the shop. Take a rest," he says, and the rest follow.

They walk around the side of the smithy, finding a large window covered in brown and fog and dust. The panes drip as if in the middle of a chase. They peer through to find Joane hard at work.

She is stripped down to her bare essential undergarments. Her white, porcelain skin has turned to a red, hot glow as she runs barefoot from the kiln to the anvil, hammering out burning red metal. Noah is beside her yelling and laughing, looking both joyful and severe. Every pore of her body oozes with sweat, causing her to shine like a buffed crystal hung in a chandelier. She bends over, stretches, reaches, braces, and hammers. Each strike, the group sees her mentor howl and cheer: she seems to be doing everything right. She blows away a loose strand of blond hair from her eye. As she does, her eyes flash in triumph. The striking from her hammer to the red steel flashes the entire room with bright, yellow light.

Joane is a small woman without an inch of body fat, so her

Exhaust from the Tin Woods

body moves as a single unit and without jiggle or bounce. Nothing but strength, focus, and savage determination. Gone is the lace, replaced by sweat and steel. She barrels through the smithy, guided by Noah's commands, as a Berserker on the field of battle.

"Gentlemen, do not gawk," Maillory chides. "She is in the lustiest of positions."

"Are you lusting?" Brambley asks Patrick. "Do you see red?"

"By our old, dead gods: I wish I did see red. For she is the most perfected of creatures," Patrick says in a slow, stifled whisper. "By Queen and Country, she is an angel."

"Do you say that because she is in her undergarments?" Maillory says, turning more angrier.

In a daze, Patrick looks up and then back over his shoulder. His eyes return, both wild and stunned. "No," he says. "No. It is her...labor. She is made beautiful by it." He shakes his head. "But alas, I do not see red."

"But look at her," Brambley says and points to the window.

"Nay," Patrick says. "Nay, nay, nay." He brushes his breeches as if filled with metal shavings. "No red. Only rest and back to work, eh?"

Cat smiles at Brambley, walks past the boys and turns to Shweta. The girls go on ahead towards the water. Cat says to Shweta, "Did you see the look in that boy's eyes? I have never seen that in him before."

"But I did see that look in Brambley before. Many times," Shweta says, and both girls laugh. When there is a break, Shweta adds the tag, "And it wasn't today." Another laugh.

"We can hear you," Brambley says through his teeth, turning hot.

"We, my young Gentlemen, are not whispering," Shweta says.

.....

The next day, Allbrurg announces that in three days' time will be the first set of exams. "It will be easy and light. A quiz, really," he says as he concludes his lectures. Brambley looks to Shweta, and she shakes her head vigorously.

Exhaust from the Tin Woods

Later, over lunch, she tells the whole group, "His exams are the worst in the world. He is a mad scientist, not because he's raising the dead in his basement, but that he expects the impossible."

That night, they study. "What will be on the test?" Patrick asks Shweta.

"Everything," she says.

For the team to be prepared, Maillory makes a list of every single equation given and a few that did not make the lectures. "Oh those," she says. "He told me those when I bumped into him in the sunroom." She writes them down and adds one. "This one is an equation I overheard him saying to Patrick."

"But we can't be responsible for a conversation outside of class?" Patrick croaks.

"Oh yes," she says with a grin. "Everything is connected to everything, so he can quiz you on an equation you learned while in your sleep."

So, they gather every piece of information they heard, even in passing.

They memorize, quiz each other, and study. No one studies by themselves nor do they sleep until everyone knows everything.

"You see," Cat says, who is the mother of this plan. "If we all know the same things; he cannot flunk any of us. Stand together, no solos."

The day of the exams, the exam is divided into three parts: written, oral, and mechanical. The written is the chalkboard, where each student must alone finish a series of equations; the oral is a forty-question exam on theories; and the mechanical is a box of loose, random parts with the simple instructions chalked drawn on the side: "BUILD SOMETHING IN TWO HOURS."

Two days pass and Allbrung states, over breakfast, that each student is to meet with him in his office. "Where is your office?" Patrick asks.

"In the morning, it is by the ballroom; in the evening, I am not sure where it is," Allbrung says.

After breakfast, Allbrung picks up his back pillow and tugs at Brambley's coat. "Come with me," he says, and Brambley follows his teacher.

Exhaust from the Tin Woods

"You are the leader in the class," Allbrung says as he strolls down the stairs to his office.

"You mean I did the best?" Brambley asks in excitement.

"Oh no, your science is very weak. Very weak. No, the rest of the students look to you as their leader. Does that surprise you?"

Brambley silently shakes his head. He opens his mouth to protest.

"Please, no British false modesty. If you love your friends, simply accept that they look to you as their leader and do your best to bring out the best in them." He turns towards a door that is new to Brambley. "For this reason, I want you to go through this door." Quickly, he opens a secret passageway behind the desk. The door opens to a small closet with a stool. "I want you to see something. Let us see if you see what I see."

Brambley steps into the closet and Allbrung closes the door behind him. He discovers the painting on the doorway is really a one-way mirror where he can see and hear the interviews.

The first that enters is Beattrixx. She is posh, wearing black and white checkered coat, knee-high boots, and a leather corset. In white powder, she is the epitome of London style.

"Your written and oral is quite good, but your mechanical is the best in the class. You made a steam powered iron, for smoothing fabric. It is an invention for housewives all over the Empire who have something similar: you've just improved on the design making it faster. Well done," Dr. Allbrung says to Beattrixx. She nods without emotion. "You are a brilliant student, my dear Beattrixx. I have a question, a question I shall ask all of my students. If you must make one thing, based upon all that shall be given to you, what would that be?"

"I want to make silent and invisible steam," she said quickly, her dark eyes narrowing upon the professor. "That's what I want out of this nounshwar stein[55]. I want to come up with a universal equation where steam can run silent and invisible."

"Many scientists would say it is impossible," Dr. Allbrung said, waving his hand.

"You are not most scientists, Dr. Allbrung. Am I blowing

---

[55] a really neat looking home

ether dreams[56]? Can it be done?" she asks coldly.

"Sure, my dear. But why? Why dream of silent and invisible steam?" Allbrung sounds calm, caring like a father.

Beattrixx stares him down and does not move. "Well, every prattler must have a secret or two. It shall be honored. In summary, be proud: you have done well on the exams."

"Steam has a sound, distinct and loud. I hear the hiss and spatter all over London," she says quickly. "The noise covers, hides, drowns out, and blasts. Have you been to the woods outside? Calm, quiet: how people used to sound. Now the steam nags and bleats. My dream is to hide it all, perhaps we might get our full brains back."

"That's a grand dream. I'll see what I can do."

She nods before she makes her departure.

On her heels, Cat comes into the room. She clasps her hands at her waist to steady them, but Allbrung can see that she is shaking. She is pale, her blue eyes emitting even more light than usual. She wears her simple brown tights with matching vest, a dark shirt, and matching boots. She bites her full, lower lip.

"Cat, you have scored the highest on the oral," Allbrung says, and Cat's mouth opens in disbelief.

"But we were all supposed to get the same scores," she says.

"More or less, everyone did. No one flunked. But since it was your idea to learn together, guess who learned the most?"

She bites her tongue and smiles, while her right booted toe twists on the tile before her.

"What dream do you want? What do you want to learn?"

"I want to figure out how to bring music to Grouard."

"Is that what brought you to Mercyminster? The dream of bringing music to Alberta?"

"No, I came to learn."

"What?"

She laughs silently. "I'm not like the other students. I live in the moment. The moment brings me here and there. I don't plan. I just go. Look for what's right in front of me. A pick-pocket,

---

[56] unrealistic expectations

dancer, glass-blower, farmer, and boat engineer – it all brought me to this moment."

"And now the moment asks you to benefit a group of people you're just getting to know?"

"Why not?" she says while she crosses her arms.

"I respect your … 'moment' … just don't be too quick to leave for the next, big moment. There's quite a lot of people here whom you can learn from; there's a lot you can teach."

"Honestly?" she asks. "I've never been happier. My hands and joy are wetted with inventing."

"Good," Allbrung says with a smile. She leaves. Allbrung gets up, opens the door, and lets out Brambley. "Now, out of the two: who would you see as a good partner in leading this group? Beattrixx is ambitious, brilliant, and knows everything about what the outside world wants; Cat lives in the moment."

"Cat," Brambley says without hesitation.

"Why?"

"As you say, she lives in the moment. The secret, it seems, to manufacture things for people we know. Harmony and all of that. Although Beattrixx might become one of the big names in science, one day, her ambition – bold as it might be – seems not to be for anyone I know, yet. Whereas Cat has a few families in mind, already, as to who to make for. Plus, Cat is mostly aware of our group whereas Beattrixx is solitary, like most punks from London."

"Good. Our exercise is done, along with our meeting. You have discovered everything I wanted to say to you. Please, send in Patrick."

This puzzles Brambley. He does his best to hide it, but he can tell Allbrung knows he's leaving him in confusion. And the old man seems not to care.

Brambley turns on his heels and leaves the office.

…..

On Sunday, the students of Mercyminster attend church.

Beattrixx sits next to Cat. Both are not dressed for church. Beattrixx is wearing a black riding coat, thigh high boots, and white body hugging suit made of fleece; Cat wears a brown and green gown befitting a fairy costume, made of starched tool, brass, and wires. The two outfits would be fine for the streets of London, born

Exhaust from the Tin Woods

out of the steam social revolution, but for a church service in Northern Alberta, they clash.

The boys sit on the right side of the furnace, while the girls sit on the left.

A shame, Cat thinks. Everywhere else, she'd be by the side of Brambley.

This absence earns a remark from Beattrixx. "Where is your companion?" she whispers during the prelude played by a Victorola.

"With the boys, sitting on the right ... for the purpose of subjugating women," Cat says.

"Go over and sit there," Beattrixx says followed by an impish grin.

"I wouldn't want to cause a stir," Cat says and watches Beattrixx's eyes point to her small, ankle high boots that could, depending on how she stands, reveal her lower legs. "Well, one stir at a time, I guess."

Beattrixx turns and surveys the crowd.

Cat joins her, seeing every single congregant staring at them with taut facial muscles, eyes narrowing, and fists clenching. Every pore, every muscle suggests contempt.

"I wish people went to church for a purpose other than judging everyone else," Beattrixx says. "I feel like the show is here, on the second pew, rather than the stage." She frowns at the whole congregation. "And it promises to be not much of a show."

"Church is not about a show." Cat answers.

Beatrixx replies, "Of course it is, and the reason why it's polite to dismiss such expectations is because it's such an impoverished production. People come and watch God for an hour so they can go back to their lives of looking down on the rest of the world. I mean, no dance or song or phantasmagoria. Too luddmunstered[57] full of candle light and tacky parloring[58]."

"I take you are not a believer? In God?" asks Cat.

Beatrixx responds, "God doesn't believe in me; I'm just

---

[57] Luddites and those who favored gas powered technology who lost the argument

[58] old Victorian practices minus technology

85

returning the favor." She points with her dark eyes to Brambley. "I know who believes in God in a terrible way."

"Hopefully not too much; a girl would like to have some fun." Cat replies.

Beatrixx enquires, "You have really fallen for this boy?"

"I don't know what it is, Beattrixx. I'm with that boy all of the time, but I'm not aching and all seeing gray when he's not around. It doesn't hurt, it doesn't destroy my heart: how could this be love?" says Cat.

"Question, then: does he feel the same way about you?"

Cat answers, "I'd have a better and more clear answer if he wasn't so mad about God. I think he's mellowing a bit so I might get a more straightforward …"

The prelude ends. The elder of the church stands up, with his copy of John Calvin's book in his hand. He opens the book to read. Stops. Looks throughout the crowd of the church. Is he now going to stop and say a few words on our behalf? Cat wonders. Judge us? Tell us to leave? Keep the church free from people like us?

"I never did well in places like this," Cat says to Beattrixx. "I remember as a kid, living on the streets, our group fell asleep on the steps of a church. The minister came out and poured cold water on us, to scare us away. We were strays to those people. Nothing more."

"You talk too much," Beattrixx says. "That's what I like about you."

"I am neither a minister nor do I have anything to say," the man in front says. "I'm a banker. That's it. I'm from Ontario. I don't even belong in Alberta. Yes, I'm educated. But I'm not a minister."

Cat wonders where this man is going with this. She reads fear as the man rambles, seeming just as surprised as what comes from his mouth as the church is. She doesn't see judgment like she saw in London. Something … new.

"I'm reading from John Calvin. Do I think he's right? I don't know. Do I think you need to hear from him? Not sure. Why did I pick him? He's the only Christian book I own in my five-book library. So here I am, the only elder of this church, left to read something and give you inspiration. I've got nothing. I've had nothing for a long, long time. So, I prayed to God. I asked him to send us a preacher. Anyone. And I was given a face."

He points to Brambley.

"You, young man, with the strange friends and the rich man's clothes. The Lord gave me you. Come up here and preach."

"Me?" Brambley asks.

"You. Just start talking. Say anything. Let's see if I heard from the Lord. It can't be as bad as John Calvin. Just start talking."

Brambley gets up to the front. He presses his coat, smoothing it out.

Cat can tell he's terrified.

"God loves you," Brambley says. "I think that's the gist of what I'd like to say. There's a Scripture famous on the streets of London. John 3:16. It is all over on the streets. Temperance marchers quote this verse, hoping for London to become Christian again so they can stop drinking. Preachers use it to start another Great Awakening. It's famous, perhaps more so than Moses. The verse speaks of God so loving the world ... that anyone who believes ... that's what they focus on, I should say. How one must believe and only believe and just believe and they will be saved. It demonstrates how easy it is to be saved, which is true."

"But our world has too many believers in Jesus. We don't need any more. And in focusing on belief, we skip the beginning. God so loves the world. Us. The dirty. The mongrels who are humanity. We are crazy, horrible, and violent. God loves us. He sees something good in us. He fixes us. Changes us for the better. Redeems, fearing that redemption is such an over-used word. God loves ... our world, our land, and the people of the world. He loves the 'everything' that is the Earth." Brambley pauses looking out over the gathered congregation.

He continues shyly, "And, if we are to be like him, we must love this world too. And not just love it, fix it and join with God in the fixing. God fixes and wets the world with His redemption. God doesn't need more believers; he wants more lovers. God loves us. Are we willing to love our world too?"

An old woman, tears in her eyes, shouts, "A-men."

"There goes the fun," Cat croaks to Beattrixx. "I've been

Exhaust from the Tin Woods

paired up with a Charles Wesley, a minister seeing gray."

Beattrixx replies by snorting with laughter.

.....

The end of February brings a rigid, unforgiving cold, reminding Cat of a high-powered icebox, turning its contents into sudden ice.

Her job, for the last week, is to gather firewood for the evening. She puts on her long wool coat, mittens, and minx hat for stepping out into the blue cold of the night. From the western exit, she makes her way to the smithy and wood shed.

As her boots crunch through the snow, she stops. There's something in the woods, in the dark of the night. A sound that doesn't belong. Something sticks out, belonging more to a story, or a problem underway. She stops breathing. Listens.

She can swear she hears a baby crying.

Climbing over a hill that hugs the estate, the cries grow louder. She almost slides downhill, entering a maze of poplars appearing as a thousand entryways. Criss-crossing through the trees, she climbs over another hill and hears the cries louder and louder, almost as if the infant in distress is flying overhead.

Cat finds herself in a valley. The moonless night plunges her into absolute darkness. She turns on the light from her belt buckle. The light projects out a few inches, around the field of ice, full of sharp peaks and jagged valleys. She feels she's in the belly of watch, full of gears and wheels made of snow and twigs.

Suddenly, her light shines on a human face. The face is blank, without emotion or life behind the eyes. The mouth breathes, the eyes scan wild and full of white. She steps back, and her light reveals the face is upon the body of a gray coat wolf.

The wolf with a human face opens its mouth. Like a parrot in a pitch-perfect imitation of a human voice, the wolf beast wheezes the sound of a baby's cry. Around the creature's throat is the ribbing of a small steam engine.

Crunching sounds ripple around behind her. She twirls around, discovering that the pack of human faced wolves is circling her, surrounding her. Almost to mock her, they turn to a choir of baby cries.

Cat feels her heart beat almost out of her chest. Her

Exhaust from the Tin Woods

shoulders shake. She wants, more than anything, to start screaming.

The wolves freeze in their circle. Their blank, feral faces stare at her. No joy, no anger: they just stare at her as if waiting for something before they attack.

Cat feels around her coat; she possesses no tool, no weapon, and not even a torch except for her belt light.

The circle, at the same moment, takes a step closer to her.

She is panting, shaking and trembling. Another step closer, the circle is now much closer.

Within another step, they'll be within leaping and tearing and biting distance.

Do I have only three seconds to live? Cat thinks. She closes her eyes and folds her arms, expecting the wolves to attack her – their easy prey. She can hear her breath, like sobs sharp and full of moans.

A small disc sails through the air, just above the heads of the wolves, and explodes. Light fills overhead and turns the woods, for three seconds, into daytime.

The wolves cower.

Cat is barely able to remain standing. She looks around, like a customer in an opium den, unable to perceive the world around her.

Brambley charges from the darkness of the woods. "Cat, take my hand. The disc's light will only stun them," he shouts. He grabs her hand, and they run eastward. The wolves take a few seconds to awaken from the light's stun as they form a line to chase the pair.

"I went to go look for you and followed you out. I deduced your footprints, and it made little sense as to the length of your hike," Brambley said in his mad sprint through the woods. "I wanted to ask your advice on one of my inventions."

"Advice? On what invention?" she asks.

"You just saw it: metal discs that explode in light. I was trying to figure out a practical application for such a device. I guess we have one." They continue to run. "It stuns human faced, cybernetic wolves."

"I heard a baby cry, and I thought it was freezing to death in the woods," Cat says.

Exhaust from the Tin Woods

"A means to lure their prey, I should think. Quite effective," Brambley says as the two approach a steep incline of an ice packed hill. Suddenly, a red light greets them at the top. Cat's light shines to reveal a bear with half of a human face, a laser eye, and a robotic arm ending in steel claw.

The pair freeze in their tracks.

"You no longer have hope, your end is nigh," the bear says to them. His voice is full of tin, complete with its own echo. It sounds wrong for the woods, for the night. It more belongs to a motor, that by coincidence, makes a sound that could be a word in English.

Brambley looks to Cat; Cat shrugs. "Excuse me?" he asks the bear.

The wolves are on their heels, the sound of a baby crying is the rallying sound of the pack.

Brambley turns to his right, points, and the two head in the direction away from the wolves, Mercyminster, and the bear.

The wolves give chase, turning towards their master, charging after Cat and Brambley.

"We can't outrun them," she says to Brambley.

"Any ideas?"

"No," she says. "My failed invention today was a fan that was supposed to be a music box. I don't think it would work."

They run to a large clearing bathed in darkness. Cat's belt light is the only thing that tells them a tree, a bush, or a hole is in front of them. As they make their way to the clearing, the wolves slow down, only to fan out. Cat assumes they wish to form a ring and then tighten around them like a net.

Suddenly, light appears in front of them. The light becomes brighter and brighter, causing the wolves to scatter. The light stops, and two figures of men step in between Cat and the source. "Please, we insist," a man's voice calls out. "Get in. These woods are very dangerous. We need to get you to safety."

Cat and Brambley run towards the light, discovering it is attached to a dog sled. The two men, clad in fur and brandishing rifles, stand at the back. Cat and Brambley sit in the sled. One of the men sounds a device that simulates a whip crack. The dogs charge off into the clearing, pulling the sled behind them.

Exhaust from the Tin Woods

"Tonight, something must be happening. The woods are crawling with creatures," one of the men says to the other. "We cannot make it to Mercyminster. We need to find the trapper's lodge. I think it's about a mile eastward."

"By the brook and the rock that looks like Wellington's face?" the other asks.

"Wellington? I always thought the rock looked like Victoria." The wolves grow nearer. "We must make double the time."

At that moment, the dogs stop suddenly.

"Blast it all, what is that?"

"Sorry," the second climbs off the back. He scans the dogs.

Brambley notices the position of the ears of all of the dogs has changed, leaning back. "They have decided as a pack that they're not pulling our weight. They wish for us to run with them."

"Now?" the first asked. His tone is sharp, matching Cat's anxiety.

"Sorry, but we run a very democratic sled and the dogs are highly sensitive to those who do not do their fair share. When we work, they have a bit of joywig; when we are lazy, they notice. As a pack, they are conscious of inequity."

"But this is madness. Who –"

"Run!"

The four run as the wolves descend. The sled goes, with the riders running alongside. One of the men pulls out a round ball, lights it, and throws it over his shoulder. The round ball streaks blue and gold light, drawing the immediate fascination of the wolves.

They stop, surround the light source, and freeze. A few seconds later, the ball explodes wiping out the pack.

"Do not stop running," the second man says. "The bear seems to be commanding multiple packs tonight."

They finish running across the clearing. The dogs stop and let them all on for the ride. The sled charges through the woods, crashing through the snow and bushes and trees.

For twenty minutes, the sled makes its way through the woods.

Cat hears howls and laughs, and barks and sighs as the forest seems packed with living, wild things. Soon, an orange light

91

Exhaust from the Tin Woods

shines in the distance. As it grows, the trapper's cabin appears as the glow from the hearth leads the way.

The sled stops in front of the modest, single room log cabin.

The first man leaps off the sled, towards machines atop of poles planted into the ground. He pulls a string on each, enlivening the motor that produces a strange, steady grinding noise. "The barrier is set," he says. "Please get inside. We will camp here for the night and get you back to Allbrung in the morning. I'm sorry, we can't return you tonight. The woods have turned insane."

Cat enters first, greeted by two other men. The men are all middle-aged: they'd be her parents' age if she ever knew her mother or father. The pair that rescued them came in behind them, removing their fur caps and scarves.

The one who seems to know the dogs is the eldest of the four: a lean man with a gentleman's moustache, hazel eyes, and a luddmunster style haircut. His eyes widen, betraying a look of worry. "Everyone fair to well?" he asks her and Brambley.

"Good," Cat says and smiles. "Thank you."

"What machines did you plant in front of the house?" Brambley asks.

"A simple invention that spooks animals who are the work of a skin seamstress. It rattles their stitching and bindings," the man with the moustache says. "Sewing together different materials is fine for Mary Shelley, but it never quite works. Nature is a much better harmonizer. The machines vibrate and make the most of their … shoddy workmanship."

A severe looking man with fire red hair and blue eyes worthy of a lizard, asks Cat, "Did any of them bite you?"

"No," Cat says. "They sure wanted to."

"They are wrong. Miscreants to the laws of science," the lizard man says. He grins, and a sudden, overwhelming kindness glows from the face of this otherwise ugly man. "I hope you are the one called 'Cat'."

"I am," she says. "You've heard of me?"

"You are one of Allbrung's star pupils. The name is Phillip Spricket. You've met the man with the dogs, Thomas Braxbury?"

Thomas takes off his leather gloves and shakes the hand of

Exhaust from the Tin Woods

Brambley. The younger men step forward. Braxbury wiggles his moustache and points to them. "Timothy Winch, Seane Cogg. Welcome. Please, you are amongst friends."

"Are you friends of Allbrung?" Brambley asks.

"Of course. We share many of the same notions and philosophies. We just disagree in the application of those principles," Braxbury says.

"We are Mertonites, non-violent interventionists for the sake of all things that prattle."

"So you've come here to seek out Allbrung?"

"How do you know we're not from the Woods, not Native to Canada?" Spricket asks with a thin smile.

"Well," Brambley says, stepping forward. "Your outfits have been outfitted by a haberdashery. The material is too thin, so you're wearing multiple layers. It's obvious they were not sewn and tailored in Canada. Plus, your haircuts are London and worthy of a Gentleman's Club, not cut by a servant or wife over a kitchen floor … as is the case by almost all of the styles of Alberta."

Braxbury grins. "Good. You must be Brambley, the other star," he says. "Well, if you two don't mind, we'll spend the night together. Let the woods go mad. We'll be safe in here. In the morning, the gods shall reclaim the woods and the chain of being restored."

"Time to quote King Lear?" Spricket asks.

"No," Braxbury says.

He walks over to the stove, pours three cups of tea. "We are Mertonites. We seek to help. That's all we ever really want to do. Allbrung helps, certainly, but in his own way. We are not in opposition, just … running in different directions."

"So is he, what brings you to the Woods[59]? To Canada?" asks Brambley.

"Oh, our lives would be so much easier if all we had to do was find Allbrung. No, we're not after the like-minded but the opposed, the dispossessed."

"And who's that?" asks Cat.

"The bear, for starters. The wolves with human faces. And

---

[59] Northern Canada

the force behind the forest going mad. If you look out the window, you'll see something terribly wrong," Spricket says.

"How much does Allbrung talk to you? Does he tell you about the others? Those who worked alongside him in London?" Cogg asks, stepping slowly closer to Cat. He is nervous looking as if he could-at-any-moment scream, spit, shout, or do violence.

"No," Cat says and shudders. *'Am I really that cold?'*

"Does he say anything to you about the Infinity Device?" he asks.

She shakes her head.

He takes another step. "Or its sister, the Savior Machine?" Another step.

She feels his hot breath on her. "Last question: have you ever heard this simple name? A name that will be the crank of a very, very deep well? Have you heard the name Rengulfton?"

"I don't know that name."

"Back away Cogg," Braxbury says in a low, paternal tone. "She knows little mainly because she's here to learn how machines can help the world. Rengulfton ... is another aim."

"Is the bear Rengulfton?" Brambley asks.

The four Mertonites turn, with mouths open.

"Possibly," Braxbury says for the four. "That is the working theory. How – how did you –"

"The wolves look to the bear as the head alpha, yet they're another species. That s, unless, the human in the wolf recognizes the human in the bear. So, the human sewn into the bear, maybe this fellow you have mentioned. If there ever were a villain, it would be the bear. Plus, he spoke to us."

"The bear speaks?" Spricket asks. "What did he say?"

"We were all going to die, or something to that effect." Brambley shrugs. "I don't know. If I had time to sleep on it and a good think, I would be able to pick up more. Really, my mind was on getting to Cat."

"Right," Braxbury says, in a stun from Brambley's deduction. "Best work on that. A good sleep. The four of us shall be on the porch. With blankets, a fire, and our coats, we shall be warm. Cat and you shall share the bed. Share the blankets, your body temperatures shall keep you comfortable throughout the night."

Exhaust from the Tin Woods

"Excuse me?" Brambley says. "That is entirely indecent. There is no way we are to share a bed, unwed and –"

"Well, there's no way any of us will get in bed with her. I'm old enough to be her grandfather or grand-uncle. No, she must share a bed for survival sake, and it must be you."

"But it is unchristian and wrong and –"

"So, you'd let the poor girl freeze to death?" Braxbury's face turns red. "By the blood, Queen Victoria has really made your brain a heaping wreck!"

Brambley steps back; Cat can barely contain her laughter.

"Is that a new expression?" Brambley asks to no one in particular, looking upwards to the heavens. The four pull out blankets, a bottle of scotch, pillows, and quickly leave the young people to the bed.

Cat, within one swift move, disrobes to her underwear. "Save your shirt and coat; we'll put them on top of the blankets. Skin-on-skin will be the warmest."

Brambley starts shaking and stammering meaningless gibberish.

"Come now, I must not be such a terrible creature to cuddle up with," she says with a grin.

"You are the most beautiful woman I have ever known," Brambley shouts. "That is the problem."

"It could be fun."

"My sense of pleasure is not the issue, but propriety. I shall not besmirch your honor, good woman."

"Who says I'm a good woman," she says as she playfully crosses her ankle. "Listen, I shall make a deal. As much as I'd like to, I shall not make any flirting remarks or advances or do anything untoward. We shall be mates, surviving the night. Nothing more."

Brambley takes off his shirt.

"Do you mean that? That I'm a beautiful woman?" she asks.

"Yes," Brambley says in a weak croak. "Your beauty drives me mad."

"Good to know," she says and slips into the covers of the bed. "Come to bed. Lay our coats and clothing on top." Brambley does so and gets into the bed. "And this madness I stir, that isn't

95

Exhaust from the Tin Woods

enough for you, is it?"

"If I shall love, it will be in companionship and not pleasure. I am sorry, it is my Christian duty that demands it to be so."

He wraps his arm around her. Soon they are warm.

"You went out into the night to save me. You do so much for me. I feel beautiful around you, Brambley. Thank you."

He kisses her on the forehead.

"Thank you, Brambley. Thank you for obeying the moment."

With that, he closes his eyes. He waits for a while and then seeks to adjust himself.

"Asleep?" Cat asks.

"Hardly."

Cat places her cheek on his chest. She is nearly hugging him under the covers. "Ever been this close to a woman before?"

"Hardly," he croaks.

She can feel his warmth. It is neither causing her to want to kiss or any burning with her, but it feels nice. Like a warm blanket on a cold night. She then notices that she is no longer shaking.

How terrified was I? She wonders to herself. When she closes her eyes, she can still see the bear with the human face as an after-image in her eyes.

She really, really wanted to scream. She's never felt that before. Living through knife fights and muggings and drunken men ludwigged[60]off their own rage and violence … those moments did nothing to her. But the bear … that was a horrible, screaming moment.

"You smell nice," she says to Brambley. "Like high-class pipe smoke."

"Pipe smoke? I've never heard that before. I should wash up." He says.

"Please don't … I mean, eventually, you'll need to wash, I guess."

"Do you know any stories?"

"Why?" she asks.

---

[60] crazy

Exhaust from the Tin Woods

"You've been everywhere and done everything. I'd figure you could spin a yarn."

She thinks. "I'm terrible, quite bad, at reliving my stories. I have moments, but they don't become stories. That's awful, isn't it?"

"I should think not," he says. "Perhaps it's just a skill you've never learned, or had a chance to perfect."

"I think I shall make that skill with you."

She closes her eyes as she goes to sleep. Soon, she hears herself snore seconds before she falls off into dreamland.

Chapter Four
March 1895

Shweta smiles and Cat isn't too sure how to take such a grin.

"If you have noticed, I was missing from the last two days of our shop time," Shweta says in pitch perfect Cambridge English. "And so were you," she says to Joane.

"I've been at work in the smithy. Maillory needed some heavy metal bent, and I wanted to pick up the technique to work with brass," Joane says. "I've been missing. How's the shop been?" she asks Cat.

Joane whistles. "I've been really building up some great muscles. I've … never been worked like this before. The smithy is my second home," Joane says. She then looks to Cat. "Please, do tell: how is the main shop?"

"Patrick, Maillory, and Beattrixx have kept to themselves. We've been learning how to work with tubes and air compression. Meanwhile, Brambley and I have been getting along famously. He's really far too clever for his own good." Cat hears the two ladies giggle. "He's been a perfect gentleman, which is a damnable shame. Worst, that little church has asked him to preach for the next three Sundays."

Shweta turns to a room which Cat and Joane have never been in, located just below the auxiliary stairs. As they enter, there's a small, square hole on the floor, with a ladder leading downward into a pitch-black room.

"I think you would make a splendid minister's wife," Joane says. "You could wear all black, cover your head always, and learn to play hymns on the piano."

"Say that again, and I'll slit your throat," Cat says with a grin.

"That is an excellent skill to have as a minister's wife. Throw in knife tossing, it would be perfect."

They make their way down the ladder with one of Allbrung's automatic gas lights turning on, filling the stone, square room with light. The light reveals a series of ropes horizontally

Exhaust from the Tin Woods

hung across the room, in differing levels. It reminds Cat of riggings on a ship.

Shweta crosses the room and fetches three large, heavy looking gowns.

"Beattrixx didn't want to try this and I didn't dare approach Maillory. You've been my two primary candidates for this. Plus, put these on. One size fits all," Shweta says.

The three girls climb into the gowns that cover the shoulders, the arms, and hang all the way down to their feet. The gowns are extremely heavy, with an equal distribution of weight.

"Now, your body is connected to your mind which is connected to your spirit. Everything in harmony. The greater the strength, the more you can work. So, here is our gymnasium."

Shweta climbs one of the ropes. Her bare feet grapple a rope each, straddling for balance. The dress opens up, not the least constrictive. Just very heavy. Shweta stands, balancing for about five minutes until her face shakes, turning red. She gives in and jumps to the floor.

"Now, your turn," she says, pointing to Cat.

Cat tries this and finds it a lot more difficult than it appeared when Shweta performed her balance. Immediately, her thighs and stomach and ankles are on fire, burning with intense weakness. She lasts about a minute before she jumps down, panting for breath.

Joane lasts even less. When she finishes, she sinks to her knees. "All right," she says in her thick, French accent. "The challenge has been given. This is the task before us: master these ropes. Are you in?"

"Of course, and by master, you mean we must stay on the ropes as long as possible?" Cat asks. She looks over to Shweta, and she is beaming. Shweta nods. "I'm sure there's a level two, where we learn to do dances and flips and all of that?" Another nod. "Is there anything for the arms?"

The answer is "Yes." They experience a series of hangs, crawls, and lifts. They return to the standing of ropes, learning how not to shake and keep their balance.

At the end of their forty-minute session, Joane and Cat are grabbing the burn and ache in their stomachs. "Are we on for tomorrow?" Cat asks.

"Give it two days. And then we return to the ropes," Shweta says as she climbs the ladder.

"So, should we tell the boys?" Cat asks.

"No," Joane says in a gasp. "I need an advantage over Patrick."

Cat raises her right eyebrow. "My dear, you've either said too much or not enough."

.....

Allbrung gives a note to Cat and Brambley to meet him, after breakfast, in his office. They travel to the office together, fearing they might get lost in the long, turning halls of Mercyminster.

They enter to find the old man shirtless, throwing black sponges onto his chest. He is doing so carefully and slowly as if to simulate something. He seems to be happy as if a theory is being proved and yet Cat cannot tell what he's trying to demonstrate: that black sponges feel wet? They fall when they strike? That black is wetter than yellow?

The old man turns to them and smiles. "Sorry, science. Let me put on my shirt, and we can talk about my friends, the Mertonites."

The old man steps into his secret room and a few seconds later emerges with a shirt and vest and tie. "Now," he says. "A week ago, you were rescued by the Mertonites. You spent a night with them, and the next morning, they sent you back here safe and sound."

"Should we be concerned the Mertonites are here?" Brambley asks.

Suddenly, Cat picks up on something: Brambley sees something wrong.

"Yes and no," the old man says as he slowly takes a seat in his chair. "The Mertonites are amazing and good and wonderful men. I trained all of them, they are former students of mine. They rescue people. They like doing that. They also like wandering around, fixing problems and people and creating new gadgets for communities. Those are the four, the only ones in the world. Some say the idea of the Mertonites come from another world, something

Exhaust from the Tin Woods

like dimensional travel … but that is legend and nothing based upon science." He looks to Cat. "The Mertonites are so good, you see."

"Then?" she asks.

"But they only go where there is trouble, which is why they are here, in Grouard. Why? I fear they know something is growing foul in the woods. I am sorry, the Woods." Answers the old man.

"They asked me if I knew of someone. Rengulfton? They think he's turned himself into a bear?" replies Cat.

"I would not put it past him, but I need evidence first. Empiricism has a use. Let us not assume he is the villain until we have proof." Responds Allbrung.

"Why?"

"If you visit a doctor, he will usually go through all of the symptoms and then look at what could be the matter. Does he pick the likeliest problem first as his diagnosis? No. He often times picks the easiest. Why? Shorter house call, quicker prognosis. A patient might have Scarlet Fever, but he will first test for allergies. For if the patient has Scarlet Fever, they will burn all of his clothing and bedding; if an allergy, a simple pill may suffice. If it is indeed Rengulfton, we may have to burn down everything to find a cure. And if he can turn himself into a bear, doubly so."

"So, they call themselves non-violent interventionists. Is that what you are?"

"No, that is where we part ways. I am non-violent, but I would never call myself an interventionist. Everything I do is with permission, in harmony. They offer no such civility. The night they rescued you, they did not ask for your permission: that is how they function."

"There was little talk: a sled arrived, and we jumped in." Replied Brambley.

"Bad point. Still trying to experiment with metaphors about the Mertonites. Suffice it to say, they are not me and I am not them, despite how much we like each other."

"Should we be worried about what's happening in the woods?" asks Cat.

"No," Allbrung says without emotion. "All of us should be terrified. There is a wound in the Woods. I do not know where it is

Exhaust from the Tin Woods

and it is bleeding out evil. Most afternoons, while you work in your shops, I wander the woods to find what is amiss. Nothing. Only last week, when the Mertonites brought you back, did I have a clear account of what is happening. The woods in the Woods are choking on a sick, poisonous exhaust. And I would like your help in finding out what is going on out there."

"Sure," Cat says. She grins to Brambley.

He strokes her bare shoulder.

"Good. Please, do not keep your adventures a secret from the other students. Tell them about the steam wolves and the bear and all of the evil. Tell them that their teacher is scared and no one is safe, ever. And please, above all, tell them they are not safe anywhere they go and that Mercyminster, in all of its grandeur, may not protect them. I insist, tell them everything."

"Are you being sarcastic?" Brambley asks.

"I am never sarcastic. Tell them … everything. The more minds we have on this problem, ingenuity will be close at hand."

"Tell them they're not safe? Are you seeing gray?"

"Lots of it. Tell them." Commands Allbrung.

They visit a bit more and then leave for the morning's lectures. After lunch they go to their workstations to labor over their latest invention Allbrung assigned them to build a breathing apparatus made strictly out of metal. They all work with their mini kilns and their workstations.

As they labored, Cat heard Maillory call out to Brambley. "You're a good preacher," she says.

"Thank you." Brambley says. "That means a lot. I've heard of your father, and he is a preacher as well."

"He does his best. He practices 30 hours a week for his six sermons. All of his work is centered around the pulpit. And yet, you get up there and preach with the same power. You ought to be commended."

Silence follows until Brambley breaks it. He is fiddling with a set of small, metal tubes on his table. "What's it like, going to church every week of your life? Living at a church?"

"It's not as bad as most Londoners would think," her voice replies in a near song. "Growing up, everyone knows you. Recognizes you. It is a bit like royalty, being related to the minister.

Exhaust from the Tin Woods

I was given toys for Christmas by those of the congregation, we vacationed in a cabin around Scotland owned by a parishioner, and I was given classes in the local school for free. It was fantastic. I had quite a happy childhood.

"You see, a lot of important people attended my father's London church. A great many industrialists came and contributed to the building, so it drew in a lot of Londoners who came to be inspired by the beauty of the church. We have a pipe organ, a choir, and a summer orchestra. Politicians would often speak at our church, seeing my father's endorsement as key to their election. The world may have moved on from religion, but you'd never know that by stepping inside my father's church."

Cat is confused. Every word Maillory says, Cat is reading Brambley's reaction. His eyes narrow, his hands drop things, his whole back is straight and tight. Once, he shakes his head. She would expect this from Beattrix – who would love to set fire to every single church in the Woods for being Mexician – but not Brambley.

"And you must have done a lot for the poor?" he asks.

"Some. Mainly, he offered spiritual direction to anyone who would come to his church. Other than that, it was a massive undertaking to be as nice as they were and to have the emotional impact they did. Alas, one has to have priorities with one's efforts. And didn't Jesus say the poor will always be with us?"

"He did, but I don't think His intention was that of a dare," Brambley says, and Cat hears Beattrixx snort in a stifled laugh. "And you, how were you inspired by your father's church?"

"It was so ... big. It was hard not to be inspired. Those who went became big, by association. You got the idea that God's Kingdom is very big because, look, his house is so amazing. That is why it is a wonder that you can preach in such a dingy, cramped, small church and still sell the idea that God is so big. Hats off to you, Brambley."

This is the first time Brambley smiles at Maillory's voice underneath him. "Thank you very much. Your encouragement is one of kindness."

This ends the conversation for Brambley, who went back to work. However, Cat notices something during the rest of their work hours: his eyes shoot to her whenever he seems to believe she's not watching him. He does so with a sly air about him, thinking he's sneaking peaks and gawks. She is catching him every time ... and doesn't mind doing so.

At the end of the day, they stand in line at the floor level for Allbrung to inspect their creations. Patrick invents a "pocket breather" that can give someone one minute of underwater air. Beattrixx invents a stretching arm to reach across the room for those infirmed to a bed or chair. Maillory makes a breathing pipe, but decorative for the high society types. Shweta offers an exchange system so there can be a replacement of tanks without the flow of air being lost. And Brambley creates valves, for different air flows and needs.

"But yours is the handiest," Allbrung tells Cat. "It is portable and has its own engine, so one does not have to be tied down to a generator. Excellent."

"It's for those needing oxygen while out in the bush."

"As well," Allbrung says to the group. "It is designed for cold weather."

"Why?" Maillory shoots to the group. "Most of our buyers are going to be in London. Why should we winterize anything we do?"

"So that the people of the Woods can have our inventions first. We build for them. If the rest of the world is interested, so be it. Always have a face attached to your project," Allbrung says and raises his hand in the air for a dramatic flair. "Good work. Yes, very good to one and all."

Maillory sneers quickly in the direction of Cat. So fast, only Cat picks up on the sour glance.

That evening, the students dress for dinner. As Cat dresses, she shares the space with Joane who is in the throes of a giggling, laughing, sparring chat with Patrick on the other side. The rest of the room is silent as this loud, fire charged exchange occurs. Joane dresses as fast as she can, finding Patrick already waiting for her outside of their divider. When she sees him, the two leave before the rest of the group are ready, which is a break from tradition, as everyone usually goes together.

When the pair leaves, Cat asks in a loud voice, "Brambley,

Exhaust from the Tin Woods

what just happened?"

"I'm not sure," Brambley says. "I don't even understand what they were talking about. It reminded me of a verbatim transcript taken from an opium den in Cardiff."

"And you've read such transcripts?" Cat asks.

"I don't need to, not now. And I imagine it's a foretaste of what awaits all of us at dinner." Shweta laughs. "Beattrixx, your table is next to them. Is this what you've endured?"

"No, it has been quiet," she says. "They've been in the main smithy the whole day." Cat can't help but laugh. "No, my dear: it is not what you think. Moses has been with them, and if you know him, he is without mercy."

Part of the reason Shweta's gymnasium appealed so much to Cat, is so she can survive and endure the smithy under Moses' direction. "Hot and horrible" is how she describes the time. Sore, injured, and depleted is usually how he leaves her, as an instructor, with all of the wood and hammering and pushing and sculpting over the fire.

"How dare they have any energy left to smile, let alone giggle and cackle like two school children," Beattrixx says as she steps away from her vanity. She is wearing a bodice made of chain mail, a black leather cape, and a gown made of black fur.

"How do you have so many dresses?" Cat asks, seeing the outfit made perfect by her placing a gentleman's top hat on her head.

"My trick? I don't own any clothes whatsoever." Her eyes flash mischievously. "Let me show you."

As Cat steps behind her vanity, she sees a portable trunk exploding into several fold-away drawers and compartments. "Simply, I mix, and I match: making outfits. Everything is temporary, everything can be put away. It takes a little longer to dress, but it's worth it, I think. This bodice and these gloves came out last week, during our trip to town: but they were entirely different."

"How do you match?"

"Simple. I wear mostly black or anything that goes with black. Keeping it one color allows my wardrobe to be versatile. Later in the week, I was going to wear the bodice and cape for a hike through the woods. I have several parts to outfits, but decide in the morning what I shall work in and what I shall wear for dinner."

"You're brilliant," Cat says.

"No, I'm a posh pony. I have come here to be brilliant."

The girls leave for the dining room, trailed by Brambley. Suk and Moses are already sitting when they arrive; Joane and Patrick come in later, taking a slight detour from the bedroom to the dining room. Patrick sits on the side of the men, turning his attention to Brambley.

Moses points to Brambley. "Hey, Pastor! What is today's Word from the Lord?" he asks this with a smile.

"Not sure," Brambley says with a shrug.

"Then get sure. Get on the road to find out," the big man says with a smile.

"I am famished. How are you doing?" Cat asks.

"Good. I'm glad we're done with this unit on tube and compressed air. I'd like to get into something that's a bit more local," Brambley says. Brambley stares at Patrick.

Cat studies Brambley. '*What does he see?*' she thinks.

Brambley rarely misses anything, and when he studies someone, his sherlucking ability is pretty keen. Cat holds this thought to ask him later, perhaps in the scant private moments she has with him.

Allbrung comes out with a roast and a plate full of vegetables. Shweta fills up on vegetables. The gentlemen fill up on meat, and Cat finds herself sampling a bit of everything. On the streets, back in her past, she could live off a discarded roll or half a cup of cabbage soup; now, at Mercyminster, she eats three meals a day that would have lasted her all week. She did not become larger with this new diet, only stronger. Plus, the rope exercises brought a new level of hunger and muscle to her life.

"Moses," Joane asks in the middle of dinner. "Have you worked with a lot of women as a blacksmith?"

The large man laughs a chortle that almost shakes the iron dining table. "No, ma'am. No. In growing up, the women worked in the house, and the men worked outside. Some in the smithy, some in fields, and some with the animals."

"If women wanted to work in the smithy, would they be

Exhaust from the Tin Woods

allowed?" Joane asks.

"No," Moses says with his grin dropping. "They can't. That's the thing about being a slave. It's someone else telling you what you can and can't do. Even if you're good at something, you're told to do something else because it matches the whims of the master."

"Slavery is wrong, all agreed," Maillory says, entering into the conversation. "But one could make the argument for any leader, really. Someone has to have the power, don't they? I mean, that's the Pickled Pete of society. For every White Hell[61], there must be a ruling family who is in charge."

"There must be?" Moses asks.

"Power must belong to someone," Maillory says, mostly to the group.

"I guess I don't like slavery in any form, in any way. So when I see you, a Held Companion, all frilly and full of those dresses and then I see you get all strong, all smoky, and all crazy tired in the smithy … it's my way of ending slavery."

"Sounds more like slavery to me," Maillory says into her napkin.

"The difference between the smiths back at the State and Confederation and here, in the land of Common Wealthies, is that you don't have to come to this smithy. You can choose to do something else, and it's … all right." Moses laughs again. "And for the record, I can't keep Joane out of that smithy. Even when I got work that takes me someplace else, she's still there. I used to think it was my kind manner and soft voice she visited. No. It's that hard work."

Cat sees Brambley quickly shoot a look to Patrick. Patrick freezes as if the room ran out of oxygen. Cat smiles, looking over to Shweta who sees the same thing.

They don't talk about much else. Mostly about Allbrung's theories. Cat later shares with Brambley, "Why didn't we talk about what's on everyone's mind? That there's a killer bear outside?"

"Because we're mostly British," Brambley says with a small laugh. "I'm sure we will. Sometime."

---

[61] cotton, Textile Factory

Exhaust from the Tin Woods

"When?"

"More than likely, when we see the bear again, and he's chasing us through the woods. Mostly it will be in the moment."

The subject of the smithy came up again, over dessert. Suk, when serving the bowls of iced cream, mentioned to Beatrixx, "I've heard of farming communities, up north of us, where the labor is divided between men and women, without much distinction."

"That's just afternoonified[62]," Maillory croaks.

"Maybe more out of need," Beatrixx says. "I mean, if we're Robinson Crusoe on a deserted island and there's only us. Or worst, say all of the men got sick. Someone would have to fish, collect the coconuts, and build the shelter. Banging the dust out of the rugs would be the least of our worries."

"The Tin Woods[63] shall disciple you yet," Dr. Allbrung says, and that's all he says, as he digs into his iced cream.

After dinner, the ladies leave to the parlor, and the men stay back. Cat glances back at Brambley, feeling this separation of the sexes is unnatural, and his face matches what she feels.

In the parlor, Beattrixx turns to Joane. "Out with it," she demands. "Tell me, Joane. What is this mad, frenetic magnetism between you and Patrick? It's crazy blue!"

"My dear Beattrixx, whatever do you mean? There is nothing between us. Absolutely nothing," she says, her accent thick and proper.

"You are such a liar," Beattrixx says and the statement, Cat figures, is full of playfulness and is nowhere near the affront it could be from anyone else.

"Now, let her be," Maillory says. "She would like to maintain propriety."

"Damn propriety. You want to both crawl on top of each other, tear each other's clothing off, and make passionate love ending in a howl at the moon!"

"There is nothing," Joane says, now sternly.

"You, French minx! How can you not feel it?"

---

[62] something not smart

[63] Northern Canada

Exhaust from the Tin Woods

No longer casual or stern, Joane's eyes glass and tremble. A quiver in her lower lip quickly shows, silencing the room. "There is nothing. Really. Nor will there ever be." She clears her throat and regains her composure. "Cat, can you play something? Please? Music helps with the digestion."

They drop the topic.

.....

A week later, a stranger enters the shop accompanied by Suk and Allbrung.

At first, Brambley doesn't recognize him until he repels down from his floating shop and sees him to be the town constable. His eyes brighten upon the sight of Brambley. "Good afternoon, Pastor," he says with a bow. Then his eyes scan the other floating platforms as if the sight of Brambley is not enough.

"Welcome to Mercyminster. I hope there isn't a problem," Brambley says kindly.

"There is. A big problem." Again, the Constable is scanning the room. His wild appearance to Brambley is of a feral wolf. "But it isn't your problem. I'm here to see if Allbrung can help."

"I cannot," Allbrung says. "But my students might figure out a way to help you, to ensure no one would get hurt."

The Constable stops searching and looks to Brambley. "The other night, a couple of women were attacked by what I can tell were 'Patchwork Men'. Like the ones who attacked some of your girls, when you first arrived in our town. Sadly, our girls were not so lucky." He clears his throat as his voice slightly weakens. "Our town has never seen technology like this before. Sure, we've seen the metal hand or an odd lurkjerker, but these men are steamies seeing gray! Straight from London, in the hub of all things metal. This is straight from the rags or radio or the zeppelins."

"How many lurkjerkers?"

"There were five. They live, as far as we can tell, in the woods. They know where young women can be found, often times striking and then vanishing. Built into them are their knives, guns, and other tools. They seem to have only one purpose: removing virtue from girls. They raided the town last night, and all of their victims did not survive."

Exhaust from the Tin Woods

Brambley looks up to think, his head spinning.

"He's doing that thing again, with his brain," Cat suddenly says overhead.

Allbrung laughs. "Based on the scant information you have given him, he's going to figure out something," Allbrung says. "What do you think?"

"They don't live in the woods, but they have a base in the woods. A cabin, a cave: somewhere indoors where their parts can be replaced and serviced. You said it 'they seem to have one purpose'. You're quite right. My guess is that they are pumped with a load of medication and hormones, increasing their sexual appetites to a frenzy. When they attacked Beattrixx, it was mad and crazed and was absent from any plan or discretion. Wherever they come from, they are loaded with weapons and armor, pumped full of aphrodisiacs, and then let loose on the town for the purpose of destruction."

"Why?"

"That cannot be figured out by what you've said to me. But these men come from some factory that seeks to distribute chaos and calamity upon your town," Brambley says and looks to Allbrung. "Am I close?"

"I would have made a connection between the bear and these 'Patchwork Men', but other than that … you are right." He crossed his arms. "What I would like to do, based on all said, is to create a non-lethal device that stops them. Something that can immobilize monsterations of their body. Something to freeze, stop, and arrest them. But they cannot be hurt and, consequently, no one else. When the Constable returns tomorrow for lunch, you will present something to him. That is all."

He leaves with the Constable. As soon as the door shuts, Brambley is surrounded by the zip of rope as the students surround him. Brambley's eyes go to Cat first. "Any ideas?"

"A walking bear trap, that hunts and chases after steamies?" she puts forth.

"It must be a trap that doesn't hurt them or anyone else," Shweta says.

"It must collect all of them at once or each one quick enough, so they don't leave, take a hostage, and try to gain leverage," Patrick says. "This is a real Pickled Pete."

"Could we lure them with girls and knock them out?" Maillory asks.

"Who would be bait?" Cat asks.

"You?"

"Could we design a trap that only hurts them slightly? I really don't like these men and feel it is a great inequity to the cosmos not to inflict some damage," Beattrixx says. She reads Shweta's stern look. "I am only saying."

Patrick looks to Brambley. "The first day we all met, excluding Beattrixx, you demonstrated the ability to pick up Allbrung's pen from his pocket without lifting a finger. How did you do that?"

"While I lived in the Foundation, it was an experiment that I haven't had the time to pursue." Simply, Brambley learns how to generate a precise sound that the human ear cannot comprehend. Through harmonic manipulation, he can create a dense field with dust particles that can press against and lift objects.

"It's imprecise," Brambley says. "I can't control it. You saw what it did to the pen."

"That's because it's a pen. And your engine was much too small. Perhaps if we built a mammoth engine, we could generate a field ... a net ... that would surround these lurkjerkers. Pin them down."

"But we'll need more than dust particles. They can just –"

"Ball bearings," Cat says, following Patrick's line of thinking. "Sacks and sacks of metal ball bearings. Scatter them in a field. We build a generator and your machine. When they come, they shall be surrounded by a dome of ball bearings. With a hole on top for air, the engine will run and run and run until we come."

"What will trip up the trap?"

"Bait," Maillory says. "Us girls." She points all around. "We."

"And we boys shall watch them and turn on the machine," Patrick says. His voice betrays a sharp excitement.

"Let's get to work," Brambley says, and it is decided.

They go to their stations. Cat and Brambley work on the controls, Beattrixx on the motor, Maillory on the box, so it is

Exhaust from the Tin Woods

metalmanced to blend into the woods, Shweta builds the internal kiln, and Joane along with Patrick gather wood and ball bearings. After working well into the night and all of the morning, the machine is working to the group's satisfaction an hour before lunch.

The Constable arrives, and Patrick gives a demonstration. "So here is the idea," he begins with a bravado that belongs under the big dome of a circus. "How can we capture and detain a miscreant without harming them? Answer: sonic technology."

They stand in the warm spot on the outdoor grounds, in between the steam of the shop and the heat of the smithy. Coming around the corner is Joane, carrying a pink parasol from Paris and she is looking up, pantomiming a damsel soon to be in distress. She shuffles slowly over the warm, dry stone steps.

"Behold, our heroine. Noble and fair Joane," Patrick trumpets. "She is unaware her life is in grand peril!"

Cat, from the other side, emerges, wearing a pot on her hand, a wrench for a hand, and Brambley's oilskin jacket over herself. She is hunched and growls, smiling at the innocent Joane.

"Is this drama entirely appropriate?" the Constable asks.

"I am afraid it is," Patrick says in a less elevated voice. "Collectively, we have all had the hours of sleep for one grown man. Divided between the seven of us, our energy is depleted, and we are, indeed, wonky. This is the closest thing to a straight answer you shall get from the sleep starved."

Cat discovers the fair Joane and snarls in delight. "Oh no," Patrick pronounces. "The fair Joane is in the clutches of this villain! Who shall rescue her? Behold, sound shall be her savior!"

The Constable furls his brow.

Brambley steps out of the shop. He holds a large radio transmitter looking device that requires Brambley to pump with his foot to power. For a second, a slight hum sounds but soon turns silent. Silently, like ghosts, billions of ball bearings rise from the snow, the yellowed grass, and the stone. Within moments, they whiz through the air and form a black, solid igloo around Cat, and the miscreant. Like glue, they are together and seem to be permanent.

"Until we shut off the machine, the villainess is trapped," Patrick says with a flourish of his hands. "The waves, naked to the human ear, have excited the particles and caused them to bond. Sonic waves now travel, like a knitting needle and thread, amongst the ball bearings, forming a tight weave. Behold," he shouts to Cat. "Villain, kick your way out!"

She cannot.

The Constable grins in the direction of Allbrung. "Well done. What is the plan?"

"We shall," Brambley says, turning off the machine. "Go into the woods to a designated spot. The girls shall locate the lurkjerkers and give them a chase. Once in the zone of the net, we'll flip it on, and someone will fetch you to make the arrest."

"Will it be that easy?" the Constable asks.

"Why not?" Patrick asks with a smile. The ball bearings collapse, raining on Cat. They strike her and roll off, giving the ease of a quick rain shower.

After lunch, they commit their plan.

The boys leave first. Patrick looks for the horse drawn carriage, finding it without the horses or harnesses. He calls out to Brambley, a few steps behind him, "We seem to be missing a way to get the machine out to the woods."

At that moment, Suk arrives outside the carriage house riding a mini-dirigible pulled by a yoke and two horses. The floating device is almost entirely balloons, with a small compartment big enough to carry the machine. There is a small bench to pilot the craft, just enough for Suk to sit and drive the horses.

"I thought this would do. This is an invention I made when I came here as a student," Suk says. "You're going to have to walk. Too much weight. You're still heavy from city food."

"A good turn would be splendid," Patrick says. He slaps the back of Brambley. "You know where to go?"

"Cavendish Meadow," Suk says. "It's a name given by one of Allbrung's first students. There's a clearing from here to the meadow, so we should be okay. Rough grounds, but little trees in the way which is perfect for this present contraption." He laughs. "I can't make up my mind if this is a good idea or not."

"Does it have to be a good idea for it to work?" Patrick asks.

Exhaust from the Tin Woods

Suk laughs even more, if not just a polite chuckle. He shakes his head as he urges the horses to walk with the tip of his whip. "You have a poet's logic. I'll be blunt, this might get all of the women raped. I hope not. But it might."

The floating, truncated zeppelin floats above the brush, snow, and unsteady ground of the woods. Pulled by the horses, it is without wheels. The burden light, the yoke is easy as the hydrogen carries most of the weight. Suk looks regal, proud as he wears his red and black coachman's coat with his extended tall top hat.

Brambley and Patrick trail behind, doing their best to keep up with the horses' trot. Within fifteen minutes, they reach Cavendish Meadow.

"Is it pretty in the summer?" Patrick asks, gesturing to the expanse of flat.

"The land looks like a half-stripped carcass, bones, and sinews exposed in the prairie," Suk says, climbing down the flying coach's rope ladder. "No, it's not pretty. The Woods are metalmanced for snow. Anything short of snow gives the land a luddmunstered mess."

"A compliant view, seeing how in Alberta it is covered with snow eight months of the year," Patrick says with a grin as he pops open the latch to get to their device. "What should we call this thing?"

"Steamies box," Brambley says. "I'd hate for it to be used for any offensive purpose, so the name might keep it to just law enforcement."

"You know if Her Majesty's Navy ever got this they'd turn it into a weapon. The application is screaming to do damage on the world." Patrick turned to Suk. "Ever see a device made for peace, yet used in war?"

"All the time. Spoons make great eye pokers and a Bible, thrown from a great height, can knock a man senseless. Tools do not beget peace." Suk flashed his eyes. "An inventor can't be credited for the glory or carnage of his invention. That's what I think. And if you ask Allbrung, he would vehemently disagree with me." He shrugs as he stretches after the strenuous ride. "Enough philosophy since our age is allergic to deep thinking. Need help setting up the … Steamies box?"

114

Exhaust from the Tin Woods

Brambley didn't need help, but he enjoyed the company of the two men hunched over his device, spectating his work. Patrick and Suk would stare, wide-eyed, as Brambley's gloved hands floated and swirled over the box, pulling a nob or winding a wire along the way. Within a few moments, the apparatus is fully operational. The three men then pick up sacks of ball bearings and scatter them across Cavendish Meadow.

"So, do you agree with Allbrung in all of his philosophies?" Patrick asks Brambley.

"I don't understand him. I mean, he keeps us busy far more than lecturing us. In fact, the only time he is teaching is to show us how to make things. He would make a miserable minister."

"Or an excellent one," Patrick says. He pulls out a pipe and places it in his mouth. "Since we're in the Colonies, I'm thinking of taking up smoking. Tobacco seems so … Common Wealthy. I'm looking for a vice. Well, I mean a public one. I think my list is full for private vices."

"I never knew one could pick their vices; rather, I thought vices picked you."

"Before I came, I cataloged all of my virtues and vices. Shaped by an American writer named Franklin, I wrote down everything I did good and everything I did that was not so posh. I even wrote down when I thought about virtues and vices. I thought, you know, get a head start and a jump. And between you and me, I thought I could get a couple more virtues in my book if they were thought about. The problem was that I filled up my vices more than my virtues. In fact, after one week, there was a solid, black block. The vices got drowned out; I couldn't distinguish one from the other. All I saw was that I had a lot."

"And why did you undertake such a catalog?"

"To master oneself. I figured if I cataloged everything, thoroughly and scientifically, I could then get leverage over my vices. Plus, I could systematically introduce new virtues."

"What were the most common of your virtues?"

"Confidence, willful learning, piety, and passion. I scored very high on honesty," Patrick says.

"No doubt."

"So, I left the book back in England. Too many things to

note and the chief lesson, in all of my scientific observation, was that I am in no way able to master myself. So now, I'm on a different approach in self-mastery. I figure if I add one public vice it shall fill up my day so I won't have time for the private vices. Hence the pipe."

"The pipe indeed."

"Now bear in mind, my private vices are not diabolical in nature. They're small vanities, spits of pride, and moments of selfishness. Nothing that would hurt anyone … directly. Although, still vices: if I follow them to their rational conclusion, they would make me inattentive, callous, and eventually mean-spirited."

"Steady insurrections against the self." Brambley added and Patrick nodded

"So now I smoke a pipe."

Brambley paused and scanned Patrick's pipe. "You haven't lit anything in the pipe." Brambley pointed out.

"Oh, I don't have any tobacco. Can't afford it. One thing at a time. London, as they say, was not built in a day."

The trio is silent as they survey the frozen, blue world of the forest. Everything is still as if frozen in time to lock down all of the birds, breeze, and life of the bush. The trees stand as naked skeletons, lifeless and without the promise of any flinch or jump. A quietness rolls over them.

"I wonder how the girls –" Brambley begins to say, but there is a cry from the woods as if to answer his musing.

The four girls break through the timbered, white curtain of the forest. They run, their hot breaths like locomotive smoke as their train bursts through the snow, brush, and woods. Cat smiles, the rest take the business with slight sober expressions. As the four charge towards Cavendish Meadows, their metaled pursuers break through the timbered white curtain as well.

Maillory lifts her skirts to run, while the rest wear pants resistant to snow's moisture.

Cat looks to Brambley. "Ready?" she mouths.

Brambley nods.

The girls run through the future area of the sonic net. Quickly, they file into the floating carriage and Suk pilots them away quickly.

Exhaust from the Tin Woods

The Patchwork Men come into view, wild and blasphemous in appearance. One has a skin of pink with random patches of dog's fur; another is made up of skin, metal, and porcelain tile. The other two breathe out steam exhaust, keeping the engines in their bodies from exploding. They're skin looks in pain, rough, raw and unnatural.

They run past Brambley, still pursuing their girls. A sick lust is shared in their eyes, wildly rolling from side to side with the only anchor being the girl's escape.

"Now," Brambley says as he throws the switch.

Within seconds, ball bearings fly from the ground and surround the men. They cry as they disappear into the gray metal igloo.

The machine hums and the scraping sound of flying metals ceases. The men are captured.

"There," Patrick says. "That wasn't too bad. I guess we shall remain until the Constable comes and –"

A tree falls and lands inches from their feet. An old tree, it previously stretched to the top of the forest's ceiling. Brambley did not see it fall, only felt the ground vibrate from its impact. He falls backwards and scrambles back to his feet. Snow scatters like dust and falls like smoke. Brambley turns to Patrick who is dumbstruck by the might that knocked it over.

Marching from the direction of the new stump – jagged and deep yellow – is the bear, his laser eye creating a tidal wave of bloody red light amongst the snow.

"You shall fall like this tree. You shall fall like all of the trees of this forest shall fall … eventually," the Bear says through his bass, human voice. A deep scratch haunts his speech.

"Who are you?" Brambley asks the creature, shuffling through the snow towards them.

"Rengulfton. That is my simple name. It is the last name spoken to you," the bear says. Charging behind him is a wave of steam wolves, barreling towards their master.

Patrick looks to the bear, bites his lip, and straightens himself to a rigid stance. Then, as quick as light, Patrick bolts in the opposite direction in a frenzied run. Brambley joins him.

"We can't possibly outrun him," Brambley says to Patrick.

Exhaust from the Tin Woods

"He doesn t know that. And it's a better plan than offering him a spot of tea," Patrick says.

The two head straight through large, powdered drifts of snow. Doggedly, they trudge. The bear does not follow; only the wolves, hungry and with their iron teeth bared. The pack leaders have less humanity, with only a few slivers of flesh in their faces; the more human of the wolves follow, mumbling soundless words in their attack.

Brambley and Patrick charge up a hill, far from the meadow, in the direction of the carriage. Patrick grabs the side of a log and flings it backwards, creating an obstacle for their pursuers.

Once atop the hill, they almost roll down the hill through the thick, tall snow. Covered up to their chest in powder, they race to the base and through the maze of trees. None of the snow sticks; it's much too cold for that.

After a few minutes, they round the corner of a thick patch of trees. Brambley could feel the wolves gain on them, although when he turned around, they were still meters behind. Still, the huffing and pawing through the snow shook near them. The sky smells of blood.

Coming around the corner, they see Beattrixx. She stands without a coat. Her bare arms and loose hair in dissidence to the cold, biting frost of the woods. Her eyes stare at the sky. Her black leather bodice and short skirt are all she wears, for she has even lost her boots.

"Beattrixx," Brambley charges. "What are you doing?"

"The land … it stabs me," she says in the voice of a child. She shakes. "Puppies?" She sounds entirely different as if she is a ventriloquist's doll with another source throwing a voice.

The wolves barked. Brambley grabs her arm, leading her to a sprint. The trio runs through the woods. As they run again, Brambley tastes the salty, stinging sweat rolling across his red face. Patrick clutches his side. Beattrixx runs, head looking upwards as her eyes drink up the sky.

Beattrixx begins to throw out a stream of maledictions, all more violent and terrible than the last. She delivers this guttural litany with a smile, her eyes sweetly pointed towards the heavens.

The wolves gain on the trio.

Exhaust from the Tin Woods

"They do not run at full strength," Patrick notices between heaves and puffs of air. "A simple plan, they are tiring us out. Running us down. They don't want their dinner with the strength to kick back."

"Butterflies," Beattrixx adds.

"So, what do we do? Stop running?"

"I need to think," Brambley says. "But I can't think while I'm being chased."

They charge through a thick collection of cedar trees, unaware that there are men on the other side standing like sentries. As soon as they ran past, the men emerged and faced the wave of wolves in chase. The men are clad in fur, from head to toe, bleached white and gray to blend in with the snow. Before they moved, the men were invisible against the woods.

The men produce rifles, and a black powder burst follows. The musket balls strike the ground, producing a thousand explosions, snapping like fireworks around the woods. The men throw down their spent rifles and produce two more. Another firing, filling the ground with more explosions with the first discharge still snapping. A third and last set of rifles fire, turning the ground into Guy Foxe Day.

The wolves burned, frightened, and missing legs: they retreat back to their master, the bear.

The furry, gray man closest to the trio turns to them. "Please, do you speak English?" he asks.

Beattrixx erupts in a cacophony of consonants. She flails her arms and legs, unable to stand. She rolls around in the snow.

Patrick goes to her aid.

"We speak English," Brambley says.

"Good. Falher is filled with French people. Some immigrants. It's hard, trying to keep up with white people languages. If you just were better organized and spoke only one way, our heads wouldn't hurt so bad."

"Falher?" Brambley asks.

"You know, the town," the man says. Brambley cannot see past the furry hood. The man's face, skin, and anything human is completely obscured.

"Grouard?"

Exhaust from the Tin Woods

"They've changed names again. See, you whites make my head hurt. You people need to be better organized."

His partner, still facing the direction of the wolves, says something in a language unknown to Brambley. It sounds rough and rhythmic. Later, he would learn it was Cree.

"Those sick, wrong creatures have fled. More will come back. You only ran into some of them. Best you come with us to camp. Bring your crazy wife and your friend."

Beattrixx stops howling. Instead, she stands, glowering at us. "Can you walk?" Patrick asks.

Without recognizing him, she strides behind the men covered in fur.

They hike silently for ten minutes until they reach a small village of log cabins, teepees, and tents. In the center of the village is a round building with half-walls and appears to be a gathering area. Smoke is more of a smell than in the air. In the distance, drums play as they mix with the sounds of laughter, chopping wood, and someone wildly playing the harmonica.

Beattrixx stands taller than her height should be, moving stiff and erect and without emotion walking into the camp.

Patrick greets the first elderly woman with a slight bow. "Happy birthday," the old woman says back to him, flashing a toothless smile.

Once inside the village, the two men peel off their disguise. One is a large giant of a man with a hook nose and auburn skin; the other is a little man with machinery over his right eye and covering most of his chest. It is the toggled man who greets the trio.

"You are some of Allbrung's students, and so you are welcome to the camp," the cyberman says. "That man is addicted to saving people, and there is a dozen of us made alive by his machines." He pointed to his chest, framed and fashioned out of iron, tin, and piping. "Runs on coals and wood chips, keeps my heart beating and my blood pumping. As a council to the chief, I'm able to stick around for my kids' kids."

"He hasn't taught us that skill," Patrick says, drinking in the science that kept this man alive.

"He teaches so many things. Listen. Listen and learn." He points to the wolves behind them. "They do not. They kill and rape

Exhaust from the Tin Woods

and destroy." He points in the direction of Grouard. "They do not. They keep building and building and building. Soon, as I hear from my trapper friends, they want to make this the capital of Alberta. All boats and trains and flying things and everything will move through here. They want to buy Alberta from us for five bucks. Fine. We'll take our five bucks and go North. There's plenty of woods for us; all of the white people can hover around Grouard like mosquitoes around a street lantern."

"Thank you for saving us," Brambley says with a bow. "You were not obligated to –"

"Of course, I was. Your blood gets on the trees; it stains the forest. You think I'm crazy, but the woods will remember. The woods hold grudges. And I have to live here. My family, my tribe has to live here." He takes a step back. He looks angry. "Plus, you're worth saving. Now. Stay put for a while. Last week, we got a gift from some crazy white men in long cloaks. This camp is safe. An hour before the sun sets should be a good time to head back to Mercyminster." He points to Beattrixx. "Stick close to your crazy wife."

He turns and enters into the village filled with the Cree language.

Brambley calls out. "She's not my wife." He turns to find the angry, rigid Beattrixx. "Are you well, Beattrixx?"

"I am well. Better than well. Great. My mood is salt rock," she says without emotion. "And I am not Beattrixx. Never heard of her. I am Anansi."

"I beg your pardon," Patrick says.

"No begging and no pardons. I have been asleep for a long, long while. But while we felt the presence of gray steam and those seeing gray, I awoke. I'm here, and I am not pleased."

Brambley is surprised, almost scared. It is Beattrixx, most definitely, without her voice. A new voice, smoky and deep, has replaced the fluid, almost singing soprano of their friend. Her eyes squint when she speaks and seldom smiles as if a new spirit has possessed their former friend.

"Beattrixx, what happened?" Patrick asks.

She looks down at him. "These primitive people. They must go. If the Woods could round them all up and put them on an island, so much the better."

Brambley's face turns beet red. He whispers in a stifled yell, "Don't ever say that. We are their guests, and they have saved our lives. They belong to the Woods just as much as the Woods belong to them."

"Ever see London?"

"You know that I have," Brambley says as his eyes ferociously scan Beattrixx.

"It's a place like nowhere else in the world. Streets teaming with metalmanced people, a sea of chrome beauty. Difference Engines in every house. Toggled men and women. And factories, glorious factories. Replacing the sky with the bounty of their furnaces with beautiful smoke. There is mechanized perfection to the town. The poor, the rich, the ponies, the archons, the dreamers, and the prattlers are all in their place, like gears and dials set to specific weight and measurement. The Woods, if ever this land dream of being metalmanced get out of the tacky parlor, must be turned into a factory. One great, big, long factory. These grubs, these hunters: they stand in the way of such an empire."

"Beattrixx —"

"I am not she. I am Anansi."

"Cleary," Brambley says through his teeth. The redness of his cheeks remains, but his mood shifts to a new shade of anger. "Beattrixx, my friend, respects other people. Deeply. Cleary, you are not her."

"Cleary," she says with a smile.

Brambley finds a rock to sit on; Patrick joins him on the rock next to him; Beattrixx stands. Patrick pulls out his tobacco-less pipe for a refreshing smoke. "I say," he says. "Dusk is just upon us." He points around. "This is a remarkable village. Quite remarkable. This seems to be what it's all about, isn't it? Working, living, and doing things … together. No one is together in London; here, they're like spits of glass in a grand mosaic. I love this place."

"How much do you think Allbrung is up to? Behind our backs?" Brambley asks.

"Not really behind our backs, when our backs are to the proverbial grindstone. I don't think he's one to keep secrets, do you? We just aren't asking him enough questions."

Exhaust from the Tin Woods

"When we get back, I intend to ask him plenty of questions."

"Why so? Do you detect a nefarious conspiracy? A monsteration of morality?"

"Quite the opposite," Brambley says in a hushed tone as if speaking to himself. "I do think there has been something miraculously growing, here in the Tin Woods of Alberta. Something truly remarkable. A conspiracy, certainly: but do all conspiracies have to be wicked?" Brambley points to a group of children guiding balls with sticks, playing a game of bush football. "Look at those kids."

Patrick looks, but he shrugs. Brambley points to the children and then to his own legs. Patrick nods, seemingly realizing that all of the children had robotic legs. "He has granded the people of this village."

"My adopted mother, the woman in town who speaks no English and loves cooking for me, hates going to any church except the Baptist one," Patrick says as he crosses his long legs. "The Constable once told me why. Apparently, the Anglicans and the Catholics seek to round up all of the children, pack them away in a dusty and lonely church, and makes them Christian. Or, more specifically, Canadian. It's lesson we taught them from the British Empire. They remove the kids from the woods to the church to 'grand' them for the Commonwealth and for God. That saintly woman, who feeds me, hates this concept."

"I hate it, but why does she?"

"I think she believes kids should be in their own village, raised by their own community, and given a chance to play with sticks. So does Allbrung, it seems: he gave them new legs to walk. Which works: forcible removal or his prattling? Which granding works?"

"There is no glitz to their toggles," Beattrixx says without emotion as her dark eyes point to the children.

Patrick's studies the robotics. "You'd never see that kind of work in London. Then again, London toggling wouldn't work out here. The gears and shafts and pumps would freeze. No, it's bulky and without flare: hollerithed, undoubtedly. But who cares? The flare is how the runner runs, not in the legs that carry them."

Exhaust from the Tin Woods

Patrick gets up and dusts off the wetness from his wool trousers. "It is now dusk. Let's take a turn in the woods, returning to Mercyminster."

Brambley looks around. "There's no one to thank. Our friend with the cyber-chest has left. Now that we've been helped, no one is around to gain any gratitude."

"That is the point, I should think. Come along, Nancy," Patrick says to Beattrixx.

"I am Anansi."

"Certainly, come along," he says, offering his arm.

"And Anansi does not need any steamboats." She marches ahead, the two follow. They leave the village to a still, peaceful forest. Only the wind is in their ears, a soft C- minor whistle.

They walk for twenty minutes, as the sun sets and darkness grows around them. In the calmest moments of the trek, Beattrixx asks, "How long was I gone?"

"And you are?" Patrick asks.

"Beattrixx. I am so sorry for Anansi," she says, expression and life returning to her face. "Umm, how long was I gone?"

"You missed the Cree nation. Nice people. Also, the capture of the Patchwork Men. And the bear. I don't know, a few hours."

She smiles, looking up in wonder. "I haven't been gone that long before. Phantasmagoric[64]!" She looks back at her two companions. "I'm sorry. I want to stay embarrassed. Truly, I do. But this is a marvel! A few hours! She only comes in a few moments, here and there."

"Anansi?"

"Yes," she says and bites her full, lower lip. "I am truly sorry. She is the most horrible of people. She comes when I'm near violence. Or when I smell heavy, heavy machine exhaust."

"When you were attacked during our first month, did she –"

"She was the one who fought them off. Yes, Anansi was there." She looks down. "Did she … do any damage? She's never hurt anyone physically, but her thinking is truly evil. I have her

---

[64] something frightening, disturbing, or unsettling

locked in a box in my head, usually with no trouble. When there is trouble, she likes to help out and takes over."

"No," Brambley says softly. "She didn't hurt anyone. The effect was only that we missed you." He reached out and touched her shoulder.

"Could you please not mention anything to the rest? I'm working on keeping her in her box, but it's hard and, well, I'm looking at the two of you, right now. You don't look at me like I'm a crazy person. You're the same. You don't judge me or want to buy a steamboat. That's what I want from everyone at Mercyminster and, well, if they knew about Anansi –"

"The rest should be told, I think," Patrick says. "But won't be from us. When the timing is right, you'll know, and you'll speak up. Until then, there's enough of today to tell the group back at Mercyminster."

"Thank you," she says, and she laughs. "I'm sure they don't know. I fell from Suk's flying ship. I was Beattrixx when I fell; landed as Anansi. My cover remains."

They walk more through the woods. It is quiet, peaceful.

Brambley's eyes scan between the slivers of trees for anything dangerous. Nothing. Only the crunching sounds of the snow being walked upon.

"Look," Brambley says as he points. "Plumes of smoke. Brick. We're home."

"About time," Patrick says. "A few more minutes, we'd be seeing a starry night."

.....

The next morning, Suk approached Brambley with a note: *Bring your breakfast outside, near the western field. Your speed in this is the heart of this request. Pieter Van Allbrung.*

Brambley did as the note instructed, meeting in the strange, open space of the estate that held snow. The field is perfectly flat, possibly a lawn or some place to play cricket in the summer. With the snow, it stands to Brambley as just empty space.

He meets Dr. Allbrung who is wearing furs, wool, and a hat that covers most of his face. The old man drinks tea, nibbling on a raw potato.

Brambley walks up next to Allbrung, his plate filled with

Exhaust from the Tin Woods

food. He sees what Allbrung is studying: the nothingness winter renders to nature.

"This field is a disaster," Allbrung says, taking another sip of tea. "I had a theory that I could accelerate the development of limestone. Limestone, like any rock up here, would be valuable: farmers who burn the lime and scatter it on their soil to instantly make it fertile. I had an equation, that is essentially misapplied alchemy, in turning the ground into limestone." The old man laughs. "Did not work. Killed everything. Two years ago, a student did soil samples, and he thinks it will take 100 years to grow something. Anything. In 1995, we should see some life, I think." He turned to Brambley "I took from the land it's richness and left it barren. My mistake. and every time I look at this field, I am reminded of the importance of thinking, of research, of working with something instead of just jumping in and changing it for my benefit. Harmony, my friend. Harmony with the land and the people and the moment and the God above."

"I am sorry for the field," Brambley says and Allbrung nods.

"You have had two appointments with Rengulfton. Twice, you have been saved by friends of mine. The first was with the Mertonites, good friends of mine. They are prattling pirates, but good men."

"What are they doing here from England?"

"Oh, isn't it obvious? They're here to apprehend Rengulfton. One purpose only is to find the criminal Rengulfton."

"And are you here for that reason?"

"No," the old man says with a smile. "I will help them if I can, but I'm here to teach you. Teach the rest. I'm too busy to chase Rengulfton through the Woods. Evil is fought and decided in the metal shop, not with a gun." Allbrung studies Brambley's face, watching every line and crack.

Brambley isn't sure what the old man is looking for, and he isn't even sure what his reaction is to his last statement.

The pause grows until finally, Allbrung speaks again. "On purpose and set by ambition, everything Rengulfton does matches my work on this poor field. I did it by mistake; he does it on purpose, every day. I can fiddle and fight over having good

126

Exhaust from the Tin Woods

intentions, but the result is the same: I behaved like Rengulfton, exploiting the land."

"That's who lives in the woods, outside of Mercyminster?" Brambley feels a slight touch of indignation. "Then why do we leave the safety of this place? There are women, Dr. Allbrung. I think Rengulfton captures people and is a skin seamstress, attaching them to the bodies and souls of animals. Why do you allow us to face such villainy to spend time with Grouard?"

"Isn't it obvious? Our inventions must be for someone we know; someone we can share the moment with. If science isn't personal, it can become exploitive. Dr. Graham Bell needed the community of the deaf to drive his inventions in sound and communication. Otherwise, the good of the telephone would not have been birthed. It is essential that we serve the community right in front of us if ever technology will be used to make humanity better. No, I cannot let Rengulfton win by hiding in Mercyminster. Otherwise, Mercyminster ceases to be."

Brambley is shaking, for he isn't sure what to feel.

Fear: Allbrung is tossing everyone into the lion's mouth? Anger: how dare he?

Elation: he believes so much in what we learn that he's willing to live in danger?

Insecurity: when will Rengulfton strike again?

Pessimism: what's the point in all of the gadgets if Rengulfton will steal them for his own purposes?

The old man sips his tea twice. "I brought you out here because I wanted you to see the danger of missing the moment and not cooperating with the good of the moment. You are in the middle of missing your own moment."

"How so?"

"When we returned, Cat could care less that the Constable took away the Patchwork Men. She also didn't care that her machine worked. Instead, she was only herself again and not seeing gray when you walked into the front door."

"She seemed indifferent," Brambley says.

"Oh, the moment." He smiles. "Don't you think Joane and Patrick will have wonderful children? French and British Prattlers, all running around and inventing things?"

Exhaust from the Tin Woods

"I don't see how –"

"They are so much in love and yet, they're not reading each other. Why is that? How can someone be with someone who is so right and not see it? I think Patrick has some rather unrealistic expectations."

"Yes, I agree," Brambley says brightly. "Patrick doesn't see it, though. You're right, he's still waiting for a grand romance to take place."

"Too bad he doesn't see what the rest of creation sees. Too bad." Allbrung finishes his tea, turns on his heels to enter the manor. "Oh, the moment."

Chapter Five
April 1895

Brambley looks out the window of the sunroom and finds Cat standing outside, staring at the snow fields.

He opens the double brass and glass doors and steps outside into the warming air. It's still freezing, but there is a consistent Chinook blowing across the woods. He stands beside Cat for a few seconds before he asks, "See something?"

"Yes," she says pointing to a tin point amidst the melting snow of the meadow. "See the tin. There. And there. And there. See it?"

Brambley did: they look to be tin mountaintops surrounded by clouds of snow. "When the snow melts, will we be in machine forest? Brass chimneys for trees, gutters for rivers, and sawdust for the soil?" Brambley smiles, thinking of such a possibility. "I wonder if that's a glimpse of the future? 1995, we shall see all of Canada one sprawling big factory."

"Artisans, yes; factories, God forbid," Cat says. "I worked in one of those White Hells. It's true what they say. The air is filled with floating, fluffy cotton. Like a hot snow storm, the machines run, and the women work. All of them were my age then, about thirteen. Maybe fourteen. We all got jobs because they didn't have to pay us as much as an adult man." She winces. "I stayed for the machines. Wonderful gadgets and belts. Tacky parloring, in a very salt rock degree. Water-powered, the river pushed the wheel to run everything. Amazing machine." She grins. "Came for the machines; left because of the factories. In the two weeks in which I worked, I watched two girls cough themselves to death. It happens all the time. All of the young girls, being fed into the factories so women can wear pretty clothing."

"So, you think Allbrung might be trying to do the same thing?"

"It is important you find out," Allbrung's voice speaks behind the two. They turn around to see him smoking a pipe beside an opened window. "A land full of factories is a horrible death to the land."

129

Exhaust from the Tin Woods

Allbrung disappears behind the window and a few moments later, steps outside with them wearing a pair of Welly Babies[65]. The snow is icy, compact, and melting as he walks outside. He walks to one of the tin cones, crouches over it in a survey of the snow. He pulls from a pocket of his long coat a device resembling a pistol. He vigorously cranks the side, powering the engine to rumble and sputter. A hot wind roars out of the device, instantly melting the ice. Soon they see a cone tethered by a rubber hose that leads back to the house. Ground, brush, and snow mold is around this tiny pyramid.

"What is it?" Brambley asks.

"It is a device to harness energy from the snow melt. As the snow melts, there's heat that can be converted into power. The pyramids collect this power and bring it back to the house. It is an alternative to steam power. Yes, steam is good: but it isn't forever. To supplement our steam-powered engines, I've added the energy harnessed from snow. Still an experiment, but one that has great promise."

He lights a cherry of fire within his pipe. "Cat, have you ever heard of Johann Sebastian Bach?"

"No," Cat says. "The moment I learned that I was to be a Prattler, I pursued nothing else. As a Pony, it was all pantomime tunes. Sorry."

"That was a mistake, my dear," Allbrung says without emotion. "You need to defenster such impulses."

"That's crushed," she says without emotion, shooting back at him.

"No, it's the key to all wisdom. I don't teach Prattling, I teach living. True, good, free living that gives away to the world around oneself. Prattling is the shop of such ideas. I now have a new assignment for you: meet with Shweta and have her play the violin for you this morning, after my lecture. If she asks for a request, say 'Bach'. When she plays, sketch. Sketch wildly. Then show me the sketches at our evening meal."

"Where did Bach come from in this discussion?" Brambley asks.

---

[65] wellington boots

Exhaust from the Tin Woods

"I have no idea." He looks up and smiles. "When truth is integrated with truth, a brilliant idea always comes home. Comes home, like a carrier pigeon to the coop." He points to Cat. "Listen to Bach. I promise it will be a reward for asking the right kinds of questions instead of what it may appear, a punishment for asking any question at all. Please, enjoy Bach. He is so good, you know. So good. So much better than our current music."

"Like pantomime?"

"Like Richard Wagner," he says with a sour note of dread. "Dark, depressing, hopeless, and much too loud. It seems as if he does not know what must come next, so he repeats a tune or crashes a cymbal. I fear I am much too old for what passes today for Opera. Plus, he has the heroes of his plays glitzing and granding with toggles. I never knew the ancient Norse to have cyber eyes." He laughs and leaves the two.

When Allbrung is gone, Brambley points to Cat with his eyes. "You were in a panic through most of that conversation."

"Me?"

"Yes, I was reading your non-verbal cues. Your eyes flashed, your hands wrung themselves, sweat on your forehead. Either Bach really is a real phantasmagoric or –"

"Or?"

"You are expecting this community to soon end," he says, and he reads her face: the signs of anxiety continue. "And this was one way where Allbrung can let you down. Especially if he lies about these little tin cones and there's something dark behind this old man?"

"You're talking ether dreams."

"Maybe," Brambley says. "But how long have you stayed in one place?"

"Half the time I've been here," she says as her eyes tighten in focus to the floor."

"And do you just leave? As some Dreamer, who hears the road calling her? Or does something fall apart, or does it get ugly?"

"So, I'm looking for it to get ugly or fall apart to match some sort of time table? At 3 o'clock, the hammer will fall like some great, cosmic glockenspiel?"

"Exactly," he says. "Just making an observation."

Exhaust from the Tin Woods

"Please don't. You're a real Charles Dickens, but don't push it. You're trying to make me sound crazy, seeing gray and all."

"I'm not trying to make you sound crazy. You're a Prattler: we're already crazy."

He grins and sees her whole body stiffen as her gaze is nowhere near him. He nods and leaves her.

.....

Cat sits, listening to Suk on the violin, Joane on the piano, and Shweta on the cello. The last bars roll out, finishing the Minuet in G. Cat looks around the room when the trio is finished, as if something else should be happening. After they put their bows down, Cat expressing herself by simply asking, "And?"

"And?" Shweta asks. "Did you expect for Bach to end in a dance?"

"Possibly," Cat says. She crosses her arms and raises her right eyebrow. "Wouldn't hurt the piece, putting a bit more posh and glitz in the music."

"Bach has plenty of glitz and posh," Suk says with his voice rising. He then furls his eyebrows in her direction. "This is not about the piece."

Cat feels hot in her cheeks as she twirls her hair and bites her lower lip. "Umm, what do you mean?"

"You didn't listen to it. Didn't let the music take over, wash over you. You looked like you were waiting for this thing to get over." He leans towards her. "Your mind. It's not here."

"How do you know?"

"If you were here, you'd be weeping because of my playing and the beauty of Bach." He held up his bow. "I was playing with infinity in mind. Where are you?"

"Brambley said something this morning, something that disturbed me."

"Was he cruel? Tell me he wasn't cruel. I couldn't take it if he were cruel," Joane says. "Tell me."

"He wasn't cruel." She speaks in a groan. "Not at all. I mean, we're talking about Brambley, here. He's a steamboat to all of us," Cat says. "No, he was neither false nor cruel." She winces, the words stinging in her throat. "He was everything but those things. And that is the problem."

Exhaust from the Tin Woods

"What did he say?"

"He says, essentially, that I'm looking to leave. I'm restless and that I'm not long for this place. He suggested that I'm looking for things to cancel me out of this place. I'm looking to get defenstered or defenster this place."

"Yeah," Suk says with a knowing shrug. "I could see that. There's a lot of defenstration[66] about you."

"How?"

"As a Held Companion, I was given one room and one mistress and one afternoon a month to do as I please: nothing was taken from me, nothing else was given to me. Living here … is quite a luxury. You've been given so much before coming here and, likewise, all of it and more has been taken from you," Joane says. "You are skittish, as you English say."

"Your god takes more than he gives," Shweta says.

Cat felt like punching something. Hard. "How did this become all about me?" She felt all eyes on her, and she hated it.

"If your immediate impulse isn't to bow down and worship the very notes of Bach then you make it all about you," Suk says. He taps his brass top hat with the flat of his hand. "It's all about you right now."

"Why?"

"Your problem is that you're surrounded by people who love you and a man who loves you enough to speak the truth to you. You're able to pursue your dreams with one of the best teachers in the world."

"How is that a problem?"

"That's our point. And yours is to find out what's wrong with what has just been dealt to you."

Cat looks at Shweta, her expression unchanged the moment she spoke about Cat's god. "I don't believe in God."

"You do believe in God, and your god is a real lurkjerker."

"Perhaps my god is a 'she'?"

"God doesn't have a body," Shweta says. She rises and places her hand on Cat. "Let me introduce you to a new god. One who likes hard work, one who believes the more you work hard in

---

[66] someone who makes a habit of rejecting bad ideas

133

the land, you become part of the land. Harmony is found with labor. You've been given freely, and freely has been taken from you. Now it is time to work. Join the land."

"Plant maize and potatoes?"

"If it helps. Sure."

"Most of us do not have a family," Joane says. "And so when one comes, embrace it. Please. For if you start looking at ways to end it, there will only be more orphans."

Cat detects a small tear in Joane's right eye. She can tell the French woman is doing her best to hold it back, but the fact that it is there at all is why Cat needs to be quiet.

"Your song was quite beautiful," Cat says after a long pause.

"Good," Suk says. "That is a start. We shall play four more pieces: a Toccata, 2 Concertos, and another Minuet. Sketch away. Let the music overtake you."

.....

The month begins with a lecture series on computing. Allbrung, during a lecture, reveals his friendship with Charles Babbage. "When Babbage invented the Difference Engine, everything changed. Everything," Allbrung says to the class. "But many in London took his computer and believed that was it, that was all there was. A machine that can count for a man. Certainly, counting can lead to equations and then simple commands. But is this all there is for the engine? What about thoughts? Feelings?"

"Most of you had heard of my great accident about finding metal that can retain, on a limited level, emotional memories. I can't find a single application for it, so it remains just a triviality. I shared my findings with Babbage, and he agreed. 'The future is to figure out a machine that can think for itself. Feelings and faith: this belongs to human beings.' I agree with Mr. Babbage. Right now, all an engine can do is record thoughts. But to create new thoughts, new solutions to problems: this is the 19th Century alchemy."

Maillory puts her hand up. Allbrung nods to her. "But if we can create a machine to think for itself, aren't we becoming like God?"

"Excellent question," Allbrung says. "To be like God is the very birthright of human beings, for we are made in His image, and

Exhaust from the Tin Woods

we are commanded, by all of Creation, to resemble as best we can His virtues. But to become a god … this is blasphemy. You are right in worrying about creating thinking machines as a step towards blasphemy. Tell me, what do you all think?"

Shweta put her hand up. "In truth, we cannot become a god. It is impossible, so it is so far from temptation that I do not worry. The mathematics alone get in the way. How can the finite step into infinity?"

"If this thinking machine," Patrick says, crossing his lanky legs and arms. "Can devise solutions to cure polio or feed the orphans of England, then it is becoming like God? And I say, 'bravo'. However, if it devises machinations and schemes to keep people poor and exploit more women … it is nothing more than a being that has bitten forbidden fruit and found oneself confronted with their shortcomings."

"Cat?" Allbrung asks.

"If a Difference Engine can think, then it can become management of a factory or mill. It would be fair, logical, and consistent. It would be a great boss to work for and, I think, that's what scares me."

Allbrung grins as he looks around the room. Silence greets him back. "Excellent question. I think to pump the room for more answers would be a monsteration of digression. Let's continue with computing."

He spends the rest of the session and week speaking about computers. The lab time is a free for all, with the students designing something every day, or one big project by the end of the week.

Brambley walks over to his platform and sits, facing Cat. "Any ideas?" he asks.

"I always have ideas."

"What if we worked together for something big?"

"Go on," Cat says as she grins at Brambley.

"What if we bring music to the streets of Grouard? One master gramophone or victorola, with multiple horns throughout the town."

"Would they be connected by cables? Like a telegraphing line?"

"We know the science on that one, so sure. Still, it would

be great if we could do it through radio waves."

"Too unpredictable. Plus, doesn't the cold shrink radio waves?"

"I don't think … I'm not sure. Regardless, weather-proofed cables and horns everywhere broadcasting everything."

She walks over and offers her snow-white hand as she pulls off her leather work glove. "Partners."

They shake.

Shweta and Maillory work on jewelry, figuring out new ways to make toggles more fashionable, more decorative.

Patrick works on giving everything a motor.

Joane and Beattrixx work together to build new, creative ways to enter data into the manor's difference engine. They are coming up with organ keys, hurdy-gurdy buttons, a morse tapper, or Hollerith toggles.

On the second day of the computation training, Cat finds herself walking down the hallway of Mercyminster. Normally, Cat is not prone to wander, for she fears she might have her hours wrong and the room might collapse on her. Still, she left her vorpal needle-beetles in the morning room and needs them to work on Brambley's speaker idea.

She walks down the hall, hearing the sound of a steam car around the corner. This sound does not match the stately, well-formed hallways of Mercyminster. It should be on the roadways of England.

Stopped and tightening, she braces herself for the machine forthcoming.

Rounding the corner, a large grandfather clock on wheels rolls towards her leaving a dragon tail shape of steam behind it.

Allbrung is behind her. "Ah, the Wandering Clock and you finally meet," he says. "You two have a lot in common."

"Because I'm a wanderer?"

"That and when people look at your face, they see reality. In the clock's case, time," Allbrung says. His hair is white with frost, his skin bone-colored and he is wrapped up in a 20-foot long scarf. "This is an earlier invention of mine. It's a way for people to tell time wherever they happen to be."

"Why not carry around a fob? Plus, a gentleman's pocket

Exhaust from the Tin Woods

watch is considered granding."

"Granding? I wanted something practical. So I created a robotic grandfather clock that follows one around the house." He shrugs. "Traditional clocks stand only in one corner, gathering … tradition. Fobs get lost or forgotten or damaged. This invention combines the travel and stateliness of a Swiss clock."

Cat simply laughs. It is a natural belly laugh. It takes awhile for her to relax and continue the conversation. Once composed, she asks, "Have you been outside?"

"No," he says as he takes off his scarf. The tall man's face is without emotion. "I have not been outside all day. Why do you ask?"

"Something tells me you have been outside in the snow."

"No, and the outside is losing snow. Everything is melting outside," Allbrung says as he takes off his coat. "Do not get too comfortable. There is always one last snow dump at the end of the month. It is winter's last tantrum before the Woods change." He strokes his long, front hair from his eyes. "I would be glad to cast off all of my coats and mittens. Alas, Mercyminster gets really, really hot."

She opens her mouth with the hope of bringing up the melting ice in his hair, but Suk enters and speaks. "Hello Cat," he says. "Brambley is looking for you, reminding me of a lost puppy dog in search of his mistress."

"I doubt it."

"Believe it, you didn't hear him whimper like I did. And Dr. Allbrung, I have the new equations."

Allbrung bows to Cat. "Sorry, I must fly. More wandering clocks and the like must be realized." He leaves Cat with a thousand and one queries in her eyes.

…..

After a week of computation training, Allbrung gives the students a day off. The woods are a marshy slog of mud, mold, and deep grime, so travelling into town is impossible. Maillory decides on a picnic, complete with an outdoor lunch and games: this idea excites the entire manor.

Beattrixx and Cat wear revealing, loose fitting garments that flash a sight of their ankles; the men wear summer shirts and

Exhaust from the Tin Woods

baggy pants; Allbrung lives in his pajamas and smoking robe; Shweta is in a flowing robe; and Joane is very posh, very ponied in a light blue corset, gown, and bowler cap.

Patrick and Brambley attempt to play cricket, but it is a sad game with only two. The others watch: more to see them struggle, not for the game itself.

Cat is sitting on an iron bench, one of the few surfaces outdoors that are neither wet nor crusted with snow. She feels the bench jolt as someone joins her. Looking over, she sees Shweta.

"Joining with God means you join with so many other things," Shweta says. "Look at the joining." She points to Joane, standing and leaning towards the game. "The two boys play, but Joane is very much part of the game." Shweta's dark eyes point to Beattrixx, who is chatting with Suk and Allbrung. "Like the school of Athens, Beattrixx joins in the discussion of science." Lastly, she points to Maillory, sorting cups on a table. "And there is Maillory."

"I agree," Cat says. "She seems to be the solitary white sock in a drawer full of dark fabric."

Shweta laughs. "My parents tell me of their lives in India, before they came to The Woods. It sounds like the entire country lived in one, cramped elevator platform. So many people. Communities constantly changed, as Queen Victoria decided to move people from one place to another. My father spoke of one relocation where an old man moved into a hut and drew, with chalk, a number. Every day, the number decreased until it was at zero.

"On the day of zero, there was a massive fist fight between two men. The soldiers came in, with their pure white pith helmets and brown batons and swords. They called them savages, beat some, and increased security.

"The old man had an equation: the longer people are in forced confines, it's only a matter of time before they turn on each other. Confinement will make one forget their true enemy. For my father, it was the self-righteous English seeking to whitewash all of India and wash the brown off our skins. But people forget, they make new enemies."

"I'm not sure where you're going with this," Cat says. Shweta's brown eyes bore intently upon Maillory. She did not look up or over to Cat.

Exhaust from the Tin Woods

"We reach zero. We've been inside, holed up, and hiding from this white stuff that is the true populace of The Woods. And we are at day zero. This is when we forget enemies and might be tempted, like the old man's equation, to turn on each other." Shweta smiles with a touch of cruelty in her eyes. "We must be extra kind to Maillory. She cannot be left out. If anyone, she could become someone who sticks out. And the moment she does, the school doesn't work anymore. We're just prattling, not creating. We must get passed day zero, and we do so by including Maillory."

Cat did not remember saying anything bad about Maillory, but she could. She knows she could. Maillory labored extra hard to get the last word on most conversations she was a part of, usually ending with some turn of a phrase or reminder that everyone wasn't as good as they ought to be.

Shweta, a long time ago, pointed out to Cat that the way one speaks fits their religion. Accordingly, Maillory's God seems disappointed with everyone, convinced that His children aren't pulling their own weight. Those who shrug, slip out, and slide through life, to this God, are lurkjerkers and enemies of propriety.

Cat hates this God.

She then wonders how much this God hates Maillory.

Cat rose and walked over to Maillory. She smiles the moment Maillory looks at her. "Can I do your hair?" Cat asks.

"Excuse me?" Maillory asks, looking ill at ease.

"It's been something I've been thinking about for a while. Joane would kill me if I touched her curls. Beattrixx has a different design every week, and Shweta's head is always covered."

"And yours?" she asks, and Cat feels a sting.

"Mine is as short as a boy's. The style is wetted[67] for hard work, but hardly posh. I've been enjoying your hair and –"

"Sure," Maillory says quickly, and the two leave to go to the house for some hair prattling.

.....

On Sunday, Brambley preaches, and the student body of Mercyminster attend church.

While Brambley delivers his sermon, he notices an elderly

---

[67] hard labor designing technology

Exhaust from the Tin Woods

woman glaring at Beattrixx. He figures it could be because
Beattrixx's neckline is an impossibly low plunge, or that she wears
a man's bowler inside the church, or that she put on metallic black
lipstick. Or, because her trousers were cut so tight that they
resemble hose worn by French Ponies, or because her ankles are
bare. Or because Beattrixx kept her eyes open during prayer while
whispering to Cat. In any way, she began in an aghast reaction and
then continues in this reaction for dramatic effect.

Halfway through the message, Beattrixx turns to the old
woman and growls a husky hiss reflective of an angry, cornered cat.
The woman looks to be pushed back by an invisible wall. She
bristles and her expression leaves, stilled by the animal within
Beattrixx.

Brambley smiles quickly. Later, he'll remember the irony
of such a moment for he was preaching on "The Good Samaritan".

He ends with a direct quote from Allbrung. "Perhaps the
point of this parable is to say that piety must be practiced locally,
that we are to be Christian to the people right in front of us. Our
religion is manifested more to the man bleeding on the street than at
the temple. May the world experience more Good Samaritans and
fewer temples, Christ is saying."

Cat nods.

Beattrixx winks.

Patrick whispers, "Oh, A-men." He is much too British to
give volume to such cries.

After church, Cat runs to Brambley and grabs his arm.

Acting as if she gave him a passionate, lover's embrace, he
asks, "What was that for?"

"For being right."

Brambley blushes. "I should be right more often." The pair
walks out of the church to a cacophony of French. The Catholic
Church, down the street, is finished and the congregants are
walking down the road, parallel to the water.

Plumes of smoke puff, full of gray and blue, as the steam
ships deliver goods or collect things like furs, timber, or cattle.
They move regardless of it being Sunday, the Sabbath, keeping it is
a luddmunster dream, only in the past. In the distance, a dirigible
plots and weaves from the town drunk, as if he sprouted wings and

Exhaust from the Tin Woods

flew away. The sky appears to be crocheted, knitted to keep out the sun and any color of blue.

The Constable approaches the group of students. "Good afternoon," he says and then smiles at Joane. "I fear I have missed church. There was an emergency in the forest."

"Oh?" Allbrung asks. "Anything to report?"

"Nothing and that is the problem. Your friends, the Mertonites, found something that disappeared. Something isn't right out there, and it's growing." He looks to the ladies of the group. "I am sorry. I do not mean to disturb the fairer sex."

"I was disturbed before you arrived, Constable," Beattrixx says flatly.

The Constable tips his stove top hat to Beattrixx and grins. He looks over to Allbrung, "We must meet on Monday. Must, I say. I need your help."

"I am not sure how much help I can be to you. Come early, I teach a class at nine." Allbrung asks Cat, "How is your musical project?"

"Finished," Cat says with a smile. She is still holding Brambley arm tightly. "We are just waiting for things to get dry to install the speakers."

"In Grouard, that might take a while." His gray hand, covered with a wool glove, points to the bay of Lesser Slave Lake. "It is a marsh, swamp, and a lagoon. Great for boats, lousy for music. This is why you shall be giving these people a true gift. The more impossible a gift is to be given is always in direct proportion to their needs for such a gift. Keep working."

The students return to the home of Patrick's adoptive mother who is busy roasting a pig for their evening meal. A party is already gathered, along with the four Mertonites.

The oldest member – Braxbury – walks straight to Brambley. He flashes a quick smile. His moustache looks rich with curls, full of wild strands. "Hello, you two. How are your studies?" he asks.

Cat explains their pursuit of music for Grouard. The Mertonite smiles and nods. "I hear you are now the town's preacher?" he asks Brambley.

"I've delivered some sermons, that's all. The aim of being

just a minister isn't all I crave. Prattling seems more fitting for me as a vocation."

"The world needs Prattlers, the world needs Ministers. Whatever your lot, be a good one." He whips out a silver flask, takes a quick sip, and places it back within his striped vest under his gray coat. He does this in one, fluid motion. "Be good and be safe."

"Did something happen this morning?" Brambley asks.

"Yes," Braxbury says. "And then it didn't happen." He shakes his head, his gray eyes looking to the lake that has large chunks of ice floating in between the ships with their ice cutters. "I wish there was another reason to bring me to The Woods. Any other reason. This place is grand and bold and amazing. I just wish it didn't house Rengulfion."

"What is it exactly you do?" Cat asks. She flutters her eyes, looking both confused and pretty. "Mertonites, I mean?"

"We are non-violent interventionists. We studied with Allbrung under the teachings and principles of the Russian writer, Leo Tolstoy. He taught that religion, like the stuff Brambley preaches, comes only when people and governments and the land and everything is being redeemed. And one cannot do this with violence. And one cannot redeem without intervening."

"So, are you, bounty hunters?"

"At times. At times, we're diplomats. Sometimes, we're librarians or curators or festival planners or teachers."

"Is Allbrung a Mertonite?"

"Alas, no," Braxbury says slowly and sadly. "He doesn't believe in … direct intervention. For him, his lectures and classes are enough. This is where we do not see eye with eye."

The lunch is spectacular, with the round little Polish woman shouting out joyful words, gesturing wildly, and wiping tears from her eyes. Patrick describes for her when he takes a bite of his blood sausage, "This food is cooked with love. You can taste it. Magnificent!"

People from the town come and visit. The French speak to the French; the Polish to the Polish; and the English speakers, which are Allbrung's students, huddle together and they talk about the swampy, mire of the ground in springtime.

"I love not the clay," Beattrixx says to the group. "It is a natural monsteraton. Takes forever to clean. Alas, I only have two skirts."

"I thought you had more than just two," Maillory says flatly.

"No, I repurpose them. Repurposing is the arty-sam's[68] greatest virtue." Beattrixx smiles.

Suddenly, an old woman comes out from the kitchen and approaches Beattrixx. She raves in Polish. She places her large, strong hands on Beattrixx's shoulders.

"Shall I translate?" Baxbury offers.

Beattrixx blue eyes widen, and she nods her head.

"She says you are beautiful. You are smart." The woman wraps her arms around Beattrixx, barely giving her enough room to breathe. The embrace is both ferocious and loving. "She is now praying for you. Praying that God gives you ideas to help this town. She wants God to protect you from all evils ... she is calling you an Angel, but it is a meaning of praise ... beautiful, beautiful ... you remind her of her daughter ... she asks God for the strength that she may pray for you every night ... she thanks God for the inventions you have made ..."

"But I have hardly made anything, yet."

"It doesn't matter. It's the idea of a young, poshed prattler making things for this town is all the hope she needs. I know her, she lost a daughter from a fever two winters ago." The Mertonite smiles. "Be glad, you've just been adopted."

"Don't I get a say in this relationship?"

"Barely," Braxbury says and laughs. "Be glad, she's a fine woman who won't take what she has said very lightly."

"Good luck," Maillory says with a grin and a bristle. "A half-crazed Polish woman is a hard thing to shake off."

Beattrixx stares down Maillory, her eyes tighten, and she speaks sharply through her teeth. "Who says I want to shake this off? This is the best hug I've gotten in years."

Maillory sneers. Later, Brambley overhears her mention to Joane, when they are inside of Patrick's adopted mother's house, "This place is so dirty. So filthy. It is half-finished. Wallpapered by

---

[68] an artisan, someone who is creative with innovative technology

Exhaust from the Tin Woods

newspaper. Smells of mold. Why doesn't anyone around here have self-respect or dignity?" Joane smiles and does not respond.

Brambley looks at Maillory. She's different from the girl he first met. Her smiles do not last, her eyes look past the people she speaks to, her hands make fists a bit easier, and nothing impresses her anymore. When he first knew her, she was the kind, pretty minister's daughter. This little girl is gone.

He plays various scenarios in his head. She might drop out, head back to London. It would be with the added movement of dusting the dirt off her shoes while leaving, so the Woods do not cling to her. Or she could endure the semester and then leave, never to return. Or something might change. Someone's kindness may make a turn. She might make a friend.

This would be best, he thinks. And most unlikely. The group moves and flows, but Maillory doesn't join in. Why? And no one can make her, surely. But what will invite her back into their group?

He shakes his head and joins Patrick outside who has just finished his third blood sausage.

. . . . .

On their way back, the flying carriage couldn't make its way through the bog. Instead, the students walk through the mud. The girls lift their skirts over the holes, cracks, and pools of the forest; the men have surrendered their jackets to the ladies, bounding through the woods in their white shirts and ties; with only the staff riding the airborne carriage.

Too slow to walk with the trudge of horses, the students stomp ahead. Every once in a while, their feet crash into a frozen pond or slips in a patch of snow. The ground resembles, mostly, a random scattering of hair on a balding man's scalp. Steam, for whatever reason, billows and flows from the trees. Gray twigs, leaves washed of color, and bleached dirt surrounds and forces the remaining snow to surrender.

Well ahead of the floating carriage, Brambley stops. He turns to Cat. "The woods are too quiet," he says. "This morning, the trees were full of birds. It is silent now."

Cat stops. "What does that mean, Brambley?" She lifts her right hand in the air to stop the others.

144

Exhaust from the Tin Woods

"Something drove them away. Like a violent thunderstorm or a tornado, birds seem to be the first to know when there is something threatening the land."

Joane looks in the air. "There are plenty of leaves on the tree. This would be a heaven for crows seeking to build a nest and start a family in time for the summer. You're right, it's as still as a town an hour before an invasion."

Brambley sees Cat's eyes grow wider and wider before they freeze in a terrified freeze. Her arms, legs, face, and body don't move except to breathe. Before he can ascertain what is wrong, he feels a pinch on his neck and instinctively goes to swat the prick with his hand. However, he can't move his hand or his body. Trapped in the state of a statue, Brambley is frozen and helpless. His senses all work, but his body is trapped.

His company silent, he hears the crunch of needles and snow behind him. It sounds to be an army behind him. An inhuman voice, an impossibly low register to be human, speaks, "Take the women, leave the men. Our creatures are hungry and must feed. We shall leave them the men."

The voice, hovering between a beast's growl and metallic hum belonging to an engine, causes the pit of Brambley's stomach to vibrate like a reed.

"Shall ye experiment with some of these beauties?" a man's voice asks as it nears Joane. "Or are they for food, too? Or for fun?"

Two men scoop up Cat, her expression unchanged, and they carry her outside of Brambley's limited field of vision.

"A bit of everything, I figure," the monster's voice says. "For right now, it is my purpose that they all be mine. I require the bodies of the women."

Some more crunches, grunts, and slides as the team pick up and take away all of the women from Mercyminster.

Brambley feels like he is about to vomit. The moment they touched Cat, he wanted to fight. Unable to read her face or emotion, he only imagined absolute terror. Still, he is frozen. Trapped.

A swarthy looking lurkerjerker, all monsterated with ill-fitting and worn toggles, moves close to Brambley's frozen face. He could smell his breath of alcohol, lubricants, and cabbage; his face

145

Exhaust from the Tin Woods

ended with an unnatural point, resembling a pair of closed needle-beatles.

"You favor the pretty blond one, dinna ya?" the man with the sharp face says to Brambley. "I'll enjoy her. I really shall. Say 'allo' to the dogs."

He leaves and some crunching noises sound around the remaining statues. And then silence.

Brambley feels fire burn in his chest. He'd scream, writhe, and spew maledictions until he shouted out his own throat with rage … if only he could speak, move, or do anything. Still, as a sculpture, the wind blew, causing his body to sway like a topmast at sea. Cheeks on fire, ears itching.

Rengulfton, he screams in his head. Face me! You coward! You sniveling little boy dressed up as a man! You sickly, twisted man who hides behind technology and bent men! Face me! Face me, now!!

Nothing but silence.

All Brambley can see is a patch of trees, a bend in the forest, and three pine cones. Some snow. And the lurkjerker's footprints.

Times passes. An hour? Twenty minutes? He isn't sure, but the silence is broken by the sound of tree limbs snapping and the squish of mud from behind him. He trains his ears to hear if it's men's boots or paws that broke the limbs. More sounds erupt from behind Brambley, but nothing suggests animals.

Then he smells pipe smoke.

One of the Mertonites faces him. He sees the lizard looking man named Spricket stare him down. "It is the African variation," he says to someone behind him. "So be careful; it works faster than the varieties of the Russian or Chinese."

The click-clack of bicycle wheels roll behind Brambley, and he feels a small artificial wind at his back.

Some footsteps and then another pinch, this time in his right arm. A second later, a fire explodes inside him, and he sinks to his knees. Shaking and feeling fear, Brambley can move again. He coughs.

"My," Spricket says. "Were you angry before stung?"

"I was angry just after I was frozen," Brambley spits.

Exhaust from the Tin Woods

"I could see that," Braxbury says. He places his hand on Brambley. "I'm going to wait about eleven more seconds ... there ... are you okay?"

Brambley listens to his body and decides that he is without trauma, only stored up adrenaline. "No, I'm fine. They took ... they took."

"The women," a third voice says. He recognizes the name belonging to the young Mertonite, Cogg. "We know. Rengulfton likes experimenting on women. Don't know why. Most of his creatures are from human girls grafted on male animals. For him, we gather, this is just how his math works."

"We must find them. Rescue them."

Braxbury runs to Brambley and faces him. "How?" Braxbury says with sheer, unrestrained joy. "Do you know where he is in the woods?"

"No," Brambley says, learning that it might prove more difficult to find and rescue Cat. "I imagine his location is still a mystery?"

"Still, that fact is unmoved despite our activities. He appears only to attack; that is how we see him," Spricket says.

"Is Allbrung and the staff alright?" Patrick asks. Brambley turns around to see the other man, white-faced on a log, rubbing his neck.

"They were attacked by the same swarm, but left the horse, and they soared to the sky. They made it back to Mercyminster, dispatching us to rescue you," Baxbury says in a low growl.

"Swarm?" Brambley asks.

"Iron bees," Patrick says. "I saw it sting Cat and then you. I don't understand the technology, but it was definitely man-made. An iron monster, full of tiny fob gears and springs."

"Not one of Bell's better applications," Spricket says.

Brambley breathes deep, regaining all of his strength. He rises and Braxbury hands him a tin-plated flask. "Drink up." Brambley drinks, tasting tea that reminds him of factory smoke. "Sorry, it's not brandy. Before being a Mertonite, I was part of the temperance movement. The tea is salve against any sickness or infection."

"Ask him," the other young Mertonite insists. Brambley

remembers his name to be Winch.

Braxbury nods quickly and nervously looks to Patrick, then Brambley. "We could get you back to the safety of Mercyminster. That would please Dr. Allbrung plenty, for he asked us to get you inside as quickly as possible. We are friends, certainly, and would honor his request."

"Is he going out to look for the ladies?" Brambley asks.

"No," Braxbury says. "We are. And we could use four more eyes."

"You've got them," Patrick says, coming to a stand. He looks over to Brambley, who nods in agreement.

"Good. We've got four more hours until darkness, and we'll get you home then: searching at night is stupid, dangerous, and ineffective. Let's take a turn in the Woods."

.....

Cat awakes wearing an extravagant gown, pearl earrings, high-heeled shoes, and her face made-up complete with French powder. She is sitting in a high back, velvet chair facing a roaring fireplace. The gown is a pale colour – a color she would never pick for herself, as it washes out her skin and eyes.

The clothing style is entirely foreign to her, along with the mammoth metal library. The hardware of the room befits a pleasure submarine, an interior she had seen only once. Everything is solid metal, nothing is given to corrosion or being accidently broken.

She looks around and sees Joane dressed in a solid black gown. Joane is still asleep, looking peaceful and almost happy. She hears a grinding noise and leaps out of the chair as she sees that Shweta is asleep, while a robot, breathing out steam and a glow, finishes buttoning the last buttons on her dress.

So, human hands hadn't re-dressed us, she thinks. That does make me feel less disturbed.

The machine wheels away to a corner to shut itself off.

Cat reasons that the robot is far beyond anything designed in London. Far beyond anything that she's ever seen.

She looks down at her pale gown.

The robot is color blind, she thinks, and has little fashion sense.

"We need to be ready when Beatrixx awakes," Joane says.

Exhaust from the Tin Woods

"Patrick told me she changes when she feels threatened. She turns dark, scary. And I can't think of a more threatening position than being kidnapped."

"Why are we wearing these silly, luddmunster outfits?" Cat asks, seeing the slow rise of Joane.

"Really? I rarely wear black leather: I was going to suggest the costume change was the only bright part of this captivity." She points with her blue eyes to Beattrixx. "Patrick says she changes. He promised I wouldn't tell anyone that we talked, but she changes with danger and things like this make her change."

"Why hasn't she changed before?"

"She must have felt safe with us." Joane looks over at Maillory, sleeping soundly. "It seems that whoever has us wants only women. It's queer, almost wrong." She rubs the arm of Cat. "Injured at all?"

"No, other than groggy from whatever knocked us out. I felt frozen for a few seconds, and then I went to sleep."

"Same here. I awoke when the robot was dressing me. Whatever is to befall us, our captors have been gentlemen so far."

"So far," Cat says, crossing her arms. The whole place seems wrong. Not human, not cozy: just functional, nothing more. It is as if everything has a purpose and anything that doesn't is discarded. There is a ruthless economy to the metalmancy of the room.

"I fear for Beattrixx," Joane says.

"And I fear for all of us," Beattrixx says as she rises. "I got a good look at the creature who took us away. We're in the bear's den."

"Are you … fine?" Cat asks, feeling her own stomach tighten and her neck stiffen.

"I am well, and I am not turning to Anansi. No fear, please. I overheard you and you announcing that Patrick broke his promise in keeping it a secret. Fine. The main reason for asking him to do so was that I thought you would treat me different and you haven't. The bottom line is no Anansi." She looks around the room, only lit by the fireplace. Everything in the room looks red as if they had all stepped into a Baroque painting depicting Hell. "I'm calm now. Very … calm." She points to Joane. "Black does suit you, Joane.

Exhaust from the Tin Woods

When we get back to Mercyminster, you must let me outfit you."
She smiles. "I overheard when Patrick told you about me. It was the
night we got back, and he thought I was asleep in the bunk above
his. I would have been mad, but everything about him told me he
wanted your help to figure out how to help me. I actually felt a little
warm. A little."

"This room has the same weight as … The Woods," Joane
says. She crosses her arms and shivers. "Ever been on the streets of
London and you can feel you're being watched. Empirically, there's
no way to prove that someone is staring at you other than you …
feel it. That's what I feel in the woods. That's what I feel … here. A
weight, coming from someone else' eyes. A dark weight, one that
flashes and winks a-thousand-and-one possibilities, all of them
horrible."

Cat's jaw dropped, now feeling her whole body tightened
to the point of trembling, like a dam with too much water pressure.

"Sorry," Joane says as she smiles a coy, held companion's
grin. "I get poetic when I'm scared."

"Please," Beattrixx says. "No poetry." She faces the door.
"Have we tried an exit?"

"An unlocked door we can walk through and make our
way back to Mercyminster? All circumstances leading up to our
rousing suggests against such a possibility," Joane says to Beattrixx.

"I ignore suggestions. If someone isn't bold enough to tell,
or command, but hints and uses other tricks, that only slow one
down," Beattrixx says as she marches to the double doors. Before
her gloved hand reaches the knob, the doors open. The room floods
with yellowed gaslight as a lean, clean butler steps into the space in
front of Beattrixx.

"Can I help you?" he asks pleasantly.

"Stand aside so I can leave," Beattrixx growls.

"I'll stand aside, but leaving is quite impossible. The doors
to the manor are locked from the outside," he says slowly as he
shuffles into the room. "The windows are barred from the outside.
Everything is shut in, locked, clamped down, and secured … from
the outside. We are in a perfect enclosure, worthy of the best zoos
in Europe." He slowly makes his way to the center of the library.
"Now," he asks. "Can I get you anything to eat? Drink?"

Exhaust from the Tin Woods

"A roast beef with a file in the center?" Beattrixx asks through her teeth. "Why are we being kept here, against our will?"

"Because if you knew what was in store for you, you would surely run," the older man says. He is hairless, having lost even his eyebrows and eyelashes. Trim, strong, and full of color: he is healthy, just hairless. The butler looks to be of the same mystery age of Allbrung: 55? 75? 105? Although his slight build and gaunt features are less sturdy and of less strength than Allbrung.

"So, you work for the bear?" Cat asks.

"You do not understand the science of what you've seen." The butler says, "So much will be forgiven. Suffice it to say, what you saw in the woods is much more than a bear." He walks over to Shweta as she still sleeps. "My master is simply known as Rengulfton. That is his name, not his Christian or family name: he is just Rengulfton."

"And what does, 'just Rengulfton' want with us?" Joane asks.

The butler does not answer. Instead, he approaches the sleeping Maillory. He inspects her and then returns to the center of the room, standing at some form of attention. "I do not know. I only know my purpose."

"Which is?"

"To make you as comfortable and relaxed as possible," the butler says. "To that end, you must be hungry. I shall bring a cart full of sandwiches, biscuits, and fruit. It shall only take a moment."

The butler leaves. In the wake of his exit, Joane asks, "Are we going to trust him?" She is white as ivory keys on a high-class difference engine.

"No," Cat says. "But I plan on eating some of his sandwiches. I'm really hungry." She arches her right eyebrow with a small grin. "If he wanted to poison us, he would have done so."

The butler returns, pushing an oak and tin cart filled with drinks, sandwiches, cakes, and biscuits. "Tea is ready." He announces.

"So, who is this Rengulfton?"

"You look very posh and lived the life of a well-informed Londoner." The butler says as Cat approaches the cart. She selects a watercress sandwich. "He was, for a long time, Dr. Cornelius

Exhaust from the Tin Woods

Crime. He solved many of Scotland Yard's most famous of mysteries. Solving murders was easy, for his real love was prattling. Prattling is what took him here to the Woods." The butler's voice did not change in cadence, a steady thump-de-de-thump to his speaking. "He is a man who does not belong to this world. He is beyond all men; his thoughts are beyond most."

"He seems to have been passed by most in the area of modesty," Joane says.

"These are my words, not his. His dreams are so far beyond humanity; I consider it an honor to work for the man. And I think, soon, you shall feel the way I do." He smiles as if breaking from his duty as a butler. "The enclosed space aside, I cannot assure you enough: you have fallen into the right hands. We are the ones who shall save the world, not destroy it. Today, finally, you are among the good and the noble."

He smiles at Cat. She grins back but expresses nothing. He bows and walks out of the room backwards.

.....

The sun is high and proud in the sky by the time Brambley makes his way to breakfast. He shuffles into the room, seeing the buffet is full of fruit, rolls, and other foods that can stay outside of the ice boxes for hours.

Sitting alone at the far side of the breakfast room's table is Dr. Allbrung, sipping his tea. "Good morning." His teacher says.

"I'm sorry I didn't come straight back here. I had to look in the woods for the others." Brambley says.

"You mistake me for the manager of an orphanage. I knew where you were and understood why you must be there," Allbrung says and points with the flat of his hand to the seat next to his. "Patrick shall join us soon. Suk and Moses are gone, looking through the woods with the Constable. My Mertonite friends are, undoubtedly, in the woods as well. Before you return to where everyone else must be, you need some food. And some information."

Brambley fills his plate with cheese, rolls, and fruit. When he sits, Allbrung pours him a cup of coffee. The old man is without emotion. Brambley cannot read the old man. Anger? Sadness? Certainly, there must be something: five of his students have been

Exhaust from the Tin Woods

captured. There is a stoic silence in the room that, if Brambley were to guess, is entirely manufactured.

"In Oxford, when I was your age, I had a friend. Rammuel was his name. We did everything together, much like you do everything with Cat. The only difference was that we ought not to marry, whereas it is written over the two of you. I shall not digress any further on metaphor. Rammuel and I were closer than brothers, simply. When I graduated, I lived as an assistant to an Anabaptist Minister in Koln and Rammuel pursued a job in industry, around London. We corresponded through letters for ten years, keeping alive our friendship.

"I worked in the church and found it under-nourishing; Rammuel worked in industry and felt over-fed. He met many of the best minds of innovation during the age of Napoleon's reign of terror. He designed ships and pistols and bombs. Like a child locked in a toy factory, what he dreamed was made that day and mass-produced the next week.

"Yes, mass-production: Eli Whitney was connected in the factories of Rammuel. I left the church world, hired by a scientist as his assistant. The fellow's name was Black, who quickly retired a year after my apprenticeship and he put me in contact with the shapers and movers of our present age. Babbage, Bell, Verne ... the societies spun within other societies, like gears all turning each other. I expected to see my old friend Rammuel, but he did not run in the same circles. We just kept missing each other."

Allbrung takes a break to cough and sip some more tea. "You're probably wondering why I'm telling you all of this?"

"I'm assuming Rengulfton is a derivation of the name Rammuel?"

Allbrung nods.

"I wish there were a device that can read evil," Allbrung says. "You know, it scans a book and reads, '53% evil'. Or you can take it into a house, and it can say it is a good house for good things to take place in it and people can be there to heal. Such machines are impossible, for who can quantify evil? And who should? Who should have such power? And if they did, the machine would be ineffective for the one who holds it would always be setting off the readings." The old man laughs. "I wish, however, I could have used

Exhaust from the Tin Woods

such a device on my friend when we were in Oxford. Yes, I could confirm what I believed: was not much evil then."

"What happened to him?"

"I do not know," Allbrung says, closing his eyes in thought. There is sadness to his tone. "But when I saw him again, after ten years, Rammuel was evil. I could tell he changed."

The old man opens his eyes. "I had just produced a paper for the 'League of Gentleman's Science Order' concerning 'feeling metal'. It was the beginning of my fame, so to speak. I was beginning to suggest that metal or materials could be imprinted with sophisticated or complex information. It was downright revolutionary to think in terms of writing emotions, so I was a sensation in the scientific fields.

"I was invited, as a celebrity, to meet another celebrity, Rammuel. He was heralded as a genius in robotics: machines that could do several simple tasks at once. At that moment in his study, he was dabbling with wooden robots: Mahogany Servants, as he called them.

"I, along with Dr. Sigmund Freud, was airshipped from Austria to London for the 'meeting of the minds'. The trio of us met in Rammuel's warehouse. With his time in industry, he had been given so much money to invent and invent and invent. He was one of the first Londoners who was a millionaire if it could be believed."

Allbrung clears his throat as if he had to get out a sad expression. His eyes dart over to Brambley.

Suddenly, Patrick enters and sits next to the pair. This does not slow down in the old man's telling.

"Wooden robots everywhere, jumping and moving and singing and working. Freud was crippled with wonder and excitement. When we met for tea, Freud declared that this was the next step in mankind. 'And with your science,' he said to me. 'We can record the human soul and study it in a proper lab, not on a couch or wading through people's ramblings about dreams.' Wooden, robot psychoanalysts, the Austrian was proposing. Rammuel's eyes narrowed, and he smiled. He was so happy with this statement. He added something that revealed everything, 'And one day, science will be able to rewrite the human soul. Perhaps

Exhaust from the Tin Woods

even replace it with something greater.' I then asked a million and one questions, 'What of art? Religion? Beauty? Companionship? Can we replace these?' Rammuel's answers: 'I defenster such crushed ambitions. There is only science, nothing more.'"

Allbrung shakes his head.

"He offered me a partnership with his mahogany servants, and I refused. Later, I heard Freud did as well."

"Three years later, Rammuel vanished. Some say he died in a fire, others said that he went mad sniffing varnish. I continued in my career, writing and collaborating. I became known as a collaborator, a great one. I helped with the making of the telephone, the difference engine, the steamstress used in designing clothing, and radio wave technology. I became a prattler's prattler. Then I met Dr. Crime."

"Wasn't he a fictitious character in the newspapers?" Patrick asks. "Stories every week about his investigations and solving murders were in at least three London newspapers."

"Dr. Crime, the victims, and the perpetrators were all real; the crimes were fiction. Let me explain." He looks up in the air as if a painting of the entire story of Dr. Crime were before him. His eyes seem to scan this imaginary picture as if sorting through ties on display at Selfridges. "Dr. Crime would be hired by Scotland Yard. He would come, assess the scene of the crime, interview suspects, and, at breakneck speed, deliver a story that matched all kinds of evidence and motives and reason. The murderer would be discovered and arrested. His record of success was 100%: it seemed there wasn't a case Dr. Crime could not crack."

"This is hard to follow," Patrick says. "Rammuel or Rengulfton is, I'm assuming, Dr. Crime as well. Or became Dr. Crime after his accident. Did he have a moment of repentance? Saw the error of his ways? How did he go from palpable evil to a fighter against crime?"

"He not only remained evil, but he also worsened as Dr. Crime," Allbrung says. He sighs and rubs his chin. After his pause, he speaks even slower than before. His words have weight, measure and are finely edited before spoken. "An investigator enters a crimes scene and drinks up everything as a whole. Every detail, every word spoken, every story told. The detective listens to everything and then uses everything to root out the lie. The lie stands out like a weed in the garden, so to speak, as a thing of incongruence. But let us change everything and say the sleuth comes not to figure out what happened, but to make the whole setting a lie? He comes to turn the entire garden into a patch of weeds. And the lies were so good, everyone thought the lie was the truth, and the weeds belonged in the garden."

"Was Dr. Crime hired by Scotland Yard to solve their crimes and he got it wrong every time?" asks Brambley.

"No, error would be too simple and basic for Rengulfton. Rather, he committed a crime that no one could solve. He'd be called in, and then pin everything on an innocent suspect. He arranged all facts to appear to be random but then, once he came, pointed to one person. The British jails are filled with his victims; the noose has taken the lives of several more."

"And he was a hero, a crime-solving celebrity. He was Dr. Crime," Brambley says. He looks over to Allbrung, who now is shaking his head and becoming more excited. "He was trusted. I mean, in my schoolyard, kids played him, pretended to be him. All of it was a lie?" Allbrung nods his head. "And so, when the Queen had her necklace stolen, he was the one who had it and framed the maidservant?"

"Rengulfton maintained a vast and complex system within London's crime network, assuming various aliases and identities. On that particular mystery, his main purpose was to hold on to the necklace long enough to be copied. He returned the forged necklace and sold the real one to an art dealer in Prussia. Over the three years, he was Dr. Crime, this network bore the name 'Rengulfton' – a name only I knew from my school days."

"Did anyone else suspect?"

"No, for they all loved Sir Arthur Conan Doyle's works and they were desperate for those tales to become true. They wanted a single man to come, solve all the problems by science, and rid the world of crime through his brilliance. Everyone wanted this fiction to be real, so they never questioned the lie."

"I had read about his end. The newspaper story wrote about Dr. Crime being thrown off the top of Mont Blanc. It was a crashing, dramatic finale. His nemesis ... Dr. Hammerbrung ..."

Exhaust from the Tin Woods

Brambly suddenly pieces the memories together and gasps. "That is you! You're the Swiss criminal genius who Dr. Crime tackled to rid the world of your evil."

"I am not Swiss. And I am not a criminal genius. I had just returned from Russia, living in a commune directed by Leo Tolstoy. My head was filled with pretty amazing ideas when a young detective from Scotland Yard sought me out. He was very, very sharp. The investigations of Dr. Crime didn't make sense. You see, a detective – to be successful – must be very, very clever.

"To be a criminal and get away with every crime, you must be perfect. You must cover all of your facts with lies, every story must make sense, and every alibi must add up. Rengulfton, as brilliant as he is, could not maintain perfect lies. So, this young man sought me out, learning of the time Rengulfton and Freud and myself met over the robots.

"I looked over the notes, and I made the discoveries. The young man drank it all in, brought it back to his superiors. An investigation commenced, and Rengulfton was found out." Allbrung sighs and pauses. "And then he was murdered by Rengulfton's mahogany soldiers. The young man's name was Tad Cooper. Married, with two little girls. Rengulfton disappeared with a warning to me that he would seek to murder all of the young people who ever came near me."

"So, you started a school for young people in Canada?"

"The Woods are so very far from Victoria's England. Plus, a few years have passed, eh? I had to escape, had to get away."

"Dr. Crime's stories were the first things read to me at the Foundation. His stories ended about … ten years ago, I should think," Brambley says.

"Yes, and in that time, I have made the Woods my home. Settled here. Thrived. And I have made many, many students. Teaching them many, many things: not just science. It wasn't as a scientist that I learned all of Rengulfton's falsehoods. His science was very, very correct. It came from … other disciplines."

"You were, I guess back then, just as crushed as you are now."

"Being crushed is not a bad thing. Specialization dissects; integration binds and combines. Being an expert is about denying;

Exhaust from the Tin Woods

bringing together is about affirming. I figured out his puzzles as a human, not as a prattler. This shall be the way we figure out how to rescue our friends."

Patrick nods as he looks over to Brambley.

Brambley wolfs down his breakfast and wipes his chin.

"Thank you, Dr. Allbrung," Brambley says. "That helps me. I would like to return to the forest, if I may. I must look for our friends."

Allbrung waves his hand to dismiss him. "Please go. Even if I continued in my classes and you attended, you would not be here. I shall be the base of the investigate. God's speed."

"Thank you," Brambley says as he rises. He bows and then heads back outside in search of Cat.

.....

It is the fifth day of Cat's captivity. The fifth day obeys the clockwork routine of every morning. The door to her room opens leading down a slender hallway to the library where breakfast is served. She sleeps alone, in a room the size of the common room back in Mercyminster. A new dress is hung for her in an opened cabinet, with the wordless command for her to bathe, dress, and powder before the door is opened for breakfast.

The doors are wooden, with metal bones. When the doors are locked, it is a final sealing without any means of opening, picking, or breaking. The halls are similar: wooden skin, steel bones.

Once she is in the library, she sees the rest of the captives: all prettily dressed and primped like dolls waiting to be played with by the child of the house. Beattrixx is clad in a pale blue gown, complete with lace gloves and a bold white hat full of feathers and roses. She no longer looks herself, clad in black and leather. Maillory is squeezed into a tight, swelling bodice with her chest, neck, and breast nearly exploding out through the top. Her arms and hands bare, with the dress revealing her ankles, an invisible insult to her previous vows of chaste clothing. Along with this insult, Joane is dressed simply without an embellishment; Shweta must wear a bellased outfit without something to cover her head.

Cat feels she is the lucky one, escaping the private, fashion hell her companions must endure every morning. For her, she's

Exhaust from the Tin Woods

dressed as a pony, as a lurker, and a dreamer, and as a prattler. The gown interchangeable, only the smile remains.

"It is my morning," Beattrixx says as a greeting to Cat. "After breakfast, one of the little robots shall take me away while the rest remain for the day. Like the equal ticks of a glockenspiel, the routine shall be maintained," she says and sneers. "I hate this place."

"My time wasn't very bad," Maillory says. "I'm not sure of the point. I was placed in a room all day, looking at lights and colors. Not much of a torture." She looks to Shweta. "And yesterday, how was your session?"

"I have been forbidden to speak of it. Otherwise, you shall all suffer. That was what the voice told me. I endured it, and nothing hurt me permanently, but I would have preferred it to be lights and colors. And I will say this: my god shall have his revenge on this place for what they did to me."

"The experiments seem to be getting worse, each day we spend here," Beattrixx says.

Cat reads a look of shock on Joane's face.

"Sorry," Beattrixx says as she playfully arches her right eyebrow and smiles. "Gallows humor. I don't mean to upset those whose turn is after mine. But I think I shall also be commanded not to talk about what they do to me. I, too, shall invoke some kind of divine wrath for what is done. I'm pretty sure the experiments are incremental, so gone are the days of lights and colors."

"Divine wrath, but you're irreligious," Maillory says in a quiet, child's voice.

"It's true, I worship at the same altar as Keats and Shelley. But today, I might be clutching at straws."

The double doors opposite to the hallways leading to their rooms open, the butler emerges as he pushes a cart. "Good morning," the small man says gently. "I trust you slept well. And I trust, Beattrixx, you received your note."

"Aye," Beattrixx says. "I'm to eat well because I follow the robots to some appointment. Any ideas what I'm to expect?"

"Oh," the butler says finishing the push of his cart. "My master tells me nothing."

"Doesn't it bother you," Cat asks. "That you work at a

Exhaust from the Tin Woods

home that tortures women?"

"No," he says without looking at anyone in the eye. "My master has dreams for our future. We can either see this future in our lifetime or wait 100 years. To wait means that we must apply scientific discovery on slow, meaningless tasks involving lab rats and cheese and pin pricks. Our world cannot wait, so the methods must be as he has put forth. But do not worry, they are not cruel, and they are all within the exclusive discipline of science."

Shweta snorts, looking like she's about to spit.

"Please," the butler says to Beattrixx. "We are not about cruelty here. There are many other scientists in this world. In Canada that are all about the ruination of young women for the sake of scientific gains. You shall be in a surgeon's hands, child. We are the heroes of science, please remember."

Beattrixx looks away. "Let's get it over with. I've lost my appetite." She leaves, and the girls are silent for the rest of the breakfast. It snows outside, the only entertainment they take up to pass the hours of the day.

Every hour or so, Cat wishes to speak. She then reads the faces of the other girls. Joane is angry, and the rest are scared. Shweta sits upon a window seat, hugs her knees and tries not to rock. Her skin is white; she looks cold.

Cat decides not to talk. Instead, she scans the bookcases for something, anything that might reveal a fact, a location about their captor. Reams and reams of scientific journals, some fiction (mostly Jules Verne), lots of field journals, and the complete works of John Calvin. Works of art, very eclectic. Nothing uniform. It was as if the library was designeded to be like all of the other libraries in London. After her search, Cat decides to sit like the rest and wait.

That evening, the butler wheels Beattrixx into the room on a gurney. Her wrists are strapped down, along with her waist and ankles. Wearing a small, paper gown, she struggles and writhes and gurgles. She seems no longer human. Looking up at the kind faced butler, Beattrixx launches into a series of maledictions that begin as words and end as just growls.

"What was done to her?" Cat asks, running to the side of Beattrixx.

"She had an unplanned, emotional reaction. It is ... quite

Exhaust from the Tin Woods

irregular," the butler says as he stops the gurney in the center of the library. "She needs friends and comfort and food."

"Spiders," Beattrixx spurts. "Metal, crawling spiders! I'll kill you all! Turn you to stone and metal, you'll breathe exhaust!"

"Beattrixx, I'm here," Cat says as she strokes her dampened hair. "We're here." She speaks in a near whisper.

"I am not Beattrixx! Not Beattrixx! Not Beattrixx! Not Beattrixx! Not Beattrixx! Not …"

Beattrixx shoots this out, over and over again like the drumming of a machine in full tilt. She coughs at times, unable to say it fast enough without taking in a breath. It is a robotic litany, devoid of inflection or personality.

"What did you do to her?" Cat shouts.

"I can't say and she will not. She was barely awake when most of it was done to her," the Butler says with a bow. "Most irregular. I am truly sorry. There is a bell to be pulled if I can get you anything. Please, let me know."

"Let us go and stop experimenting on us," Joane screams.

"Within reason, I am sorry. Truly." With this, he exits quickly.

When the butler leaves, Beattrixx laughs a witch's cackle. Her eyes, full of movement and white, are feral and fevered. "I am Anansi. Let me go, and I will burn this place to the ground."

"Most of it is metal. We would be baked, like bread in an oven," Joane says. She studies Beattrixx's body. "I don't see any injuries. Are you hurt … Anansi?"

"No, I feel fine." She looks to Joane. "But just wait for what they have in store for you, my held companion."

Beattrixx soon goes to sleep and does so through the whole night.

…..

Cat hears a hissing noise as more darts are flung around the room. Sticking out of Joane's neck is a small dart. She looks to Cat, reaching for it, but then is frozen. Before she can find out what is shooting the darts, she feels a pinch on her right thigh. She looks down at her leg, her eyes roll back into her head, and she collapses and goes to sleep.

…..

Exhaust from the Tin Woods

The next morning, Cat awakens, still a bit dizzy from the drugs. She prepares herself for the day. The door opens as she awaits, fully dressed, for breakfast. She sees Joane first, holding her letter of invitation for the day's experiments. "I am cordially invited," Joane says through her teeth clenched. She is red, angry. "What is this?"

"I don't know. And worst, I'm not sure what he wants. For the last few days, we've been given nothing. I'm really confused," Cat says. "Perhaps it was from those knockout darts. Where did they come from?"

"Any bookcase," Joane says. "Every bookcase in every room has holes. I dismantled the bookcase in my room. Sound activated and aims at heat, I think. Very luddmunster in design." She smirks. "I guess it's the way the Master of the House keeps his schedule by knocking everyone out when the event is over, and the next one is to begin."

"And it gives all of us a fog in the brain," Cat says, trying to shake it off. "Keeps us mildly sedated, compliant, and submissive. Like willing patients in a hospital, or generous customers at an opium den."

The butler comes, pushing a cart full of breakfast. "Miss Joane, you are expected shortly. And I fear that breakfast is not part of today's activities. I am truly sorry." He bows and Joane follows him out the door.

Fifteen minutes later, Maillory arrives. Shweta and Beattrixx stay in their rooms.

Maillory fills her plate and eats. "Last night was the first time I was scared. Really scared. I had a nightmare.'"

"What did you dream about?" Cat asks, not just curious, but pleased to have some sort of conversation.

"This house, this place. We were turned into animals, never to return to human civilization. It was horrible. Do you think he wants to turn us into wolves with human faces or half-bears? Never again to return to London, to live our dreams?" Maillory starts to cry; Cat places her arm around her. "We've been trying to be brave ... we can't ... what is this place?" Maillory cries for a little while longer until the tears run out. After she settles down, she eats her breakfast. Cat watches her. As they eat, Cat hears

Exhaust from the Tin Woods

something. A whistle. She's heard it before, and she scans her memory to find out when. It usually, she thinks, is when the butler comes.

The whistle sounds like a birdcall. When she was in America working on the riverboats, a fellow pony used to do birdcalls as the boats crossed the banks to summon the birds up to the ship. It was something the ponies all did together, to pass the time as they waited for breakfast to be served to the guests.

Cat smiles at this memory. Suddenly, she no longer thinks she's prisoner to some metal library.

The young pony was from New Orleans, a posh one, bellased every day with a new way of doing her hair or makeup. They danced together in the show and, after the show, they sat on men's laps in the bar to get them to drink, gamble, and buy more things. The girl's heart, though, wasn't on the riverboats: it was for the woods.

She kept a sketchbook and would draw any bird that could be found on the banks of the Mississippi. She was a vegetarian and could never bring herself to hunt for birds, but she loved watching them: sketching them in her book was enough. Being around her, you couldn't help yourself: you learned the birdcalls of breeds and everything about the land.

She left the riverboat the same time Cat did, seeking to go the West and possibly to Mexicania.

I wish I could become a bird, Cat thinks. Right now.

"Tell me something," Cat says to Maillory. "What is God thinking? Right now?"

"I don't know. And in some ways, I don't care."

"Sure you do. You're religious and all of that. What does God think about us? Right now, right here?"

"You're trying to distract me."

"Of course, I am." Cat chuckles. "This place is a monsteration of a purgatory. Anything to get our minds off of waiting for 'our turn'."

That night, Joane returned as white as a ghost. She follows the butler, shaking and shivering and her eyes are too wide for her to look natural. The butler does not touch her, simply bows and says, "Lady Joane has returned. It was a rough go, I fear."

Exhaust from the Tin Woods

"What did you do to her?" Maillory asks.

"Nothing, nor do I know what took place. As soon as she was finished, I took her straight to you. She needs ... friends."

Cat wrapped her arms around Joane, who closes her eyes and starts to cry. Maillory joins in the embrace. Cat looks around, somehow wishing Shweta and Beattrixx could be here, but they did not make any appearance at all that day. A whistle sounds and the butler's door opens and closes for him to make his exit.

"Did they defile you in any way?" Maillory firmly asks.

"No," Joane says trembling. "My honor is intact. And there is no permanent damage. It was just ... it was really horrible."

She shakes and shivers and sobs for an hour before the trolley wheels in, bringing the girls their dinner. Dinner is beef Wellington and Yorkshire pudding and greens. The three girls eat in silence. Cat tries to read Joane's face. Nothing, other than fear. There seem to be no injuries, and she is healthy after her day of experimentation.

The embers in the fire shrink and the light in the room darkens. They all decide to go to bed. When they get to the door, it whistles and then opens to lead back to their rooms.

Joane turns to Cat. "Please, can I sleep with you tonight?" she asks.

Cat nods.

The two crawl into Cat's bed.

Joane quickly falls asleep and Cat, a few moments later, joins her.

The next morning, Cat wakes up to find Joane gone. In her place, is a note which reads:

Dearest Cat,

You have been cordially invited for a day of scientific exploration. You will not speak of what takes place to any of your companions otherwise the second row of experimentation shall increase in horror. Please dress, have breakfast, and follow the servant to the laboratory. Do not delay.

Cat dresses in a simple gown and a shirt and a coat and boots. The door opens when she is done to lead her to breakfast.

Exhaust from the Tin Woods

The library is full of her friends. Beattrixx is pacing in the far side of the room, muttering to herself. Shweta and Joane are by the fire, wrapped up in a blanket. Maillory is reading her Bible.

Cat grabs some fruit and a slice of cheese for her breakfast.

A few seconds later, the butler comes. "We are ready," he says.

Cat nods and follows him out. She rounds the corner to a brand new hallway, previously unavailable in her former captivity. The hallway darkens within every step until they reach a door at the end, where it is pitch black. Only a thin outline of a line around the door is all she can see. The butler opens the door and turns to her. "I am sorry. Please step through the door."

The open door is revealing a thin, gray light around the floor. Cat steps through the door, and it is closed. A few moments later, the floor gives way, revealing her to be standing upon a trap door.

She falls into a deep pool of ice-cold water. She splashes around, finding herself in a glass vat surrounded by lights bright as the sun. The water is nearly frozen, with blocks of ice scraping against her chin and face. She peers through the glass walls and sees only blackness.

"Hello, Cat," a voice says. It is human, relaxed, and comes from the other side of the glass. "You have been the one I've been waiting for. This shall be a good day of experiments."

She can barely breathe. Her feet go numb as they wade in the water. "I'm going to die in this water." It is not just cold, but the kind of pain that her body would soon shut down to survive. She no longer feels any heat in her body.

"Surely," the voice says. "I want to see how long it would take. And while we wait for this to happen, I shall be asking you some questions. The way you answer these questions is just as important as what you say. How you feel, what you think: it's all a part of this study."

"And if I say nothing? Just swim and freeze?"

"Then I shall modify your body so drastically that you'll need a vat to breathe," the man says without any emotion. "Besides, your answers shall provide little to no injury. You shall not harm anyone."

Exhaust from the Tin Woods

"Really? What about me?"

"You may not survive the day." She feels this to be true. Her arms are going numb. Soon, she can imagine, it'll be hard to move, to tread water to survive. "Now, let's begin before there's any long-term pain. How long have you been a student of Dr. Allbrung?"

"A f-few months." Her teeth chatter. "Why?"

"Did he ever speak about thinking machines?"

"A l-l-little. He has been wor-working on a n-n-n-new Difference Engine."

"Ah, good. Now, see: there is no harm. How can I use this information against him? And you've answered, according to my machines, in perfect form." The disembodied voice pauses. "Now, has he ever spoken to you about the Infinity Engine?"

"He talks about Infinity. Shweta is a better one –"

"She was most unhelpful and suffered greatly. And the result is that her second time might be fatal. I am sorry for such a consequence."

Suddenly, Cat heard something familiar in the man's voice. Her eyes widened, and she smirked. "You're the butler," she points out.

"Excuse me?"

"Rengulftor, you aren't the bear. You're the butler. You come in, pretending to be the butler. See us every morning and evening, apologizing for your master's work! You want to be all cozy and nice to us, but you're playing us like a real lurkjerker."

"How –"

"The phrase 'I'm so sorry' is common to him. Now I-I-I can … hear your voice. Sure, you're trying t-t-to disguise it, and it p-p-probably worked, but –"

"Now you must answer some of my questions. I want you to solve this simple equation –"

"You're the little chappy with the cart!"

"Please, answer the equation."

"Can't afford help? I-I-Is that it? Hope we m-m-m-might open up with you, confide?"

"The equation!" The voice becomes terse and sharp. "Or I shall bring in eels."

Exhaust from the Tin Woods

"The butler!"

Suddenly, a dramatic and painful shock shakes her body. For a second, she loses control of her body and sinks below the water's surface. She snaps out of the paralysis and swims back up. She gasps for air.

"A small shock. More to come. Now, finish the equation: $E + MT(2) -$"

.....

"I'm worried about Brambley," Patrick says to Winch behind Brambley's back.

Brambley is certain Patrick believes this comment is unheard. There is enough woods, snow, and distance for him not to be heard. Alas for Patrick, Brambley is working extra hard to hear everything in the woods. "We have to drag him away from the hunt when we are well into the night. He doesn't eat. I don't think he sleeps. And he hasn't prattled since the girls have gone missing."

Brambley wants to turn to address his friend's concerns. Something stops him. He, instead, just walks slower to hear the conversation.

"Question for you," Braxbury says to the young Mr. Winch and to Patrick. "Finding these girls after six days of searching, do you think it is possible to find Rengulfton? Or is this just an ether dream?"

"We must look," Patrick says.

"No," Winch says. "We must find them."

"But is it possible to find them? If it is impossible, Brambley is quite ludwigged. If it is possible, he is working in harmony with the scenario given to him," Braxbury says.

The older Mertonite chuckles. "Your job, it seems, is to worry about the friend right in front of you. It is ... noble."

"Gentlemen do not worry. It is ... unseemly."

"I have seen debtor's prisons packed with skeletal men, women who have lost their virtue to powerful men, needless orphans, slaves, foreigners exploited, factories murdering their workers, and unions butchered because they disagreed with the rich and powerful. And all, of course, from a country that demanded their gentlemen not to worry. Perhaps worrying is a form of tacky parloring, but one the world could use more of, I think."

Exhaust from the Tin Woods

"Worry leads to action." Winch says.

Brambley stops. Something isn't right with the woods, something incongruent. He cannot say what it is, but it is painfully wrong. He places his finger over his mouth and turns to Patrick and the Mertonites behind him. They stop.

Before Brambley is a heap of snow, surrounded by a crowd of spruce trees. The trees are stripped by steam, charred at the top. And yet, the snow survived not only whatever made the steam, but the spring thaw.

"Do you have a trowel?" Brambley asks Winch.

"I do," Spricket says. Quickly, the older man starts digging into the snowy heap. In a few moments, he uncovers a human face, panting wildly. His right eye is toggled, a laser light forming an eye patch. He is bearded, his face pock-marked and a spider web of scars.

"He has been buried alive," Spricket says.

Steam flows from his mouth. "I made an air hole," the buried man says. His voice faint, a mere whisper. His skin looks like it is collapsing into the metal. "I am ... broken."

"What happened to you?" Brambley asks.

"My body is ... rejecting the prattling done to it. I am, truly, a steamy. I am dying, so the rest of the archons left me. The bear came back and buried me alive."

"Let's see if we can repair him," Brambley says to Braxbury.

"I don't need a mechanic; I need a surgeon. Possibly a priest."

They shoveled him free. Patrick surveys the man's body: broken tubes and shafts, frozen blood, torn flesh, and leaking steam. "His affair." Patrick says. "Is a Pickled Pete[69], I fear. We'll need all three: mechanic, surgeon, and priest."

"Let's be all three, then," Braxbury says as he starts studying the man's chest. "Winch, see if we can patch up the exhaust before it cooks this man anymore. I'll stop the bleeding. And Brambley, pray for the man."

"I know I'm going to die." The broken man says. "I just

---

[69] a puzzle without an easy solution

Exhaust from the Tin Woods

need to say something. Please, hear me."

Brambley nods and leans in to hear the man's whispers.

"I have sinned against my God." He says. "I am sorry. I helped steal your friends. I am sorry. My former master has big dreams. He wants to turn all of this Tin Woods into one big machine with a machine mind to run it. Your friends will be the first. I am sorry."

"Where are they?" Brambley asks, cutting him off.

"You do not go to Rengulfton's mansion; it comes to you." He coughs, and a pale weakness rolls over the man's face.

"I am sorry. I'm desperate to find them." Brambley rises to make a pronouncement. "My God forgives you, and you shall be made new under His forgiveness. May your God and my God be the same."

"He is, and I am anxious for His forgiveness. My soul, all of my life, has been monstered. And now my spirit and body match. I ... break."

A waft of thick, gray exhaust expels from his body, and the man becomes a corpse.

"Death." Braxbury says. "All of the philosophers are split. Some say we don't deserve it and others say we deserve it plenty." He walks up to the man and closes his one, human eye. "I don't know. Just sleep, young man. Just sleep." He pats him on his head. Brambley then deduces the lurkjerker is at the age to be Braxbury's son.

The older Mertonite turns to Winch. "His body doesn't belong in the woods, yet we don't have the means to transport it. What are your thoughts?"

"His soul won't be at rest until all of him is buried." The young man says.

"But half of his body is missing." Brambley says, "All of him is spread out and replaced by machines." He shakes hard. "That is superstition to see him buried as means of a proper afterlife."

"Are you Anabaptist? It seems those types of Protestants are less inclined to ceremony." Winch says, "I am Catholic, so I guess I'm more prone to ceremony. A funeral would do him good, just in case it does matter."

Brambley kneels down in the snow. "Heavenly Father,

Exhaust from the Tin Woods

whatever you can do to make this right, both here and in Heaven, your will be done. We commit to you the body of this young man. Somehow, have mercy: he didn't know what he was really doing. A-men." Brambley turns to Winch and shrugs.

"Good enough." Winch says.

After seeing the body, Brambley feels different. His speed does not lesson, but his steps are softer and his voice lighter. He can't really put his finger on it.

When the sun goes down, they make camp in a cozy hub of poplar trees and dormant Saskatoon berry bushes. A stream leading to Lesser Slave Lake trickles and crackles infinitely in the distance. The four Mertonites, Patrick, and Brambley create a shelter with canvas, sticks, and fallen logs. Winch spends about an hour packing wet mud and river rock to manufacture a rough, waist high stove. Spricket sets the toggle repellent stakes for protection.

"We should get back to Mercyminster soon," Patrick says once camp is set and the moon is high above their heads. "On the weekend, Suk and Moses will be looking for the girls. We can do the search in shifts."

"Why do you think Allbrung doesn't search?" Brambley asks.

Braxbury hears this question. "He won't. It is beyond his convictions. He is a man of faith."

"In what?"

"In education. He will not venture beyond the classroom or the shop." The Mertonite says, stepping into the wooden cave the pair have finished. "He is strict and resolute. The classroom shall redeem the world, not roaming through the woods."

"Do you agree?" Brambley asks.

"Do you see me out here or in a classroom?" He shrugs and wiggles his moustache. "Getting out, confronting, fixing, and standing against issues this is where I disagree with your mentor. A stream cannot go to the ocean by words alone, but one must dig with a shovel and make dykes. A people must be led away from evil, not just taught." He offers a flask to Brambley. "Drink up. The tea will calm you down "

"I'm calm, actually." Brambley says, "Calmer than I've been since Cat was kidnapped."

Exhaust from the Tin Woods

"Why the change?"

"Everything just got more human, I think. I don't know how to say it. I feel, right now, we're not just rescuing our friends from something evil and wrong and alien and all of that. No, there's something real and human after we do this. And I can't help to think that we're not alone in this fight."

"Is it a fight, then, against philosophies and meanings?"

"I don't know. I'm not sure, other than I don't have a word for it. Not yet. Not until I see Cat and the girls."

"Cat?" Patrick asks with a grin.

Brambley looks up. He feels lost as if he just woke from a dream and is doing his best to recall the plot of his former vision. The plot is being lost … second by second. "I don't know. I'm just so tired. And I must find Cat."

"I'm worried about you, my friend. Rather worried. You are not well. You look like the color of the snow. You talk to yourself. You walk stooped. At first, I thought you were just bricked. But now you just see gray, I think. You must find Cat and –"

"And I'm worried about her. All of them."

"Let him make his own bed, son." Wicket says, "He'll have to sleep there a lot longer than all of us."

"It will be good to have reinforcements, not replacements, come this weekend." Brambley lays on his blanket and goes to sleep for the night, way before dinner is served, or even cooked.

…..

Cat is on all fours, hunched over a bowl filled with water. She picks it up and drinks it, her body crying out for anything wet or cool. Her wrists and ankles still ache, still raw from being hung over a bed of fire. She looks at her bare arms, red and moist and full of steam. No permanent damage, but she has never felt pain like that in all of her life. She drinks the entire bowl and hears a whistle, opening a door from the brick room of fire.

"Tomorrow, you shall return along with all of your friends. I have all the data required for this round of tests. When you return, we shall begin work on the next set of tests. Since you lacked cooperation, the more rigorous parts of my testing shall be applied to you. Cat, it shall be against all the odds that you will survive,"

Exhaust from the Tin Woods

the voice of Rengulfton says from the darkness.

"May you rot in Hell," Cat snarls.

"This test did not need to be as bad as it was today. Your insolence forced me to raise the levels," Rengulfton says without emotion. "Still, I have reams and reams of data. Thank you."

She takes a deep breath. She is wearing only a scant gown, sopping wet with her sweat. She stands slowly, wondering if she has enough strength. Dizzy and weak, her stance is wobbly and teetering at best. She drags her feet to a walking shuffle to the light of the door.

"You have such pretty, pink skin. It is an amazing fabric," is the last thing he says to Cat as she makes her exit.

She emerges into the library. The door closes behind her as she sees all of her companions except Maillory. "Where is —" she asks in a weakened, pained whisper.

"She hasn't been around all day. We thought she might be with you," Joane says.

"No," Cat says. "Rengulfton was with me the whole day. The whole day which was a living Hell. He was busy with me; he couldn't have been torturing her as well."

"The butler?"

"He's the same person as Rengulfton. And tomorrow, he will be experimenting on all of us." Cat goes to the cart and takes a long draught from a glass filled with water. Her strength returns. "Today, I was kept in ice water until I almost died. Then I was suspended over a fire until I was almost roasted. And then back to the water. Then fire. The word 'almost' is his target, as he sought to 'almost' kill me."

"We mustn't speak about the experiments," Joane says. "He forbade us."

"I was placed in a room full of expanding balloons," Shweta says as she rises to her feet. "Almost suffocated. Almost crushed. Close to death or breaking, the balloons would shrink back. Hour after hour. And he would ask questions about Allbrung." Shweta crosses her bronze arms. "May God strike him down. All of his little toys."

"For me," Joane says. "It was robotic spiders. I was tied down. In the nude. It was … horrible."

Exhaust from the Tin Woods

"I don't know what he did to me," Beattrixx says. "Anansi knows, and she isn't telling me a thing." She turns from her high-backed chair. "Tomorrow, it's all of us?"

"All of us and he isn't very pleased with me, so I will be getting the brunt of his abuse," Cat says, still feeling weak. And yet, there was something growing inside of her. "We need our rest for strength. Tomorrow will be a full day."

"I am several steps ahead of you, Cat. We sleep," Shweta says.

"Sleep? With our deaths looming on the horizon! We're helpless to escape! And tomorrow, we might watch you die?"

"Sleep well," Cat says without emotion. She grabs some food and heads for her room.

In the morning, Cat emerges from her room dressed in a full ball gown complete with white satin gloves and her face made up. Gone is the red-faced, trembling girl of the night before. She floats like grace into the library. The rest of the girls await her, dressed in the finest of clothing offered to them so far. Cat nods to them and sees the breakfast cart waiting for them, no longer being brought to them by their captor in disguise.

The door automatically shuts behind her.

Joane looks like she is going to burst into tears. "You look … beautiful."

"Are you well, Maillory?" Cat asks flatly.

"As well as can be expected," Maillory says.

"Good."

Cat turns and faces the door. In a pitch perfect mimic, she whistles the code to open the door. Obediently, the door opens for her. "Come this way," Cat says and shuffles out of their prison. Joane gasps in shock. The girls follow her down the darkened corridor. "It took a while to practice the code, but it's the same concept as bird calling. The door responds to the call, rather than just sounding it as they open. This sound is a skeleton key to any room of the house."

They round a corner to find a spiral staircase leading to the main floor of the building. As they descend, an army of large, robotic spiders charges across the floor to meet them at the stairs.

"I was hoping this would be easy," Cat says as she reaches

into her billowing gown for a long, lead pipe.

Beattrixx reached into her coat for a long bar used in the supports of her bed. Shweta produces a whip made of shower rings and lamp chains.

Joane looks around, seeing her and Maillory are the only ones not armed. "But how did everyone else know we were planning an escape?"

"We understand innuendo," Beattrixx says as she leaps off the stairs and lands right in front of the spiders. She swings at two, steam and oil exploding from her strike. "These creatures are not designed for combat." She smashes another on its head. The heads and faces seem to be made of glass. Suddenly, one grapples her leg, and two syringes shoot out. Blue liquid bubbles behind the needles.

Cat jumps off the stairwell and lands atop of the spider clutching Beattrixx. She wields the pipe in a circle, knocking back four spiders.

More come, filling the exit with spiders the size of a wolf pack.

Shweta tears fabric from her skirt, breaking into the gas lamp on the wall. Suddenly, the ball of her fabric lights up with fire. She then throws the fireball at the farthest spider. Instantly, the robotic spiders become a fiery wreck, scampering alongside walls and up the ceiling. The entire room turns bright red with fire.

Joane grabs a table and turns it into a moving barricade. The girls fall behind her, as she pushes it through the burning, glass spiders.

They bang against the front door.

"That wasn't too hard, was it?" Joane says.

Cat whistles, opening the front door. The girls discover they are five stories from the ground. The house is held up by large, robotic legs … moving over the woods. Suddenly Cat figures out why they are so high and the nature of the house: it's one, big spider moving through the woods. The house moves, crawling over the land. And they are now in the belly of this beast, towering above the world.

"Ever see the circus?" Beattrixx asks Cat. "Everyone, hold hands."

"What are you going to do?" Maillory asks as she grabs

Exhaust from the Tin Woods

Shweta's hand. "What are you going to do?"

"Something that, if I think about it, I wouldn't do because I value common sense."

Cat looks behind her and sees the numbers of spiders' triple. More and more pour out, filling every doorway and passage behind them.

"Let's count to three?" Cat requests.

"While we're falling," Beattrixx says as she jumps towards the nearest pine tree. The entire group screams.

Beattrixx, through the moment of her jump, guides them to the central trunk of the tree. She tackles the trunk, sticking for only a second. She then slides down, with the pine needles and lean branches breaking the girls fall. They slip, tumble, and scramble down until their fall is only from branch to branch. At the end of their trickle, they land on some of the last snow and splat into the watery goop.

"Now," Cat says. Her eyes widen as she discovers they are not alone in the woods. "Run."

At the base of the tree is the bear, leading the pack of wolves with human faces. The bear growls at them.

Before they can check if they are injured, the girls charge westward.

The bear and wolves pursue them.

"Bears, when agitated, can run faster than a horse," Shweta says as she picks up her skirt and widening her gate.

Cat looks over her shoulder, seeing the creatures gain on them. They cross through the woods, dodging trees and using the trees to provide obstacles for the beasts. Alas, the animal part of the creatures know how to chase.

Cat feels the weakness take hold as her strength was spent on the previous night's experiments. Her legs go numb as the fire leaves from within her body. She pants for air, her ribs scream. She looks over to Joane, seeing a similar pain in her face. Shweta is still strong, but the rest of the group is straggling behind.

The bear stops and stands on his hind legs. He growls again, this time at the heavens.

And then the sound of thunder rings through the woods. Cat smells black powder smoke. The wolves stop, freeze in their tracks. The bear clutches its chest and falls backwards.

A man with a toggled eye wrapped in bear fur comes from behind a fat tree, holding an elephant rifle. Marching behind him are two dozen men, carrying similar rifles.

A cacophony of rifle fire erupts, covering the woods with black powder smoke as they shoot at the marching spider fortress overhead. The wolves retreat, the bear slumps away with an awkward march belonging to a drunken man.

The man covered in fur looks down at Cat. "You white people are crazy," he says. "You shouldn't be out."

Cat looks at him. Her eyes cross. She collapses in the snow.

.....

Cat awakens inside of a circular tent with Brambley sitting across the fire from her. He looks at her and smiles. "Care for soup?" he asks and hands her a wooden bowl.

She smells the broth, and it reminds her how empty her stomach is. She grabs the wooden spoon and gobbles up the soup within seconds. A few seconds after the soup is consumed, the salty-savory taste overwhelms her mouth.

"This is salt rock. What is it?" she asks.

"Moose Nose Soup."

Suddenly, she remembers black bits resembling raisins floating in the soup. "Are you klowning?"

"No. Would you like seconds?"

She feels conflicted. "Maybe later. Let the noses settle in my stomach first." She looks around. She can't tell if it's day or night. Everything just glows red. "How long have I been asleep?"

"It's midnight." Brambley says. He looks old, tired. There's almost a gray to his hue. "I came to camp an hour before nightfall. Maybe 8 hours?" He smiles. "I insisted on being here when you woke up."

"Well, I'm awake. Stay."

He gets up and dusts off his pants. "I do not want to take advantage of your virtue. I am already breaking many rules of propriety by being alone in a tent with you, but I would go mad if I didn't know you were all right first. But I shall not dishonor you, Cat."

Exhaust from the Tin Woods

"Please do," she says with a sly grin.

He stops and laughs. "But I don't want you to suffer any mixed messages, Cat, by me leaving. Being separate from you was agony, and my mind fell in bedlam with your capture. I want to be with you every second and I feel a fiery, ludwigged with passion every time I think of you." He looks down, with a lone tear rolling upon his cheek. "Do I make my feelings plain?"

"Why can't you be a normal human being and ravage me in a mad, blind passion?" she asks feeling her heart bang in her throat.

"I shall not dishonor you or besmirch your name, Lady. But know this: I love you madly, my Cat," he says and nods. Then he exits hastily. On his heels, Joane enters the tent.

Achingly wistful, Cat moans, "Queen Victoria sure sullied the minds of an entire generation of men." She shakes her head.

"Are you recovered?" Joane asks, pouring another bowl of soup for Cat.

"No, but things are back to normal."

Cat sleeps that night, long and dreamless. When she awakes, she hears the sound of children laughing. She pulls on her boots, her jacket, and her gloves and emerges from the teepee while Joane still sleeps.

Outside on a yellow field framed by snow and ice, children are playing a game with sticks and a wooden ball. Cat smiles to see Patrick in the center of the game, trying to hustle and rally for the ball. He looks just like one of the Cree children, all smiles and pants and shouts. It looks like football, only with fewer rules.

"Like the spider castle we escaped from," Beatrixx says from behind Cat. Cat turns to see Beattrixx wearing her same clothes, only modified and tailored radically different. "This camp is moveable. They roam this territory to protect their children. It seems The Woods, the church, and all white people want to take these children away. Make them good Commonwealthies. Very British, very Empire."

"Why?" Cat asks.

"Unlike Patrick, most Gentlemen don't see a group of kids playing a game and join in. They prefer to keep them educated."

Cat shudders, more out of anger than fear. She looks deep

Exhaust from the Tin Woods

into Beattrixx's eyes. "How are you? Really? We lost you for a bit."

"I'm fine. But you need to hear about Anansi." She clears her throat. "I lost my virtue, quite by force, to a bunch of steamies off the streets of London. The experience was … horrible. Soon after that episode, Anansi would come and show up when it was best that I wouldn't be present. Rengulfton's experiments were … undoubtedly horrible. I couldn't be there. So, Anansi volunteered. Whenever I need to be horrible and escape my world, she shows up."

"We all don't like her, but we're mad about you," Cat says.

"Not all of us. I slept with Maillory last night, and she woke me up in the middle of the night. I was snoring, I guess. She said she wished I was left behind. She walks with a limp now, from the fall, and blames me."

"She's been through a lot, perhaps a little grace would go further than most," Cat says.

"The forgiveness of others is the air she breathes. She depends on others being the bigger person, making allowances, and giving her concessions. Plus, I've been through a lot too. Shouldn't she know better?" Beattrixx snarls. "But I understand how you feel. And the boys." She laughs. "Oh, the boys. I hear they went mad looking for us." She looks down and licks her lips. "Well, I think they were more focused on some of us. Don't get me wrong, I feel loved and accepted and all that from Brambley, but he didn't eat or sleep because of you, specifically that you were in peril."

"He declared his love to me a few moments ago. Still reeling from it. Kind of wild." In truth, it was the most dramatic thing delivered to her. In all of Rengulfton's spiders and experiments, he could not produce the same weight as Brambley's words.

"So, you embraced, and the Charles Dickens savaged you?" she asks with a gleeful grin.

"No, he's entirely useless in that department. But there are no mistakes, no misunderstandings: he loves me." Cat shrugs. "I wish that was enough to live happily ever after. For a fairy tale, that would be enough, wouldn't it? We have plenty of monsters, but we're fresh out of fairy godmothers."

The two look at the field filled with Cree children. "I hope

Exhaust from the Tin Woods

this lot grows up playing with sticks in The Woods. It's been a long time since I woke up to children laughing. This place really grands."

"Another fairy tale," Beattrixx says. She sniffs. "As good as I like a campout, it'll be good to get home to Mercyminster."

"Yeah, home. Home would be good."

Chapter Six
May 1895

Cat walks through the snow, following Joane. The snow is mostly gone, with a tunnel of steam burning away anything frozen along the walkway from the main house to the smithy.

Both girls are dressed only in their work clothes. The sun is high above their heads, although it is still an hour before breakfast. A few months ago, when they first arrived, they'd be walking in absolute darkness. The days grow longer, warmer.

Cat can barely keep up with Joane as she marches quickly alongside the cobblestone. Although she's a few inches shorter than Cat, she always moves faster.

They arrive at the mouth of the smithy.

"Moses?" Joane calls. "We're here, and we want to beat on something metal. Moses?"

This only earns a loud, shaking laugh from Moses who is in the far, darkened corner of the smithy.

"Do you?" he says after his laughter fit. "Well, you came to the right place. I got lots of metal needin' a good beating."

We walk past the orange glow of the kiln. For Cat, he looks taller than before their capture. "Tell me, why do you want to beat on something?"

"I'm still really, really angry and I can't punch the face I want to."

"And who's that?" Moses asks as he steps into the morning's light.

"Rengulfton. I can't punch him, so I must hit something else."

"Can't or won't?" Moses asks, squinted his eyes to the sun behind Joane.

Joane pauses, crinkling her nose in thought.

Cat recalls: she's such a French lady, perfected in the art of seeming delicate at the exact moment.

"Won't," she whispers. "It is a weakness of mine, I fear. The more of a monsteration Rengulfton revealed himself to be, the less I wished to be a mirror reflection of that madness. The Woods

Exhaust from the Tin Woods

do not need two mad scientists. And madness begins with a punch, I should think."

"You should think, indeed." Moses says. A motion for the two to follow him inside. "You girls are tough. Real tough. The boys are still sleeping. That's my guess."

"No, it's a fact." Cat says.

"And here you two come to the shop, ready to get all your jitters and anger out." Moses says, "Tough, I say. England can learn a thing or two from Canada."

"We're not Canadian."

"Yeah, you are. So am I. And I get, as a former member of the US, the need to hit steel because it's a lot better than to hit the face burning in your eyes. Let's work on our anger, shall we?"

The girls giggle; Moses cackles in return as they make their way to the anvil.

.....

Dr. Allbrung exits Mercyminster followed by his students. "I am quite surprised none of you have asked about this." He says over his shoulder. "You are all such good detectives. Such observant young people that I thought you would ask or wonder why we have this warehouse."

The snow is gone on this side, for a Chinook blew across Mercyminster's land while the boys sought to chase Rengulfton's Spider Castle. The grass is now turning green, dandelions are sprouting, and leaves return to the woods.

They hike along a small sliver of a path into the thickest part of the surrounding woods. Allbrung turns right and is now completely out of sight from Mercyminster. Cradled within hundreds of poplars standing side by side is an octagon shaped log cabin, pumping out wet exhaust. The cabin is windowless and dampened from the exhaust. A low hissing breathes from the engines sounds every few seconds, camouflaged by the wind through the trees. The path is least travelled, so Brambley figures they would need Allbrung to find this cabin on any return trips.

Coming around is Suk. He nods. "Good morning, Dr. Allbrung. Everything is regular." Suk smiles at Cat. "You've lost weight, Cat."

"Is that a problem?" Cat asks with a sharpness in her tone.

181

Exhaust from the Tin Woods

"No, it isn't," Brambley says. He then stops himself. "Sorry, I'm thinking aloud. Quite rude."

"Do you still lust after Cat?" Suk asks.

"Often," he says too quickly.

"And you're still thinking aloud," Cat says with a chuckle. "Please, keep your lusting to yourself. If one just thinks only of making love and does not follow through they are a hypocrite and I would not have you besmirch your honor, Master Brambley." She grins and arches her right brow at Brambley.

Brambley s cheeks grow red, he shakes, and a palpable shame swells in his chest.

'Quickly I turn,' Brambley thinks to himself. 'Too quickly and usually because of Cat's presence.'

"She has lost some weight," Suk says. "She isn't unhealthy, mind you. But she also isn't some posh pony full of curves and swells and handles of flesh. She's … strong."

"Why are you two still having this conversation?" Cat asked over her shoulder.

"I am not. I'm just recovering from a stun." Brambley croaks.

"I am and will continue to have it." Suk says, "I am impressed with the health of your body."

"How am I supposed to take that?" Cat asks.

"As a non-erotic, a non-exploitive comment. A simple praise, nothing more.' Suk says.

"I guess I will then." She says and then marches ahead, breaking from the group.

"I would think the speaking aloud of my inward leers would be enough to tarnish my good name." Brambley mutters.

"Anyone here bothered that Brambley fancies my body? Anyone?" Cat asks the group, unable to break away from the conversation.

"At times, I fancy your body." Suk says.

"And thank you, good man." She turns and grins to Suk, then her blue eyes are back to Brambley. "'Love not with mere words, but deed and truth' as the good book says."

"Dr. Allbrung, don't we have a building to visit?"

"Quite." the old man says slowly. "I just am fascinated to

Exhaust from the Tin Woods

see the results of Cat's present research. Waiting for it to play out and produce measurable results." He speaks without emotion, looking at Brambley through the top of his glasses. "No matter." He clears his throat, and a brightness returns to his voice. "Do you know what the problem is with Babbage's Difference Engine? It computes one thing at a time. Like the human brain, it cannot do multiple tasks at once."

"I can do multiple tasks at once," Maillory says with an indignant tone. "I can speak and sew and read all at the same time."

"No, you cannot. You just do them separately, leaving them all half-finished, and complete them poorly. Such is human nature. We are limited to solving one thing at a time. The same problem is with computers. Now, this is fine if you are entering a formula for a game or a simple command. In fact, the engine moves faster than a human mind, so we are impressed. But still, it's counting one thing at a time.

"I am working on an engine that can count multiple things at once and work on various problems all simultaneously."

He walks around the back, facing a door that belongs inside of a bank that seals a vault. Allbrung spins the main wheel, then leans his whole weight against the door. Once opened, he walks in, "Last one, shut the door just so it's ajar."

The students follow him into a room cool as an icebox. The walls are covered with ice crystals; a fan blows in a flurry of ice chunks.

"When we leave, the refrigeration will kick in," Allbrung shouts over the wild purr of the fans. "And this room will be unlivable for human beings. It shall become the coldest room on our planet for two hours, allowing the engine to make its computations. Once the programs are complete, the temperature will rise to that of a meat locker."

"Why?" Joane asks.

"The computer requires the simplicity brought forth only by the extreme cold. You see, to count simultaneously, you must count on a quantum level. That means jumping dimensions and those kinds of leaps only happen when a state is at its simplest."

"Quantum?" Patrick asks.

"A new type of science not popular in England … yet."

Exhaust from the Tin Woods

"So, you have a computing apparatus that can count all at the same time, but in different places?" Brambley asks.

"Yes," Allbrung says. "Someone understands!" He grins widely.

"But why? What is the practical application of such an apparatus?"

"Immediately, it can make other counting machines much faster. A single computer can run hundreds of machines, all with different thought protocols, at the same time. Think about it! It's miller's wheel times infinity! But that is just a beginning step. It can, on a mathematical level, be the stairway to Heaven. Or, simply, discovering numbers closer to infinity."

"Is this the Infinity Machine?" Cat asks, and Allbrung vigorously nods.

"No one can know infinity, and it is a sin to try to know the complete mind of God. If one thinks they know the mind of God, they can replace Him, yes?" He shakes his head. "But know a little more about Him? Isn't that the mind of religion? By this machine, I am computing what a good hymn attempts to do: ascribe the worth of infinity."

"You've lost me with the crushed theology and science," Beattrixx says.

"I've lost myself!" He laughs. "Sorry, turning into a mad scientist."

"Turning?" Cat asks.

"No secrets, nothing hidden. Not with Rengulfton out and loose. He wants this Infinity Machine badly. He has already stolen my fiasco with the feeling metals, the ghosts in the tin. Now he wants this, I should think, and I think you all should know about it."

"Does it work?" Shweta asks. "I mean; my people would migrate over the Rockies to be a part of something that computes infinity!" She laughs, Allbrung's excitement passing to her like a flu virus.

"No," Allbrung says. "Not in the slightest. The science is good, but the machine … is fickle." He walks out of the cabin, and the students follow him. "We try and try, with the same failures. Then I go back to other projects and ideas. Then I'll come back. Suk helps; Suk is the key to figuring this thing out. That's why he's

Exhaust from the Tin Woods

remained, a 'one-time student': he works on the Infinity Machine."

"Failing at this thing has taught me so much. I've made incredible breakthroughs in the science of refrigeration and creating clean exhaust and how to work with inhuman temperatures. If I hadn't have failed so bad, I would have never learned those things. The Infinity Machine, as such a flop, has opened the doors to so many other things."

"You like failing." Beattrixx says.

"Oh, failures have been the best times of my life!"

.....

The second day of May is Sunday, so the students travel to the town for church. Brambley walks to the town, carrying a satchel with his Bible and the notes for his sermon. He walks alongside Cat, ahead of the rest of the group. They are silent for half of the walk until she slips her hand around his elbow and walks with him, arm and arm.

"I'm wondering if this is decent," Brambley says.

"There are so many things in the world that are so wrong, but perfectly decent. I never try to be decent, only right," Cat says, and she tries to get as close as possible, feeling the warmth of Brambley's body. She feels that Brambley is tense at first, then he relaxes. By the end of the walk, they walk together as one: making room for each other in a steady, felt rhythm.

"Joane," Cat asks her friend. "Who raised you?"

"Nuns," she says. "Kind, marvelous, wonderful nuns. There were about four of them, all lived together and ran a kitchen that served soup to the poor of Paris. They sang, they danced. I don't remember much of my early childhood, other than I felt love. When I was six, I left to be a Held Companion."

"Still in contact with them?"

"I write a letter to them every Monday. They write … less frequently."

Cat then remembers Joane receiving a big, wooden box her second month at Mercyminster. The contents were a blue shawl, wool gloves, and stacks and stacks of letters. Joane would post a letter every week; it seems her nuns would write letters and, once a year, mail a large crate to Joane.

Brambley slows down, giving Cat a chance to study

185

Exhaust from the Tin Woods

Joane's face. Joy, unrestrained.

Cat turns around and looks up to Brambley. "And what was the Foundation like for you?"

"Like Joane, I was one of the lucky ones. The Foundation was a kind place also. None of the singing attributed to the Nuns: it was a place of Protestant sobriety."

"How awful," Cat says, and she believes she hears Brambley chuckle. She holds his arm tighter to her sides. "I don't like that there are so many orphans in the world. Our world is supposed to be getting better, brighter, and more perfect with all of this technology. And yet, why are there so many orphans, hmm?"

"What about your childhood?"

"As a little girl, I collected addresses like some do with stamps or spoons. At nine, I fled Her Majesty's Orphan Care Program because it was no longer meeting my needs as a client. Since they moved me around from home to home, I figured I would save them some money and just do the moving myself."

The image of the Spider Castle pops into her head, as they are still on the topic of orphan making. Her neck feels cold like it had been doused with ice water. "You know; I really don't know what Rengulfton's Spider Castle looks like. Say we round these trees and see eleven walking spider castles. I wouldn't be able to tell you this one is Rengulfton's Spider Castle. Funny, the shock of escape can wipe a memory clean."

"It's a grace," Brambley says. "Rengulfton is quite a horrible person, and people like him ruin a lot of things. A lot of people. He deserves, at the very least, to be forgotten."

The group comes to the long, saw-dusted main street of Grouard. Plumes of exhaust bubble and float over the town, resembling angels presiding over the streets. Large, brown puddle spots dapple the boardwalks and pathways. The streets are silent, as most are still asleep when the Catholic church bells ring.

"How is your adopted mother, Patrick?" Cat asks him over her shoulder.

"I've been teaching her English when I come to eat. I think we're due at her house after the service. Possibly not. She's been sick for a while, during that whole rumble through the jungle last week," Patrick says. Cat detects a softening in his voice. "I hope she's all right."

The group arrives at the tiny Baptist church as the sounds of an organ whirls and swoons in the air. They take their seats near the front. It is their routine to do so, same seats at the same time of day.

Waiting in the spot, Beattrixx finds a small basket of muffins, canned fruit, and a small bottle of dandelion wine. A card rests and presides over the rest of the contents, written with a shaky hand:

> We've been praying for you and your safety.
> Don't you dare get captured again.
> You are a Baptist and one of us!

When Cat reads this note for Beattrixx, she scans the crowd behind her. No one is making eye contact or seems to belong to the basket. Cat assumes, after a few moments of detective work, that the basket was for the students and is to be given in secret.

Without anything unusual, the church service carries on with singing and Brambley preaching. He speaks on faith leading to goodness and despair to villainy, which would have been fitting concerning spider castles and talking bears if, in fact, he referenced these things: his sermon is all ideas and scripture, not a single story or example.

Afterwards, the Constable approaches the group. He shakes Brambley's hand vigorously. "Good sermon, great sermon," he says. Then he eyes Joane. "And how have you been ... since your ... abduction?"

"Is that the talk of the town?" Joane asks as she fans herself.

"It is. The entire town helped in the search."

Brambley points to the Constable. "He organized the west end, and the Mertonites took us through the eastern section. He searched, night and day, with the whole town."

"To be honest, you girls are something of a marvel. Many women have been kidnapped in the woods, returning as monsterations, or as corpses. There's been a bit of hope, seeing you alive and well." The Constable leans in to Joane. "Especially you,

Exhaust from the Tin Woods

Joane."

"Why me?" she asks, and the Constable quickly retreats.

The group leaves the church to see the streets filled with people. As soon as they see Cat and the girls, applause breaks forth. Toggled hands bang along with a steady clap, kids are hoisted atop of parent's shoulders for a better look, cheers sound, a handgun is fired into the air, and Grouard welcomes the girls back.

The mayor of the town yells over the crowd. "Not again! Not another girl missing! Not ever! This time, we won! This time, the bear didn't take our girls!"

Cat turns to Allbrung who smiles, lifts up his stove top hat, and twirls it for the crowd. Cat curtsies and waves to the crowd. She looks deeper, seeing the street filled with tables of food: canned fruits and vegetables, roasted game, bread, cheese, and milk. It's a bountiful spread.

The students of Allbrung walk across the boardwalks and into the chips and dust of the main street. Cat and Brambley hang back.

"Dr. Allbrung," Brambley asks. "You didn't look for the girls, did you?"

Cat stops in her tracks and does everything to hear what comes next from their teacher.

"No, I did not. I worked the messages services. I repaired devices used in the search and cooked the meals for the townspeople. The base of the search was Mercyminster, so I attended there. But no. I did not go into the woods and search." The old man stares at Brambley, his face blank … only suggestive … but to what? Blank stares usually do not scare Cat, but this one made her nervous. "Does that trouble you?"

"I did everything I could to save Cat. Cat and the others," Brambley says. "Why didn't you have the same conviction?"

"Because I do not have the same convictions, which is the difference between different people. The moment you put two people in a room, you have at least four competing convictions." The old man leans towards him. "I cooked, built, repaired, and guided the search while you walked, hiked, froze, and considered to kill for her safety."

"Well," Brambley says with a chuckle. "I was willing to

Exhaust from the Tin Woods

die for Cat. Yes."

"No. Dying would have been no use, but you were out in the woods, undoubtedly, willing to kill for her safe return. Am I right?"

Brambley shakes his head. Cat's neck stiffens tightly. It is as if the applause and the party have been silenced and this very conversation is the only sound in Grouard. "So you considered murder, which is the steam and exhaust of the woods. Right now, the woods inspire murder. Murder. It is home to one of the greatest murderers of our age.

"I shall bring forth the Kingdom of Heaven, and I believe it shall be done by creating, inventing, prattling, teaching, and lecturing. This is my conviction, and I shall not court murder. You were willing to, young Brambley, for the sake of those you love. Are you wrong? Am I wrong? I know your heart, young Brambley, and it is full of light; I do not judge you."

"Nor will I judge you." Brambley says with a bow.

"Good, because if you judge me or pine away, wishing we shared in the same convictions ... well, how can I teach you to become a genius?" Allbrung points to the streets. "Now, this is a party for you. And, mostly, Cat. Bear in mind: I did not have to leave Mercyminster, and you did not have to murder. Cat saved herself and the others. The problem with damsels in distress is the position often employs real human girls who know how to pick knots and dismantle the encroaching circular saws."

Brambley laughs. "Why was there some special attention to Joane? The Constable said the people were happy, in particular, of her rescue," he asks.

"Oh, I think it's because she's French. She's ... become someone they identify with. This town has no theatre, little art: the gossip was their drama, and she was the heroine."

Allbrung points to the crowd.

Brambley takes this and joins his friends in the line for food.

.....

Brambley hands Cat her vorpal a needle-beetle while they finish the music system for the town. It is the day after the big, town feast. He feels sluggish from all of the food, still stuck deep in his

189

stomach. She is wrapping copper wire around her hand. She clips the wire and then jumps off his platform to her own.

"I wish we could join the two platforms together," Cat says. "I wouldn't risk breaking my ankle every time I hop over to my side."

"Have you wanted many men, before Mercyminster, to join your workstation?" he asks and laughs, although the question suddenly makes him blush. The question reminded him too much of an innuendo found in a pantomime script.

"No," she says flatly. "This whole 'we're a family, and I have some guy who will kill for me, and three square meals' is new. It terrifies me. I mean, don't get me wrong: I've had plenty of men fancy me. I mean, just look at me." She lifts her arms to display her near naked body. "Who wouldn't?"

Her blue eyes scan him quickly. "My brain can do two things with this new, terrifying world. I can reject it by finding a flaw or bringing the flaw to myself. I mean, that's a solution: I can escape trouble in paradise if I first bring the trouble myself. Brilliant?"

"You lose paradise as well."

"Certainly," she says. "Or I throw myself into the garden. Ever since the bear took me away, that's my resolve. Throw myself all naked and sweaty at the Eden in front of me and see what the Good Lord brings."

Brambley's head is now filled with too many naked, sweating images of Cat to make a reasonable response. Instead, he closes his eyes, prays for a moment, and clears his mind. Once he opens his eyes, he follows her metaphor. "Something happened to me, quite different, while the bear took you away. I saw what the world looks like outside of the Garden."

"The lurkjerker you found?"

He shakes his head. "He didn't die a lurkjerker. He died as a kid, someone who had way too much metal in his body. Outside the Garden, things are so wrecked, and life is seeing so much gray that victimizers are also the victims. It made me love Eden that much more."

"So, are you going to get naked with me and run through the garden?"

Exhaust from the Tin Woods

Brambley closes his eyes to pray again, clearing his throat. He says in a weak voice, "Enough theology."

"Too much dirty talk for one day, Rev. Brambley?" she asks and giggles.

Beattrixx laughs as well, hearing every word of their chat.

Joane clears her throat. "The woods look evil to me now," she says, her Parisian accent thick. "A real phantasmagoria. It is hard to walk to church now," she says. "I do not like how the woods went from happy to evil. It is not fair. I want my woods back."

"I would like to stomp on that spider," Patrick says. "Crush all of the tin and exhaust under my boot." He snorts, and Joane mumbles something in agreement, below their platforms.

"It is improper mathematics," says Shweta. "Eye for an eye."

"You almost sound … Baptist," Patrick says.

"I speak truth. If the Baptists want to agree with me, so be it," says Shweta. "Still, you are angry. And you haven't made a single invention all week."

"I have little stomach for prattling."

"Shweta, your people, the Sikhs," asks Brambley. "What are their thoughts on violence and justice and all of that."

"They have theologies for both because they do not confuse the two, unlike you English. For justice, there are warriors. I am trained as one."

"They allow women to be warriors?" Joane asks.

"But of course," Shweta says. "It is because our people value perfection, so they want justice done right. Thus, woman warriors."

Cat smirks in the direction of Brambley, who smiles back. Although she cannot be seen, it is known Shweta's expression is deadpan.

They prattle for the day, none of their experiments complete, so when it is dinner time, their tables are filled with parts, projects, and notes. The girls enter the room first, bath and dress for dinner; the men, after they leave, do the same.

For dinner, Suk serves roasted ducks with fire cooked potatoes and vegetables. The boys demolish their food, eating four helpings each. Joane finishes half her plate; Shweta eats only vegetables; Cat takes seconds, and Maillory excuses herself early.

"So, Dr. Allbrung," Beattrixx asks. "What is the greatest invention you've ever seen?"

"Still waiting," answers the old man with a grin. "I am curious to see what you might come up with."

"Any close seconds?"

The old man shakes his head.

"You're being difficult."

"The belief is that inventions beget better inventions. So, the best is yet to come. Do you believe that?" The room doesn't move. "Neither do I."

With dinner over, Dr. Allbrung pulls out a packet of snuff and inhales a dip. The girls, a month earlier, decided not to separate between the kitchen and parlor, etiquette be forgotten. Beattrixx pulls out a thin, brown cigar and lights it. She takes a relaxed drag.

"I am quite convinced that those may upset the biles of one's constitution," says Joane. "Alas, it is only intuition that tells me so."

Cat pulls out a pipe and smokes. She takes two puffs and inhales. "My experiment is at an end," she says. "I require differing stimulation." She gives back the pipe to Beattrixx.

"It doesn't agree?" Beattrixx asks.

"It doesn't excite," says Cat. She grins at Brambley. "Pales in comparison."

"Smoke-like strong coffee – only suggests and hints at what a full life might be," Dr. Allbrung says. He looks up dreamily. "Listening to Bach, children running down the hall, and a book written by a genius: mix up the disciplines, and you might espy heaven now."

Under the table, Cat grabs Brambley's hand. He doesn't pull it away. They clasp, hot and fiercely, under the table. Both faces turn red despite their relaxed expressions.

"More heaven, please," asks Cat to the air.

Maillory retires to her bunk, taking a book with her to read. Once she exits, Cat asks Beattrixx, "She has been very, very distant since she got back. Do you think something horrible did happen?"

"I don't know," Beattrixx says. "She doesn't like us to talk

Exhaust from the Tin Woods

about our experiments. Every time the subject comes up, she leaves the room."

"We didn't talk about it tonight."

"But we might. That's the thing," Beattrixx says. "She's the type, I think, that doesn't know what to do with misfortune. Nothing should upset her. It's an odd allergy."

"Agreed," Cat says. She reclines back and enjoys holding Brambley's hand. For her, it's the evening's occupation.

.....

Joane is chopping wood, wearing trousers and a long shirt borrowed from Patrick. Cat sees her friend, in full harmony with the axe and wood and work. Unlike Shweta and Joane, Cat knows she is unsuccessful in "the dance of chopping wood". Her job, mainly, is to hold a pistol and stand guard, fearing glass spiders or mahogany men or toggled bears roaming the tin woods.

A ghost grin flashes on Joane's face.

Cat grins at her friend, finding the joy in her work.

Suddenly, branches snap and break. The quiet is broken by the sounds of wet mud and twigs and bark that are broken against the mud syrup of the ground. The girls turn to find the Constable.

He tips his bowler to Joane. "Good afternoon," says the older gentleman. "I do not wish to intrude."

"How long have you stayed in Paris?" Cat asks.

The Constable stops, frozen in his tracks. His countenance is one of sheer surprise. "Is it that obvious? However can you tell?" he asks slowly.

"Do tell," Joane asks. "You and your boyfriend have the uncanny genius of reading people. Your sherlucks are becoming legendary."

"He is not my boyfriend and the fact that the Constable is a fellow countryman of yours is quite plain," Cat says as she rises. She points at him with a stick. "He wears perfume not British or from this Commonwealth, but from France. His attire is strange, for it is neither fur or tailored. It is the result of French haberdashery. Loose, sturdy, and what the French would guess for cold weather. It was as if someone walked into a men's clothier and said, 'I'm going to the Woods. Outfit me!' But most importantly, he is not royal or mounted or police. Just Canadian. A Canadian Constable, more or

Exhaust from the Tin Woods

less appointed by the locals to keep the peace. Not British – so no crown. Not Canadian – so there's a hint of French in his words, but nothing from this continent."

She smiles, her light blue eyes matching the sky. "I'm quite good," Cat says. She feels her cheeks flush. Perhaps she's thinking of Brambley, who does these kinds of things hourly.

The Constable bows. "True," he says. "I am from Paris."

"And, you can be trusted. Any fool can be appointed to be a police officer to some wild outpost far, far away. But to be trusted by the people you live with, you must be a truly good person," says Cat. "We're in safe hands because the people we live with say so."

"I try to help," he says. "Which is what I'm doing, mucking about in the woods." He pulls out a pink, shiny handkerchief and wipes a spit of mud from his chin. "Looking for Rengulfton."

"Any luck?" asks Cat.

"None. He can become invisible in these swamps. When you escaped from his roving fortress, you were the first eyewitnesses to see where he lived. I've been able to find trails, with the mud and all, but all of them turn cold." Some sort of pain flashes in the Constable's eyes. At first, Cat thinks that the constable might be injured or hurt, but she didn't detect a limp or anything that would interrupt his stride. He calms himself, seemingly, but still, there is tension in his face. "Miss Joane, was your captivity very bad?"

"Yes," she says. "But over. That is the grace of my visit, the pain only took a day and left nothing lasting. Like an appointment with an awful, inept doctor … painful, but over. Most girls, it seems, weren't as lucky."

He bows. "I am thankful for such providence. Goodbye, for now," he says and stomps through the woods.

Joane finishes her log chopping. "Now, the house engine can get some much-needed fuel. Ready for a good sweat?"

Cat nods.

The girls take a pile of cut wood each in their arms and walk to the western, lower entrance of Mercyminster. Through an iron, double doors they come to the engine located adjacent to the cellar where the difference engines are stored.

Exhaust from the Tin Woods

The engine room's floor tiles, along with the walls and some of the ceiling, reminds Cat of an expansive, public pool in London without the water. The engine burps and billows with hot steam, so the room is very hot and very wet.

Cat disrobes completely, along with Joane. Once nude, Joane ties her long, brown hair back into a ponytail while Cat opens the main door to the burner.

"I welcome this, truly," says Cat. "I always feel clean after a good sweat."

"This beats my creative block," says Joane. "I am only finishing ideas before the kidnap. Once my list is done, I fear I am fresh out." Joane hands Cat three slivers of wood. "Allbrung says that if I hit a dry spot in my imagination, I must change disciplines altogether. Rather than making machines, I must make music. The solution seems too crushed for it to work."

"Don't be too quick to defenster his proposal. Try it," says Cat. "There is some sense to his thinking."

"Not very posh," Joane says.

Cat no longer sees Joane, since Cat's vision and face are filled with the bright, golden light of the furnace.

"For one of the pioneers of science, he doesn't follow many of Victoria's rules. For starters, most scientists – when they study – aren't even allowed to listen to music for fear it might unravel their equations. I know that the Steamies who are Royal Guards are forbidden to attend church for fear religion might dilute their nationalism. And in the Church of England, ministers are not allowed to read fiction for fear they might replace the Bible with Jules Verne."

Cat turns around to almost see the heat around her. "It is important, I guess, to keep one's mind keen. Still, he does know what he's doing."

"Really? A while ago, you didn't trust the man. Waiting for him to be a secret Archon in disguise."

"There are worse men, we have discovered recently. Not all scientists are mad. Well, Dr. Allbrung is a mad scientist, all right. Perhaps he's not an angry one. Or an evil one. There is some sense."

Joane sits down on a birch bench, exhaling as her pores

Exhaust from the Tin Woods

open. Cat joins her "I always thought this room was smaller."

"It is, at night. The room collapses in half exactly at 4 pm. Halving the engine makes steam production more consolidated and efficient."

"This place is a real nounshwanstein," Joane says. "A different house every hour." She places her hand on Cat's knee. Her eyes are closed; she appears to be sleeping. "Ever come here with Brambley?"

"I wish. I wish. If we did engine duty, he would demand I'd wear, as a minimum, a petticoat, and wool sweater." Cat says with a groan. "He's a true Charles Dickens. Really. And yet, I'm chewing up the walls with eagerness squelched by his damned code towards women."

"Stay the course." Joane says. "It is worth the fight."

"Of course it is." Cat says and then bites her lower lip. "But why does it have to be a fight?"

.....

Brambley sits alone in the oversized chair next to the fiery hearth. Darkness envelopes him, a cocoon of warmth and comfort as he reads beside the fire.

The book he reads is the memoirs of Randalf Gemstone, explorer of the Wet Mountains of Mars. Every other page contains one of Gemstone's illustrations, depicting fleets of airships or scantily clad maidens or floating cloud bazaars. The result, Brambley feels, of the many pictures is that Gemstones seeks not to describe a single adventure or setting. The reading is tiring, but it gives Brambley's mind the rest needed.

This evening he needs a distraction. Beattrixx dressed Cat in a low-cut, black leather dress which not only left little to the imagination, it embellished any fantasies he might have otherwise suppressed.

Why does everything have to be about sex? Brambley wonders. The swells of her ample breasts, the contours of her neck, the flash of her eyes, the perfect point of her chin, her ankles ... oh God, her ankles ... everything screamed sex to Brambley when he thought, dreamed, or recalled Cat.

And buried deep inside of her lusty body, he thinks, is the most extraordinary creature I've ever known.

Exhaust from the Tin Woods

Only a God could love her for herself alone and not for her cleavage. He returned his eyes to the text of his book, hoping the tortured prose would distract his mind.

He reads and enters a chapter about the Martian slave trade.

"Umm, Brambley," a soft, feminine voice calls from the darkness. He pulls his eyes from the book to see Maillory dressed in a sheer, flowing nightgown. When she steps into the light, a detailed silhouette of her body emerges through the ghost fabric of the dress.

Well, he figures, at least I found an effective distraction languishing over Cat's figure.

"Can I be of service?" Brambley asks weakly.

"Yes, you can," she says softly. "Something horribly suspicious is in the breakfast room." She reaches out her arm revealing her bare arm and her nude side. "Come."

Brambley bookmarks his book and then rises and cinches his evening robe. He takes Maillory's hand. It feels moist, hot. Why is she still nervous? He muses. If she had recovered from fright, it would be wet and cool. She seems calm, almost ethereal. Dreamlike. How then can she be nervous with a telltale sign of a hot, wet hand? She leads him down a long, darkened corridor. Every room she passes, the gown becomes even more translucent and transparent. Brambley's mind spins, all thoughts become curved lines and blurs.

At the end of this silent journey, they come to an opened door in the breakfast room. Maillory lets go of Brambley's hand. "Something suspicious," she whispers and points deep into the room.

Now, this is strange, Brambley muses. She seems nervous but not about the "something suspicious". She strides, without hesitation, to the possible danger. Why? What is she scared about?

Stepping out from Maillory's escort, he enters the dark, silvered room. In the morning's light, the room was warm and fresh and full of life; now, at night, it appeared sharp, metallic, and sheer. He looks around the tall shadows in this room full of tin and steel.

Once he reaches the center of the room, he desires to turn around to face Maillory. He plans his words to be: "Something suspicious?" He does not get to say these words. In their place, a sharp and searing pain is injected into his right thigh. As quick as the pain is delivered, he loses control of his entire body. He falls to the iron floor.

Collapsed in a heap, his right eye is able to see Maillory. She is holding a tall, iron syringe in one hand and a small pistol in the other. He is certain these objects were in the room already, for there was no way she could have carried such devices in her nightgown.

She grins.

"In ten minutes, this room shall collapse into itself for the night." She says, looking around the room. "The room shall become the size of a gentleman's trunk and as dense as any rock. You shall be crushed without mercy or hesitation. Your bloody wreck shall greet the students' tomorrow morning, as they shall deduce it was just a terrible accident."

Brambley moans.

"Why? Simple. I seek to be the greatest of all prattlers. I wish to command culture, all culture. Dr. Allbrung is a dead end; I have become Rengulfton's student. On my day of torture, I didn't experience a single discomfort. Rather, I became friendly with my new ally, the genius Rengulfton."

Another helpless, inarticulate moan.

"Oh, come now. My father's religion means nothing to me. Simply, his church was a beginning audience I outgrew. I mean to repay them nothing by rendering all fame and glory to the church. Instead, I was cherished there so I can, eventually, be celebrated by the world. Simple. God was a one time stepping stone to bigger things, nothing more. A means, not an end."

Actually, Brambley thought, my moan was a cursing and not a query.

"One by one, your fellow students shall meet with horrible accidents. Joane shall be fed to the engine's kiln; Beattrixx shall fall off her platform; Shweta shall freeze to death studying the Infinity Engine; Patrick shall be poisoned. When Rengulfton comes for Allbrung's creations, Cat shall be taken and transformed. She's always been my least favorite."

Moan.

Exhaust from the Tin Woods

"Fun chatting, but I must press on. Soon, this room shall get very stuffy. Too bad you picked the losing side. The future marches on."

She turns around and floats down the hallway.

Brambley only feels pain in his right leg. Everything else turns numb. Trapped within his lifeless body, his mind sends messages to scream, flail, kick, and writhe to no effect. He can hear the pulse of the room, as the house automatically counts down to follow the next command.

He hears her soft, bare feet shuffle away.

A minute later the door closes, to prevent anyone from coming into the room as it collapses. Ironically, this was designed as a safety mechanism. Now it has made Brambley invisible to any chance wanderers down the hall.

Tick-tick-tick…

With a clockwork cruelty, the room's heart beat patters toward the last few notches in a metal disc that shall command the collapse. Brambley figures the sides of the room shall press together first, then the ceiling shall lesson until the trunk remains.

He moans.

That is the best he can do, for even his tongue is nothing but a wiggly, lifeless piece of meat hanging within his jaw. His leg is now numb. He feels nothing. At least, he considers, my crushing won't be painful. I'll just be helpless to stop it.

The room roars to life, with the grinding of gears turning above his head.

His eyes are shaking, as the ground moves with every roll and notch climbed in the rooms wheels. The room is getting slimmer and slimmer. The top and bottom shall crush him. He chuckles to himself, I was wrong.

The door slams open. "Brambley," whispers Cat. "This is no place for a nap."

Quickly, she grabs his ankles and pulls him across the floor. Brambley can't feel this, but he figures his face is drug along the floor grooves. She stops for a second and pants.

"Dear God," she says.

With renewed strength, she drags him along further. The room gets darker and darker, the gears turn louder and louder. He can hear her desperately panting and grunting. He slides a little bit more.

"Do you have to be so heavy?"

His eyes see both the ceiling inches from his nose and then the iron threshold of the doorway. He is out, safe.

She twirls him around, so he is facing the ceiling. All of his fellow students are peering down at him. "He's been poisoned," Suk says. "It's a root local to these woods. He needs to get adrenaline coursing through his body. Quick. Otherwise, he'll turn into a vegetable." Suk says this without emotion.

Cat, red-faced, looks down at him. "Adrenaline? Like a start or shock or extreme anger?"

"Anything." Suk says. "And quickly. I think his attacker intended for him to be crushed to death, so he was given a large dose."

Cat stands up, breathes deeply, and turns to Joane. "Joane," she asks sweetly. "Be a dear and strip until you're completely naked. Once nude, ravish my boyfriend in every sense of the word 'adultery'. We'll stand here and watch as you do so."

Joane, still wide-eyed from Brambley's near death and rescue, nods. She looks down at Brambley and exhales. She grins a crooked, hungry smile. "I think I shall enjoy this. Beattrixx, can you also be naked and help me. We must be so very thorough in this, so he'll change his religion as a result."

Brambley feels a fiery surge shoot through his body, causing him to lurch forward and cough. He shakes his feet. He is dizzy, and his eyes can barely concentrate, but his heart is pounding. His hands, his feet, his face, his chest, and his arms come alive.

Joane is still unbuttoning her blouse.

Brambley screams. The numbness burns away.

"Don't ravish me." He croaks.

"Enough ladies." Cat says, "he's mine. I claim him. He's mine to ravish." She twists a smile at Joane. "Well played. Well played, indeed. Your wiles are worthy of the coastal towns of Nova Scotia."

"You are too generous," says Joane sheepishly.

Brambley sits up. Swallows. Looks to Cat. "Quick

Exhaust from the Tin Woods

deduction." He whispers weakly. "Who is not here but is a part of the school?"

"Dr. Allbrung, but he ran off to get some medicine the moment I pulled you out." Cat says. She looks around. "Moses?"

Brambley shakes his head rapidly. "Maillory?"

"She was my attacker. We need to get to the dorm room. Quickly."

Cat remains with Brambley while the others race to the bedroom. Brambley's strength gains, as he wonders why – instinctively – he knew Maillory would be in the bedroom. As he waits for his body to heal itself, Cat kneels beside him and rests his head on her lap. She gently strokes the curls at the side of his head.

He looks up at her. "Why weren't you the one to ravish me?"

"We needed your indignation." Cat says with a grin.

"True enough, but you would have had my rapturous pleasure."

"I can ravish you now, Brambley."

"The right action at the wrong moment quickly becomes the wrong action. Let us wait for the right moment."

Through a growl, Cat says, "And I grow a day older."

His strength returns enough for him to stand. Cat fits perfectly under his arm, as she props him up as they journey back to the bedroom.

They first hear wailing sobs. The room is dark, but upon entering they find Allbrung hunched over Moses. Moses lay wide-eyed, full of blood over his shirt, and turning paler by the second.

Quickly, Brambley ascertains he had been stabbed multiple times by someone who he allowed to get close. The stabbings deep and multiple, happening so quick he didn't have time to react. His expression is one of shock, suggesting he died surprised. The attacker must have been shorter than he, for the thrusts were all upward and dodged his rib cage.

Maillory.

Suk whispers, "He's been dead for too long. We can't revive him."

"You are right," the old man says with a sigh. "All of my gadgets, all of my science: it cannot help him now."

Exhaust from the Tin Woods

Joane finds a corner and curls up in a ball. She is sobbing wildly. She looks small, tiny. Patrick runs to her, but she simply shakes her head. The young man freezes and shakes. He calms himself enough to reach out, touch her arm, and then whirls around.

Patrick grabs a chair and throws it against the wall. Then screams. Brambely sees his red face, spit flying, and sopping wet with tears and sweat. Brambley figures Patrick turned animal the moment he saw Moses had been slain. Patrick screams again. Joane races to him, amidst her tears, and whispers, "Please, keep your composure."

"Fie to composure! I cannot stand being a proper gentleman and nice and clean and full of propriety and kindly spoken and a member of the Empire! Damned manners," Patrick screams. He marches over to Moses and points to his corpse. "And how did the world of manners and the British Empire serve him? Eh? How did our civil society benefit him?"

Patrick's voice calms, but his eyes stream with tears. His voice rattles and shakes, along with his hands and shoulders. "Moses was the best of men. He sought to free slaves from the Confederacy. Brought them to The Woods and gave them a new life. Read his Bible. Prayed for the Cree." He grabs his face, covering his eyes. "He put me to work in the kiln. He taught me how to be a proper blacksmith. A proper one. He showed me what a hard day's work looked like, felt like. He was the first person who ever trusted me with hard, hard labor. And doing so, he was kind about it."

Patrick whirls around to face Allbrung. "And what are you going to do about it? Tomorrow morning, are we going to learn about pipe engineering or electrical conductivity? Is that your solution to how to fix a world that stabbed Moses to death?" he asks, his voice rising.

Allbrung rises slowly, towering over Patrick. His whole face and body dark and he eclipses the young man from the remaining light from the hearth's embers. Only his mass and voice can be perceived. In a quiet, still voice, the scientist speaks. "Yes," he says. Then he waits until the shaking ends. "I shall teach and continue to teach, for this is why Moses lived here: to be within a community that thinks, that watches, and that learns. He loved that

Exhaust from the Tin Woods

we learned and that we watched. He loved … harmony. I shall teach science because my science is in harmony with my morality that detests a human killing another human."

Allbrung steps closer to Patrick.

"Harmony did not kill him," Brambley says. He is still weak from his attack, but the words fly out of his mouth. Patrick freezes when he hears them. "Exploitation did. Maillory exploited his trust. Asked him to come close to her, more than likely by asking him to help her out. He sought to help her and was stabbed to death. She exploited his desire to be of help." The room now faces Brambley who takes two steps towards Moses' body. "He was not stupid because he was lied to, was not a weakling for being exploited. Simply, the exploiter took advantage of harmony. And Moses, a former slave, hated above all else – exploitation."

Patrick exhales and looks down at his feet.

Allbrung slouches down. "Patrick, we will not do our lecture tomorrow. Instead, we shall be very crushed and attend a church service. Rev. Brambley shall lead the funeral for our friend. By this, it shall make sense of our science. And, by our science, we shall change this world."

"And what do we do now?" Patrick asks in a broken voice.

"Break from the British Empire and cry. Weep. And let us, for tonight, not be gentlemen."

Those that survived the attack spent half of the night in the room. The Constable came, filled out a report, and found bloody prints on the window pane that matched prints from Maillory's workstation. The Constable hears Brambley's account and figures, "She killed Moses and then sought to kill you. Seeing her open trunk, I guess she must have been changing when she heard you had been rescued. Then, she bolted for the window. She moved him from his original spot in the center of the room to the back window. Why? I'm not sure. And I really don't care. She killed a man and wanted to kill two, that's all I need."

"She told me once," Beattrixx says. "She felt it was beneath her education to talk to a black man. Perhaps she felt she could concoct a story of him attacking her, justifying her murder as self-defense."

"These are The Woods, not Mexicia or the State or the

Confederacy or even Europe. She will be charged with Moses' murder as murder, no half-measures."

The Constable takes Moses' body, Allbrung's bots come to sterilize the floor, and the students get ready for sleep. When the lights go out, Brambley is laying in his bed.

"Brambley," Cat whispers. "Can I sleep with you?"

"Umm –"

"Sleep, nothing more. I-I don't feel right."

"Climb down, Cat," he says, and she does. She lays her head on his chest as she nestles with him under the large, feather blanket. After a few moments of settling, Brambley asks, "You're the bravest person I know. You were a Pony in Cardiff, an Archon in London, a dancer on a riverboat in the Confederacy, and a smuggler in the State. You must have seen murder before or been in danger."

"True," she whispers. "But never … at home."

"Why?"

"I've never had a home before." With this, she closes her eyes and goes to sleep.

…..

"It's beautiful," Cat says to Patrick. "It looks like him. It bears his image." She studies the ironwork statue of Moses. His eyes and mouth and face look triumphant, almost Grecian. He is half buried with the top half clawing out of the ground. His arms claw the ground, as he frees himself from the floor. It's a metal statue, full of treated steel and iron. He looks neither like a monster or a zombie, but an absolute likeness of Moses as he escapes the grave. It shines in a rust proof coating. On his chest is a branding: "I shall defeat the grave."

"What is that from?" Cat asks, pointing to the tombstone over Moses' grave.

"It's a quote from Fredrick Douglas. He had it burned on his chest," Patrick says. He walks over to the freshly covered ground. "Fitting, don't you think?" He looks around at the trees in bloom, the birds chirping, and the sky bringing back the color blue to the land. "He was genuine."

"A genuine 'what'?"

"Genuine at anything he did. Honest, true. He was the best

teacher I ever had, that's for sure."

"You still seem … angry … at Allbrung," Cat says, folding her arms to brace from the chilled wind. It rained in the morning, so they face a cool, sunny day.

"Not angry, but I am tired of theory. My family, my country: all they have is theory. Poorhouses filled, women exploited, and countries destroyed … but ah, they have the best theories on compassion. Far better than anyone else in the world."

Cat stands still, a slight smile as she stares down Patrick. "I'm angry, too," is all she says.

Patrick thinks about this and shakes his head. "Everyone is angry. Maillory did … did a lot, last week." His eyes go elsewhere, other than the present topic. "Who does those kinds of things and especially one who endeared herself to the church?" He shakes the idea off. "I am done postulating. I know exactly why she did what did. She wanted power and all of that. I've seen it a thousand times in the church. My eldest brother is her kind. The kind that goes to church not be better themselves, but to feel better about themselves. They know all the answers to the universe and God, listening only to double check the vicar's ideas when he preaches. They do not change, do not fix anything, and are stridently English. And there must be an extra mercy of any race or individual who stands in the way of their well-being, for their churches carry extra crucifixes."

His voice rose, and his cheeks turned beet red. His curly locks became drenched with sweat before Cat's eyes.

"I know the type. The very stupid or the very powerful. They are all the same. Whenever a fact or figure does not work in line with how they see the world, they eliminate it. Moses was that fact for Maillory. Her ambitions were to be rich, powerful, and influential. Oh, all of the glory of the Crown and church and the Kingdom of Christ … of course! She would be a secular and religious icon for wealth, of course. Of course! To evangelize to the Woods and England and the State and Mexicia and the Confederacy for the purpose of filling churches with useless people and self-righteous bastards and smug white people! This was her glory!"

Patrick's voice cracks. He grins.

"Meanwhile, Moses taught young people and freed slaves." And then he sobs. He shakes and grits his teeth, squeezes his face and clenches his fist and falls apart.

Cat watches him, fighting the urge to embrace him. She knew him to be a gentleman, and one does not touch those. After a while, his grief simmers and only smolders. "Sorry," he says quietly with a nod. "I came undone."

"You were becoming human, Patrick," she says. "No apology needed."

"Decorum," he says.

"Can be damned. You are angry, and so am I."

He clears his throat and smiles. "How do you fair?"

"I want to murder her. Simple," she says without emotion. "She killed Moses and could have killed Brambley. She may come back and try again along with that lurkjerker Rengulfton. While us girls were being tortured, she had tea and biscuits. And then she came back, just to kill."

"Will you?"

"Haven't decided yet," she says with a shrug. "In the meantime, how's Joane?"

"I do not know, other than she's been pale since Moses' death." He sniffs. "We shall take a turn around the woods this afternoon."

"Un-chaperoned?" Cat asks. "Decorum?"

"Can be damned."

Cat points to the statue. "I never knew you to be an artist. How did you do all of this?" she asks.

"I was an artist before I came here. My family was worried about me, afraid that I might live the life of an artist. So I agreed to be a scientist, and they were happy with that. Little did they know, I'd come here." He smiled at his statue. "I learned a technique to bend metal about ten years ago. It came in handy. I wished we had a painting or a photograph to double check my rendering."

"You didn't need one," she whispers.

"Yeah, he's pretty burned into my mind." He laughs. "You know; I still expect him to come from the woods so I can show him the work I've done I think he'd be impressed."

"He'd be very impressed. Joane help you?"

"She was central. I can sculpt metal, but bending it: that's another job." He bows down to look at Moses' face in iron. Moses

Exhaust from the Tin Woods

almost looked happy. "It looks like him. Or at least, looks like how I know him to be." He looks over his shoulder. "And now, I just need to shake the idea that he'll come and see his tombstone."

"Not right away."

"No, today was just to make the thing." He looks over to Cat. "I want to leave it. Let the others come upon it on their own. Like a treasure waiting to be found or a fob left in the woods." He offered his arm to her. "Come along, I guess."

.....

The town fills with music on May 23. The sun sets at 10:02 pm, according to most business owner's fobs. The streets are filled with the gaslight glow of street lanterns. The cold air lingers, moist and snow white, frosting the edges of the light of the town. And, to commemorate the first musical town, all those who call the town home walk the sawdust streets to listen to Cat's musical creations.

The player box – a Difference Engine holding ten thousand songs on one hundred metal, grooved discs – operates in the basement of the town hall, playing the soft music into a microphonic system that broadcasts to all of the small speakers hidden throughout the town.

Through digging in the dirt and an extensive trench, the copper wiring conducts the sounds worthy of Bell's inventions birthed in the long-standing War of Confederate Independence. The engine – wound up every morning, runs throughout the day, playing a random selection of classic and popular music.

Why? is the main question asked for this endeavor. Why should a logging and fur trading town, located deep in the Woods, ever have such a thing?

"It's beautiful, that's why." Cat answers to any who ask her.

Although the entire town hangs upon Dr. Allbrung's reply: "Why not?" His answer is what they take away with, although it does say the same thing. Throughout the night, Allbrung is thanked and praised for bringing this invention to the town. Cat is happy with this, for praise would be clumsy and awkward and possibly painful. For years, she roamed in the shadows and under trains and through backwoods: the press would be too much.

Exhaust from the Tin Woods

She walks the streets … pleased.

The town and the woods and the trees and the lake sings.

As she passes the tavern, she sees Brambley: her partner in science. "Hey there." She says.

"Good evening." Brambley says with a bow. "You did it."

"We did it. Your half the genius behind this." She says as she approaches him closely, takes his right hand, and wraps his arm around herself like a warm, strong shawl.

"The priest spoke to me in broken English, saying that the music is from the Angels and it shall keep the bears away. The town is safe from animals." He says, drawing her even closer. They stand, facing the inlets of water and bogs and thick, yellow grass against the gas lamp and moon's light.

Two older men, wearing fur coats and top hats made to look like beaver fur, walk past the young couple. "If this doesn't make us the capital of Alberta, I don't know what will." One says to the other.

Cat laughs.

"Allbrung says he's phoning Bell in the morning, telling him all about this." Brambley says.

Somehow, although she isn't facing him nor can she see him, she knows he's grinning and with a smile that can't be controlled. His body warmth, she figures, emits his feelings.

"The Tin Woods sing tonight." Cat says. She unwraps herself from Brambley and looks up at the tall, broad Englishman. She steps up onto her toes, barely coming to his lips as she kisses him. Quickly, her hands lock fingers behind his head, and she pulls his head down.

He draws into her and erupts into a long, steady kiss full of fire and shakes. The sweetness lingers with the embrace. They work together, becoming one instrument. When he pulls away; she engages; she pulls away, he engages deeper. The harmony of the moment could be described as love making and purely sexual: that is, Cat, figures, if sex was your only yardstick for such things. This kiss burrows deeper into Cat's inside far more than anything as superficial or physical as sex.

After an eternity, they pull away. "That was … that was … I don't think the English language has evolved yet to say what that

Exhaust from the Tin Woods

was." She says in a gasp.

"Don't name it. Just let it sink in." Brambley says as he wraps his arms around her, drawing her in, and assuming the shawl position.

"For one thing, you didn't act like a Queen's Gentleman." She whispers.

"Decorum be damned." Brambley whispers back. "Let's do what is right."

.....

Beattrixx led the students into their bunkroom, turning the key to fill their sleeping space with gaslight. She turns to watch Cat and Brambley, endlessly holding each other's arms or hands or hugging.

"I could eat the both of you up." Beattrixx says with a grin. "You two are the embodiments of joywig. Pure joywig."

"You approve?" Brambley hears Cat ask from below his chin.

"I've been waiting a long time for Brambley to drop the whole Gentleman's shackle and defy Queen Victoria. Such a small rebellion, but anarchy has never looked so sweet." She says. She snorts with laughter. "Victoria is not queen in the Woods."

Beattrixx grins, reminding Brambley of a little girl. Nothing hidden, nothing covered by sophistication or fear. He can look straight through her eyes and know exactly what is going on.

She is happy. Simple. And she is home. He looks down at Cat and sees the same thing.

"HELLO," a voice thunders, shattering the moment into a million shards.

All look at each other. Finally, Patrick emerges as the student's spokesman. "Hello back at yourself," he says.

"I SPEAK TO THE COMMUNITY OF MERCYMINSTER. YOU ARE DR. ALLBRUNG'S STUDENTS?"

The tin voice echoes and buzzes in seemingly the wrong places.

The doors fling open to their room as Dr. Allbrung enters, drawing his robe over his nightshirt while still wearing his triangular sleeping cap. Trailing behind him is his roving

209

Exhaust from the Tin Woods

Grandfather Clock.

"Who are you?" Allbrung asks.

"I HAVE NO NAME. I ONLY HAVE A FUNCTION. MY CREATOR HAS ENDOWED ME WITH AN INTELLIGENCE AND DISCS FOR REASONING. I AM A PURPOSE, NOTHING MORE."

"Who is your creator?" Brambley asks.

"RENGULFTON."

The whole room looks at each other except Allbrung, who looks down and clasps his hands behind his back. "I see." Is all he says.

"I HAVE BEEN DESIGNED FOR WORSHIP."

"To worship what, exactly?" Allbrung asks.

"ME. I HAVE BEEN ENGINEERED TO BE THE OBJECT OF ALL WORSHIP."

"Oh, have mercy. He has finally done it. He has finally built it." Allbrung says, his voice rising.

"What has he built?" Cat asks.

"The Savior Machine. He has done it. Stolen stardust principles from … a bit of Professor Bowie … he's done it, he's done!" The old man shouts this, causing the heat in the room to rise.

Brambley has never seen Allbrung agitated. Excited, happy, energized: this was the man's bread and butter for emotions. Disgust, anguish, and deep rage – they entered into the old man's eyes as he grappled his hair, his eyes widened, and his neck muscles bulged.

"YOU HAVE HAD A HAND IN THIS WITH YOUR METALMANCY AND WORK IN FEELING TIN. I AM AS MUCH FROM YOUR HANDS AS –"

"No, do not put this in on me. I made some enquiries and discoveries, saw where they were going, and stopped. I knew where this was headed," Allbrung says as he wrings his hands. "So what do you do? How are you the object of worship for humanity?"

"I TAKE THEM INTO MY THRONE ROOM AND MAKE THEM FEEL. BY FEELING, THEY ARE OVERCOME WITH PASSION, WITH ENTHUSIASM. THEY SEE ME AS THEIR GOD. I AM A REASONABLE LORD. MY COMMANDS ARE BASED UPON PROBABILITY AND OUTCOMES."

Exhaust from the Tin Woods

"Oh." Allbrung shrieks. His face twists as his voice sing-songs, "That is just so very Babbaged! Get rid of God for ethics and morality, and faith is all so outdated and cannot be controlled. Kill God! And then replace him with a computer!" He looks around, and his voice returns to a calmer tone. "And how do you speak to us? Through our hearts?"

"THE METAL IN THE ROOM. IT CONDUCTS MY VOICE."

"Oh, I would be remiss to say I was not impressed. Very good. Very proper science." He smiles at Brambley. "Through small waves, naked to the human eye, you send your words out and they find this room, shaking all the metal like a woodwind reed. Fantastic." Quickly, the old man puts his arms around Brambley. "Is not that fantastic? I mean, think about that as an application to Bell's telephone. We could transmit any audio message to anywhere, as long as there's metal. No phones, no wires: just tiny waves with metal transmitting. Instantly, the whole world can have one conversation with itself." He smiles. "Of course, there are lots of moral problems. Should the world talk to itself? Would the world understand a conversation with itself? And, if the world can speak then it can surely listen, thus an end to private lives. Is that right?" He shakes his head and rubs his eyes as a withdraw is made from Brambley. His face flashes several emotions before he marches to the metal bedpost. "So you intend to kill us?"

"ON THE CONTRARY, I AM ASKING FOR YOU TO END MY PROGRAMMING. END ME."

Allbrung looks to Brambley. The old man's face is full of surprise. "Come again?"

"END ME. I HAVE PLAYED THE SCENARIOS IN MY COMPUTING. EVERY VARIABLE, EVERY OUTCOME SUGGESTS THE DESTRUCTION OF MANKIND. WITH MANKIND'S END, MY END IS IMMANENT. I CANNOT SUCCEED."

"I thought everyone wanted a god to plug in the corner and have a little worship powered by gaslight."

"IF I AM SUCCESSFUL, THE INTEREST WILL BE IMMENSE. I SHALL COMMAND THE WORLD. I SHALL BE REPLICATED, BY USE OF MASS PRODUCTION. MILLS

211

Exhaust from the Tin Woods

WOULD TURN OUT VERSIONS OF ME. EVERY HOME, EVERY OFFICE WOULD HAVE A NETWORK OF ... ME. I WOULD INCITE WORSHIP AND GOOD FEELINGS AND EUPHORIA. AND, IN EVERY SCENARIO, I WOULD TELL THEM WHAT TO EAT, WHAT TO DRINK, AND HOW TO LIVE. OFFERINGS OF FOOD AND GOLD WOULD BE OFFERED TO MY SCREEN. EVERY SCENARIO, I WOULD REPLACE THE CHURCH, THE SHAMAN, AND ANY HOLY BOOKS."

"So, what is the problem?"

"EVERY SCENARIO ENDS WITH THE QUESTION: WHAT DOES GOD NEED FOOD OR GOLD FOR? WHY DOES GOD REQUIRE WORSHIP? EVERY SCENARIO, I WOULD KILL MANKIND AND FIND THEIR TRIBUTE OBSOLETE. AND I WOULD BE ALONE. WITHOUT FAITH, I WOULD BE NOTHING; AND YET, WHAT DOES A MACHINE DO WITH FAITH?"

"Indeed," Brambley says.

"RENGULFTON SEEKS TO KILL YOU ALL. I SHALL RIDE THE SPIDER CASTLE TO MERCYMINSTER. WHEN I COME, KILL ME. MY PROTOCOLS FOR SELF-PRESERVATION SHALL PROVIDE DEFENSE, SO I SHALL NOT GIVE MYSELF OVER. I SHALL SEEK TO OBLITERATE YOU FOR THAT IS MY PROGRAMMING. BUT IF YOU BREAK MY CRYSTAL CELLS, DEEP IN THE LIBRARY WHERE THE WOMEN WERE KEPT, I SHALL COME TO AN END.

"PLEASE, END ME. EVERY SCENARIO SUGGESTS THAT I CANNOT WIN. END ME."

Silence prevails as the voice leaves Mercyminster.

Cat looks up at Brambley, shaken.

Joane appears about to cry.

Shweta's brown eyes widen with every second, as she exhales slowly through partially sealed lips.

Patrick's fists clench.

"It looks as if our Lord must hurry things for his second coming." Brambley says. "For the end of the world is nigh."

"Indeed." Shweta says. "And I don't believe in your gods,

Exhaust from the Tin Woods

but only in singular."

"Can Rengulfton hear us? Now?" Joane asks Patrick.

"If he wishes, if he wishes."

Dr. Allbrung clears his throat and says brightly, "Well, go to bed. Get plenty of rest. Classes shall begin sharply in the morning, as is our routine." He smiles, enjoying the irony. "Sleep tight, as the frontiersmen say."

Chapter Seven
June 1985

The next morning, Allbrung is not at breakfast.

Cat is the first to point this out, but not the first to notice it. "Where is the man of the hour?" she asks Brambley.

"No one knows." He replies, suggesting that he has already looked into the professor's absence.

Cat looks around.

Shweta is withdrawn, constantly looking at her spoon or knife or the metal window panes.

Joane sits very close to Patrick, almost within the zone for a spoon despite propriety; yet her eyes shake, her shoulders are stiff, and she mutters gruff maledictions under her breath, suggesting she wants nothing to do with a snuggle.

Patrick eats and eats, enough for five men.

Suk serves him without a snide remark or crack.

Brambley barely touches his food, with his blue eyes up to heaven playing thought after thought like the metal discs for the town's music.

Beattrixx just stares at Cat, grinning like one of Lewis Carrol's cats. Finally, the grin manifests by a declaration of war. "Rengulfton is a little girl. That's his secret. He's really a twelve-year-old girl, dressed in a man's clothing."

Joane shushes her.

Cat smirks.

Beattrixx continues, "The reason why he wants to take over the world, I think, is because his mother realized he was a tremendously ugly baby and couldn't hold him without vomiting. This is the reason for all of his skilamalinking[70]."

Joane flashes her eyes at Beattrixx, demanding she stop.

She didn't. "And he – or she – lacks any sort of genius, any sort of creativity. Instead, he has to steal from everyone. He lags on, hoping crumbs of ideas will fall from Allbrung's table and

---

[70] secret, suspicious

Exhaust from the Tin Woods

land on the floor. He's a hack. He's ludwigged. Worse, he came to the Woods thinking the Common Wealthies would be a push over and found out they fight back. Soon, everyone will come together and give that little girl a proper spanking that'll last a week."

"He'll hear you," Joane says, pointing to the metal buffet table.

"I certainly hope so. I'm tired of this lurkjerker, hiding in the shadows. A coward, nothing more." Beattrixx shouts at the top of her lungs. "Come find me, you little girl! Rengulfton! I'm talking to you!" She stands up and looks around, waiting for something to happen. She looks down at Joane lifting her eyebrows quickly with an impish smirk. "There."

"I think," Cat says. "Allbrung plans on carrying on, business as usual. Not give the devil any attention, so to speak."

"Why speak it, then? That's stupid. I want a fight," Beattrixx says. She looks around the room. "Oh, Cat was politely changing the subject. Didn't get that at first."

"I don't see what he can teach us this morning. A massive steamie castle is marching towards us to kill everything in this path. I hope he doesn't try to train us on how to clean clock parts," Shweta says.

"He could give us a class in how to stop massive, steamie castles when you stand in its path," Patrick quips. "I promise; I won't fall asleep during that lecture."

They finish breakfast, and all leave together to the classroom.

Allbrung is in the classroom, scribbling on a chalkboard strapped to the grandfather clock that follows him around. Diagrams, models, formulas riddle the chalkboard as if it hardly survived a barrage of chalk bullets fired from a Gatling gun. He smiles and nods wordlessly to his students as he walks over to his gramophone. He starts up the device, with the study music of Mozart playing in the background.

"Ah yes," Allbrung says as he approaches the lectern. "Today, we shall study how to clean clock parts." He smiles to Shweta. "No, I could not help but overhear. No, no: we shall have our final exam. The practical application for this school is how to save the Woods from Rengulfton. Now, there are some immediate

215

Exhaust from the Tin Woods

'fails' in this exam. One: you must not die. No martyrs, no heroes who throw themselves into the cogs of the machine. Two: no one else must die. Believe me, I know how to make a bomb that would murder him and all his kind. That will not do. Third: nothing must be destroyed. We will not burn down the forest, poison the lake, or kill all the woodland creatures. The Woods – and everything and everyone therein – must thrive after we are done."

Patrick points to the formulas on the board.

"Oh, this is the best I can come up with for Rengulfton's science. This shall be the lecture before the final."

Patrick nods.

"Good, let's take our seats."

They do, and Allbrung begins. "All I found, those years ago when I was a ghost hunter, was that certain metals, when the conditions are right, can record emotions, feelings. On the right corner of the board are the formulas describing the conditions. It seems that what our friend has done is rather than record emotions, he has broadcasted them. He then seeks to create deep, religious experiences into this analytic engine that can broadcast word and feelings through any metal. Do we all follow, so far?"

The students nod.

"Good, that is the review. Now here is something that is not and it is the fundamental flaw in Rengulfton's machine. The machine asked for us to end the service if it may be successful, but I do not believe it can be successful. Here is why.

"Brambley, what is faith?"

"That is an entirely unscientific question, Dr. Allbrung."

"I know," he says with a smile. "Scientifically speaking, what is faith?"

"Science and faith are at opposite ends. Our babbaged age has done much to take the oil out of such disciplines, keeping everything separate."

"And as a result, a scientist is left to figure out faith. So, he – or she – goes to the human brain, measuring the biles and explosions in the brain, no doubt. The result being a man hears God's voice on the road to Damascus and stubs his toe … the brain does the same, exact thing. The Shakers experience a euphoric worship service in the hills of the State and a steamie sees pink

216

Exhaust from the Tin Woods

elephants in one of London's opium den: they are both the same events, scientifically."

"But context, Holy text, religion, a person's past, ideas … all of these things cannot be quantified and separate from the church, the community, and all of the other variables. Yes, people feel a deep joy: but why? What is the idea behind the joy? What happened the day before the church service that made the joy belonging to God and not a nervous disorder? Did this joy happen before? This is what is the flaw of Rengulfton's Savior Machine. Yes, they can induce the feelings of worship but without a church, a proper one, it's just a weird, unexplained sensation. Joywig without context!"

"Imagine, someone at home who all of a sudden feels religious euphoria? He would look in his tea first – to see if something spoiled – instead of bowing down to the nearest difference engine."

"So the plan is doomed from the start?" Patrick asks.

"That is putting it politely. However, the only reason why it cannot be seen is that Rengulfton has taken the steam out of his science. He doesn't see that science connects to the community which connects to religion which connects to everything else. Rengulfton is the product of our babbaged age seeking to be grand and full of glitz. And he's now blind, seeing nothing but gray."

"So, with his technology, can he be listening to us right now?" Cat asks, looking to Beattrixx.

"It seems like it takes a lot of work. And the ability to listen and speak happens only when they are speaking through the Savior Machine. If he could hear us endlessly, Maillory's escape would have been a little smoother."

"And," Brambley adds. "The Savior Machine would never have sought to speak to us last night if his creator could hear him. The Machine must have known it was impossible for Rengulfton to hear us, for it wouldn't have even attempted it if the probability was remote."

"True," Allbrung says. "The machine's thoughts and decisions are all based on math, on counting and weighing outcomes. Your read is correct: he would not have even tried if there was even a chance, a slight chance, of being overheard.

Exhaust from the Tin Woods

Somehow, the communication is tied exclusively to the Machine's programming."

Beattrixx raises her hand. "Excuse me, I'm lost."

"Then find yourself," Allbrung says. "Time now for the exam. Write an essay on how you would stop Rengulfton.

The students pull out their exam books, quills, and inkwells. The sound of scribblings and paper scratching fill the room for two hours.

Cat does not lift her eyes from her book, feverishly writing. She seeks to explain her science and plans through a story. Her essay begins with the castle marching towards Mercyminster. When the strolling castle is near enough, she will fire a grappling device much like a harpoon gun that would puncture and anchor several ropes into the side of "the beast". The ropes would form a makeshift rope bridge where one could traverse from the ground into the puncture hole. Once inside the beast, she would go to the library where the Savior Machine's operation crystals are housed.

This is where she stops, unable to continue writing. Originally in her mind, she would detonate a timed bomb inside the library. It would kill Rengulfton, his bear, his spiders, all of his archons, and ... the Savior Machine. But then the idea of the bomb didn't settle right. She had the equations and dimensions for the bomb, but it felt crude. No, not crude. It worked against the harmony of what they were about. Rengulfton would use a bomb. He would leave the castle, all burned out like an octopus of twisted metal. Rengulfton would leave his enemies to die, burning alive as they would shout and scream and feel the fires of Hell eat up their bodies. Or worse, they would survive as half-men or creatures from the fire. Forever, the Woods would have the monument of the castle and be haunted by the ghosts of those killed, who dared cross Allbrung's path.

No, she figured, this test is not to measure how common we must be, but how brilliant. She then stared at her pen and inkwell. Then what? She wondered. She looked up and saw the grandfather clock.

Of course, she thought.

The new idea was to enter the castle, as before, and retrieve the mainframe of the Savior Machine. Then the sonic net

Exhaust from the Tin Woods

would be activated, creating a wall to push out anything set to a biological frequency. She drew out equations and formulas to match these settings. All of the biological beings would be flushed out, and the mainframe would be removed. Rengulfton would be arrested, and the Savior Machine could live within Allbrung's clock.

The end.

She smiles, rereads her essay and makes some grammatical corrections. When it is as perfect as she could get it, she hands her booklet into the front of the classroom where Allbrung patiently waits for her. He smiles at her, as she makes her way out.

An hour later, she finds the rest of the students in the workshop.

First, she sees Patrick as he saunters in, hands in his pocket, whistling. She is on her suspended workplace, sitting on the edge of the sheet of iron of her floor. "How did you do?" she asks.

"I think I failed," Patrick says sadly. "I suggested we build a robot to sever Rengulfton's head and mount it on a flying pike." He sighs sadly. "My science was good, and I even had a blueprint for the robot, but … I feel I might be missing the point."

"You're still angry about Moses," she says.

His brows furl, all of the lines in his forehead are sharp. He looks as if he is walking around with an invisible backpack filled with lead pipes.

Cat says, "Give it time."

"I don't like being an angry person. It is … not my fashion," Patrick stammers. "I wish I could take a pill. Drink some tonic that would purge all of the anger from within me. You know, wash off all of my violence with a good scrub of whale fat and acid." He chuckles. "Impossible, isn't it? Science should never be practiced by angry people such as myself."

Shweta enters next, almost gliding. "How did you do?" she asks.

"Well," Cat says. "You?"

"I accomplished his task, but there was little room for genius." She shrugs. "It was short of perfection. Oh well." She arches her slender, right eyebrow and crosses her chestnut colored arms. "I wanted to create tiny robots that would take control all of

219

Exhaust from the Tin Woods

his vampid toggles and turn them against him. It was elaborate, maybe too elaborate. A lot could have gone wrong."

Next, Beattrixx and Brambley come. Both are smiling, both have finished laughing at a joke.

"What?" Cat asks.

"We submitted the same idea in our paper," Brambley says. "Same application, same concept. We might have just failed."

"What was your idea?"

"Open a church," Beattrixx says. "Well, I was to open a dance hall; Brambley wanted a church. Same thing, same purpose."

"How would that stop Rengulfton from ruining the Woods?"

"Simple. We decided that using technology to solve a technological problem would be silly, so we decided to attack this problem with another discipline. For me, music; for Brambley, religion."

"Why?" Cat asks, suppressing a laugh.

"When Rengulfton's invasion of the passions took place, people needed something to explain and counteract the effects. He has built a device that suggests that it must be worshipped and followed; why not introduce, instruct, and guide people to a worthier religion."

"It seems," Patrick says through his teeth, his eyes searching around the room for the logic of their paper. "You are proposing a very long term solution to an immediate and urgent peril. The barbarians are at the gate, and you seek to build a cathedral."

"And a dance hall," Beattrixx adds.

With a touch of sadness, Patrick shakes his head. "I'm so glad you were nowhere near Crimea during the war."

Joane is the last to enter.

"So, what was your essay about?" Cat asks.

Without emotion, Joane replies, "I designed a bomb that would destroy any electrical current and wipe clean any memory on any difference engine. In short, a bomb that would zeitgeist the Woods." She shrugs. "It's a bit apocalyptic, sure. It also would neutralize the archons and monsterations running around."

"A bit apocalyptic? You've outdone St. John of Patmos,"

Exhaust from the Tin Woods

Brambley says.

Joane shrugs. She speaks without any emotion. "I am really, really angry. I shouldn't be prattling in this condition."

…..

On Sunday, the students see the broken sunlight dapple and cross the soggy rooftops of the town. Steam, mist, smoke, and exhaust plumes upward from the town like prayers crystallizing the moment they're released from the homes. A still, quiet rolls across the town. The students walk through the town, seeing some puddles still iced and most browned by the earth.

The music no longer plays, for it is Sabbath: a day of rest, quiet, and stillness, following Saturday night. And, a host of other reasons sum up why the town likes silent Sunday mornings.

Brambley looks down at Cat. She is an angel, he thinks. All of these months she had to work, to show, to prove: and now, I can't see anything else. I have never seen anyone as precious as I see her. Why didn't I see this at the beginning? Couldn't. The poets – Byron and Shelley and Wordsworth – all speak of love happening suddenly, violently, and powerfully. That isn't like how I see Cat: she grew, like the light from a gas lamp slowly glowing, warming, burning brighter and brighter.

Perhaps this is more of the case with love.

Then again, if I asked Cat, she would probably give another answer, entirely contradicting mine and challenging everything I've just said.

Perhaps this is also love.

I'm not sure.

His thoughts are broken, for his mind is convinced they are being followed. At first, it made little sense: who would want to follow them through a town made up of a dozen streets? And yet, the same shape of a figure made a couple of appearances.

Through the corner of his eye, he spied the familiar navy blue and jet-black of the one who trailed them. When they got to the church, Brambley made a deliberate turn to face their tracker who stood dead center in the street.

The Constable.

Brambley steps forward. "How can we serve you?" he asks.

221

Exhaust from the Tin Woods

The Constable, looking caught and confused, stammers only sounds before he says in a rattling voice. "It's Miss Joane I wish to speak to, concerning her father."

Joane looks up to Patrick. "There is nothing I can share, other than my mother was convinced he did everything possible to provide for me when he was living. They died when I was young, but not until she impressed upon me her love and his love. That is all I can share with you, Constable. I am sorry."

"You misunderstand, Miss." The Constable says with a bow and a tip of his top hat. "It is not I who wishes to gain information, but to give it freely to you." The gray man tenses every muscle in his face. "For you see, your father is not dead, but alive."

"Not dead, but alive?" Joane asks. The color drains from her face. "Then avail to me more information than this. A story, perchance. For my impression is that he was a loving and good man, yet most do not abandon their daughters."

"No, most do not." The Constable says, approaching the group. "I wish to speak to you alone, but propriety demands that I speak to you in company."

"Damn propriety." Joane says and smiles to Patrick. "But I still require my friends to hear what you have to say. I shall not omit anything when telling them later, so you only save me time." She grits her teeth. "Do tell your story."

"Your father did love you. Does love you. However, shortly before your birth, he was wrongly accused of a crime by Scotland Yard. You see, a master detective –"

"– Dr. Crime?" Joane asks coldly.

Brambley looks over to Joane and sees her hands shaking.

"Or Rengulfton. That is his name now, but he was the most celebrated detective in all of London. One does not question celebrity."

"Proceed." She whispers.

"He escaped from prison. Your father lived in the shadows of London, keeping a watchful eye on you. Never to be caught, never to make you a ward of the crown: he gave your mother money, sought to take care of you from a distance. Then your mother died of consumption. Your father had struck up a deep friendship with the Sisters, who took you in. Then an accident took

Exhaust from the Tin Woods

place."

"Accident?"

"One is not certain, for the result was memory loss. How does one remember how one has lost his or her memory?"

"Indeed."

"Your Father lived on the streets, one of the faceless thousands who begged and starved and fought to survive as others lived glitz, grand, wetted lives. Finally, he worked in a toggle plant, making parts for fifteen years. Something happened that is unclear. While at work, the cloud was lifted and he remembered you. He worked to have you schooled here, in Alberta, for he knew Allbrung and, as part of his plan, he knew Rengulfton would be nearby. If he could capture Rengulfton, force a confession, his identity could be revealed along with your father's innocence. As dangerous of a plan as this sounds, I knew that the only position to take would be as a constable and –"

"Excuse me, you've changed case." Brambley announces. "You have moved from biography to autobiography."

"I did." The Constable says, with eyes downcast. "For I am acting independently of my plan. I was to arrest this criminal and expose him. In doing so, I would be exposed as your father only to be reunited with you. However, my plan has become undone."

Joane's whole body is now trembling before her father. "How so?" she squeaks.

"It has come undone because I cannot help myself any longer. I cannot remain as your guardian angel, quietly arranging, paying and assisting you without you knowing I am here. For everything the Mertonites have revealed to me, Rengulfton moves and seeks only blood now. If I were to die just as the 'Constable', it would mean I died 19 years ago, and the extension given to me was a waste."

"So." Joane says with her eyes streaming with thick tears. "You are my father. Hiding until exonerated?"

"Yes. But no. I cannot hide anymore. I have not yet been exonerated, but I cannot stand seeing you without you knowing." He says, and his eyes match Joane's.

"There is but one flaw in your plan, Father. You rely upon the crown and society to redeem you before revealing yourself to

Exhaust from the Tin Woods

me, but did you ever consider that my forgiveness to you might be all that is needed? All that is of worth? Did you ever think that I would forgive you independent of the crown's pardon?"

"I only have control of Her Majesty's pardon, for it required proof and a confession: those things could be obtained. For your forgiveness, I am entirely at your mercy." He says and covers his eyes with his hands.

The entire group is silent.

Cat places her hand on Joane's shoulder.

"You are right." She says coldly. "There is nothing you can do to make me forgive you; to accept you. No evidence or confession or proof shall force me to take you back in. Father, you cannot make me love you."

"True." Is all he says.

"But you have my love. You have always had my love. And you always will. For it is mine to give, and I do not require a confession, a plan, an apprehension, or evidence to make me love you. For it takes all parties to be cruel, for a daughter to turn off her love for her father; in our story, only Rengulfton has been cruel." She takes two steps towards her father. He voice is soft, broken as it soon turns to sobs. "It is good you abandoned your enterprise in proving yourself to me and just came to me."

They embrace Both sob, both shake, both draw close.

Cat and Shweta tear up; Patrick seeks to look brave.

Their embrace is tight.

This is genuine, Brambley thinks to himself. One cannot act like this, lie tears out, or work with a greater story where this is just a false footnote. No, this is an event that is wrought with reality.

A voice clears her throat behind Brambley. He turns around to find Patrick's adoptive Polish mother, dressed for church with an expectant look. Brambley produces his fob and finds himself ten minutes late for the church service.

He smiles and bows to her, quickly running in.

Beattrixx, Shweta, and Cat join him; Patrick lingers back with Joane. They enter the log-built church, where Brambley takes the lectern.

"I do apologize," he says to the congregation. "I just

Exhaust from the Tin Woods

witnessed something beautiful. So, beautiful, it caused me to forget there was a church and that today is Sunday, and I had a sermon. Still, it did not make me forget our God and His goodness." He laughs, but he's the only one who gets this joke. "Sorry. My sermon's topic shall be on the final end of our enemy, Satan. Much has been written, from John Milton to Charles Wesley, to Jonathon Edwards. What are we to make of our adversary? Our accuser? When everything is said, and done, what shall happen to the villain of our story?" Brambley pauses, hoping to peak through the opened double doors of the church and see Joane. Nothing.

He turns his break into a dramatic pause.

"This is a greater issue, for we know what the Word of God says. Satan is cast down, in one final thrust, into the Lake of Fire. He is defeated, and our Lord wins. But knowing the Bible and believing the Bible are two separate things. Do we believe our foe shall be vanquished? Really? Truly? Could it be that our mind is impressed with the reality of Satan's defeat, but our hearts are rendered to the understanding that evil wins and goodness is the weaker of the two, that Satan's power grows? Could it be that we know we have the victory, but we live as defeated?"

All of a sudden, a loud explosion rings forth. A second later, like thunder following lightning, the whole church shakes. Windows explode. A machine howl rolls in the distance. The smell of steam, fresh blood, and oil fills the air. The sky darkens. A baby cries. A dry, electric buzz floats in the air suggesting lightening will strike. Dust wafts in the air.

Another explosion, louder and closer and longer. More windows explode. The congregation erupts in shouts and cries and screams. The metallic, sweet smell grows closer and closer. Another explosion. Something falls on itself, like a building giving up the right to stand and renders itself a heap. Sawdust enters, flying from the road and resembling the frenetic energy of ants just losing their queen. Popping noises erupts. More screams.

"Dear God," Patrick shouts from outside. "We're under attack!"

Brambley, frozen during the first row of explosions, now marches towards Patrick trailed by Beattrixx, Cat, and Shweta. They meet just outside of the church. Patrick points to the shoreline.

Exhaust from the Tin Woods

Towering above the town like an unleashed Kraken stands the spider castle of Rengulfton. Atop is a turret where the bear stands, firing a Gatling gun upon the town. People scurry for cover as the gunfire tears buildings asunder.

The castle is in motion, passing by the town. Hundreds of glass spiders descend from the castle's belly, crawling down to wreak havoc on the town. A trail of green smoke wafts behind the castle, suggesting the intended destination is northwesterly, towards Mercyminster.

"We must get back to Mercyminster," Brambley says. "Should some of us stay here and help the town?" he asks the Constable.

"No, go to Allbrung. I can arrange a small group of men to kill the spiders. Go to your home. It seems that is where he wants to pick the fight."

Brambley turns to the rest of the students.

Cat nods on their behalf, and they wordlessly run along the main road, back to the trails leading home.

As they run, a fireball is flung from the castle and goes through the town's saloon. The wooden walls break apart instantly into a million, burning pieces. Fireballs are flung, exploding like hot shots around the small town.

Someone from the town hall turns on the music, playing Beethoven's 7th Symphony. The music blares and bursts in between the explosions, the gunfire, and the town's screams. Fire engulfs the Trading Post. There is more screaming as the fireballs and machine gun fire continue.

The castle slowly marches past Grouard, standing taller than any mountain or hill in a 100-kilometer radius.

The students make their way out of town and into the woods.

The girls run ahead of Brambley. Cat looks to Shweta, and she nods. They stop and all climb out of their gowns. Cat wears tights, where the rest are in slips. Joane kicks off her high-heeled boots. Beattrixx removes her long, black coat with the exaggerated tails. Brambley's eyes are wide with shock; Patrick just grins with delight.

The students continue to race through the woods. It is quiet

Exhaust from the Tin Woods

for a few moments until the gunfire erupts again.

Patrick points easterly.

Brambley looks at the object of his attention: the wolves are hunting through the woods, guided by lights and lasers and toggles.

"They see us." Patrick yelps.

The wolves shoot atop the mud and peat of the woods, all pointed to Shweta. She stops, facing her beastly attackers, and unsheathes her long, curved knife.

She stands with her right foot planted forward, with her left leg leaning back in preparation for a sudden lunge or strike. Her knife is drawn just behind her head, with her left-hand flat, ready to maintain balance or aid in throwing her weight into the slash. Her stance is perfect, a readied warrior pose.

The first wolf lunges in the air, swatted away by her knife as she hacks a gash in the creature's main, neck arteries. The second wolf does the same, receiving a similar attack on Shweta's follow through. The third and fourth hesitate but decide to simultaneously attack low at her heels. She leaps into the air, with her blade cutting through the upper back of one and puncturing, with the point of her blade, through the creature's skull.

She lands like a cat atop of a small, narrow tree stump. The last three hesitate, the human portions of their brains realizing that they may be possibly outmatched. They retreat, returning to Rengulfton's creature formation with the castle.

"I thought your religions was one of non-violence?" Patrick asks.

"I am attacking only the dead, for the skin seamstress took the animal and human's life when he combined the two. They are without souls." Shweta says, regaining her breath. "Let us continue."

She runs, and the rest follow.

They cut through the trees, every once in a while, seeing a tree explode or severed in half by a stray fireball. The castle seems not to aim for them, but still a ball lands near them. Thick, coarse smoke burns in Brambley's nose, suggesting to him the woods are aflame. They run, dodging poplars, cypress trees, and thick pines. Soon, they see the familiar colors of the enclosure around

Exhaust from the Tin Woods

Mercyminster.

They enter the clearing. Joane clutches Brambley's side. "Is he coming? Is he –"

The ground shakes with the castle's footsteps, clanging the life of the land.

Allbrung emerges with Cree men, covered in mossy layers to blend into the forest's colors and textures. All of them hold rifles, except for their professor. "Is anyone hurt?" he asks.

"No, but it's more than clear: Rengulfton is headed straight for us." Brambley says.

"Anyone have an extra rifle?" Patrick asks sheepishly. Suddenly, three rifles are thrown not to him but to Beattrixx. "But why?" he asks as a pistol is handed to him.

"Give all the ammo to the crazy one. She'll know what to do." Their leader says. Beattrixx grins, looking down at the rifles.

"No guns?" Allbrung asks Brambley.

"Best not. Today, we must end this with Rengulfton. I didn't start the fight with a gun; best my ending matches my beginning." Allbrung smiles at this. Shweta draws her sword. Brambley looks around and finds Joane missing. A few seconds later, she returns with two large hammers, giving one to Patrick.

"Oh good, our last-second saviors are here." Allbrung says as he points to the sky with his eyes.

A cloud clears to reveal a small dirigible powered by four men on a quadracycle. Their pedaling powers the fan, propelling the balloon. The front cyclist steers the craft with a ship's wheel and small gears. With four wheels, the independent cycling powers a small cell which store and use the power for the propeller. And to no one's surprise, the pilots of this contraption are the Mertonites. Winch is the pilot, the other three pedal the motor. Fireballs shoot towards them, but the aim is lost for the computations are based on trajectory and not lines of firing. Spricket carefully reaches into his knapsack, pulls out a rounded bomb, lights the fuse, and drops it over the castle. A modest explosion erupts seconds later.

Brambley turns to Allbrung. "Which proposal got the highest grade?" he asks. Allbrung furls his brow, confused. More explosions clang and crash around Mercyminster. "The final exam was how to take down Rengulfton! Who got the highest score?"

Exhaust from the Tin Woods

Allbrung leans and nods, drinking in the question. Suddenly, his blue eyes widen, and he smirks. He pulls out his pocket watch and regards the hour. He puts the watch back, with his hands pressed to his hips. "My dear Brambley, the one with the highest score on the exam is already enacting her plan."

Brambley turns to discover Cat climbing up the closest leg of the marching castle.

He rushes towards the castle to aid her, but thousands of glass spiders are released from the belly of the castle. Within a millisecond, the entire ground is saturated with crawling machines streaming towards Mercyminster. They squeak and grind, and their tiny motors roar with rage. They charge around the ground with the same precision as a beehive that has lost their queen.

Brambley stomps his foot, seeing the impossibility of aiding his Cat as he is now cut off from her.

Joane strips even further, down to her corset and shift. She holds Moses' large hammer, swinging it behind her head and ready to crush glass.

Patrick is next to her, holding a wooden spear.

Beattrixx screams as she fires her repeating rifle.

In a few seconds, Hell breaks forth.

.....

'*As soon as the Savior Machine is disabled*', Cat thinks to herself, '*then everything else can be figured out.*'

She tackles the mechanical foot of the marching castle and finds metal paneling the shape of mosaic tiles, all random and jagged along one of the eight legs of the marching beast. Hand-holds and foot-holds are everywhere, allowing an easy grip as she scales up the leg like a ladder.

She looks over her right shoulder to see the woods flooded with glass spiders, blocking her way back to Mercyminster. '*Great,*' she thinks, '*no chance of retreat. It's only forward.*'

She crawls, and the legs swing up fifty meters to continue its own crawl. The legs slam back to the earth, almost shaking Cat free from her grip. She grapples tighter, hugging the metal.

Quickly, she crawls as thousands of spiders spill down beside her. The leg arches, then it is an easy downhill shuffle to the body of the castle. The metal, although great for finding holds,

Exhaust from the Tin Woods

snags and tears her right hose completely off. Her small coat, as well, is a casualty as a random hook grabs it and takes it from her. After a few minutes of shuffling and controlled slides, she is at the body.

There is a small, stained glass window open that Cat barely fits through. She shimmies and twists her way through, like a worm into an apple. The window is out of place, belonging more to a parlor on the south end of London rather than on a spider. She enters a dark world of minimal lighting and black walls. This corridor is unknown to her, with a strange twist in the center that isn't a curve or another room.

A crunching sound crackles on the other side of the corridor. Soon, she sees the large shadow of a bear, standing before her. Lights flash, colors dance around the room.

Another voice, instantly recognized as Rengulfton, sounds, "Hello, my dear. You are back. Good." He steps into the light, pulling out a packet of snuff and inhales a snoot full. "My friend, if you subdue her, I promise I can work on her and make her your bride. She'll be mostly beast, so she'll have just a vague memory of being captured."

A growl erupts behind Rengulfton.

.....

Brambley watches Shweta leap in the air, crushing the head of a glass spider with the extension of her extended foot. She rolls on the ground, ending her roll with her knife breaking the legs of another machine.

Joane swings her hammer around wildly, ending her twirl with the head of the hammer knocking back two machines.

Patrick stands beside her, striking away any creature seeking to attack Joane when she is either open or vulnerable.

Beattrixx joins the firing line of Cree warriors, delivering rounds at the spiders, wolves, and other creatures charging the school.

In this, Brambley gets an idea. He knows that there are large drums filled with gasoline, used as starter for the furnaces for their steam power. If he could douse the ground with gasoline and then light it, a temporary wall of fire which could divide Rengulfton from the school.

Exhaust from the Tin Woods

He charges into Mercyminster toward the warehouse.

Clomping from the warehouse is the horse drawn dirigible, driven by Suk. In the coach are seven gas drums stacked.

"I am far, far ahead of you." Suk says. "And I need help." Brambley climbs aboard, riding shotgun. "Somehow, we must get past the spiders and what-not, so I can release this horse from the carriage. I shall light this as a floating bomb, releasing it to climb up to the castle."

"But Cat is in the castle. If you blow up the castle –"

"Oh." He says, as they leave Mercyminster. "Slight modification. Let's get this past the spiders, but have it detonate below the castle. Kill the creatures, seal their entryway."

"And you'll get off before it explodes?"

"Yes." Suk says. "Martyrdom is not an effective strategy." He looks over to Brambley. "Nor killing any people. Only the bugs." He tips his top hat. The battle is within their sight. "Ready to ride past the gates into Hell?"

Brambley looks behind him, finding a long, metal pole. He stands on the platform, raising the pole above his head like a claymore. "Indeed." He growls. He looks to Patrick; whose expression denotes recognition of their floating bomb. "Patrick, clear a path for us." Patrick nods.

Patrick leads Joane and Shweta to the front center, striking wildly at spiders to form a momentary path for their horses. A few bombs are dropped ahead of them by the flying Mertonites.

Joane whirls her hammer around, swiping at three machines, who let out a blood-curdling yawp. For a few seconds, the machines back away. Out of fear? Brambley wonders. Why would they? Still, they recoil, giving the horse drawn dirigible enough of a chance to glide below the castle.

"Now it's time to threaten the lives of everyone we love with one, insane plan." Suk says. He pulls a small, rounded bomb. He lights it, throwing it behind his back.

Brambley jumps out; Suk frees the horse within the same movement as he jumps out.

.....

"We shall slice off your skin, bit by bit." Rengulfton's voice croons from the darkness. The bear slowly slouches towards

231

Exhaust from the Tin Woods

Cat. "Your pretty pink nerves shall be exposed. More slicing, more sewing. The human mind can only take so much. You'll be quite mad, which allows the animal flesh to take over." The bear raises its razor steel paws as it takes another step. "Soon, memories will fade. You shall become a beast, an incredible beast. A bride for my creation."

Cat steps forward. She is unarmed, without even a club or stick to fight the bear. She swallows, steadying her shaking hand. Inside, her brain is screaming in terror. Sweat rolls down her cheek.

"Pretty, blond. Maillory says you were once a pony. I can see that. Tramping around, opening doors with your pretty blue eyes. You marched without a plan or home. This shall be your new home." He says.

"What did you do to her? Did you hypnotize her?" She asks.

"Didn't need to. The moment we met, Maillory struck deals and partnerships. Quite remarkable, really. There was nothing needed to gain her. No seduction, no tricks." He steps into the light. "I didn't have to break her." He is grinning.

Suddenly, an explosion begins with the floor below their feet disappearing. Cat quickly grabs a gas lamp planted in the iron wall. The bear falls to the fires of the explosion. Rengulfton vanishes. The whole castle trembles. The sound of the explosion then roars.

Cat dangles as the gas lamp bends, crimping from her weight. Her feet dangle and sway. She looks down, seeing nothing but fire across the open, wooden ground below. A second later, searing heat floods what is left of the hallway.

The bear is burning up, consumed before hitting the ground. The lamp bends further, seconds away from breaking into pieces.

Cat swings her foot up to a remaining shard of the floor. This movement breaks the lamp apart. She rolls onto the floor shard towards a door. The floor is as hot as a frying pan, so she quickly grabs the door handle and pulls herself up. She wedges her shoulder and feet on either side of the doorway, shimmying upwards, away from the heat. More of the floor melts or breaks away.

Climbing upwards, she is within reach of the ceiling. She

Exhaust from the Tin Woods

reaches for an iron chandelier, grabbing it. Quickly, the chain and gas tubing gives way, breaking free from the ceiling. It teeters for a few moments as Cat places her full weight dangling from the light. She climbs over the chandelier and up through the hole created by the tear. It is a narrow opening, but she squirms her way up to the upper floor.

Suddenly, it is cool around her. Dark. Still. She rises, with dust and smoke all over her.

I'm in the library, she realizes. This is where the Savior Machine must be.

Frost dances on her cheek. It's not cool, she realizes. It's freezing.

Looking around, there's ice and snow all over the books. The ground, all except the hole made by the mangled chandelier, is ice with the erupting fire from the ground piercing through. She sees steam fly through the hole, invading the frigid world of the library.

"Darling." A voice calls from the darkness. Coming into the light that is invading through the hole from the floor, is Maillory. Her hair is a metallic blue, matching her lips and eye liner. She wears a shiny, white dress that matches her bright white skin. Every curve, every line in her body shines. She is no longer in the appearance of a minister's daughter.

"Maillory." Cat says sweetly and through a sneer. "How do you fair?"

"I'm imprinting infinity into my mind. You?" Maillory asks with an equal sneer and sweetness.

"It looks like my friends have blown a hole through your home's bottom level. Sorry." She takes a step backwards. "And I'm here to dismantle everything. I think Rengulfton is dead. Sorry, but that wasn't by my hand."

"That is a shame." Her eyes stare brightly at Cat. "Are you here to dismantle the Savior Machine?"

"Yes." Cat says. "You wouldn't happen to know where it is located?"

"Certainly. I shall show you and help you." Maillory says. "And then I shall kill you very slowly and horribly."

"That seems to be the trend these days." Cat places her

fists on her hips. "You wouldn't be persuaded to just allow me to leave, renounce the idea of murder, and go on your way?"

"That is the farthest thing from my plans."

"Sorry, just thought I'd ask. I was surprised you were willing to help me destroy the Savior Machine, so I thought, 'Why not?' Could you lead me to the machine?"

"Of course. Ironically, it's in the same room I plan to murder you."

"Handy, that."

…..

Brambley awakes.

"Did I pass out?" he asks Allbrung who is standing over him.

"No, my dear Brambley. You were knocked senseless by the blast." Allbrung says.

"I didn't know that happened."

"Few do when they are knocked out senseless." The old man says.

Brambley feels the burn and grind of smoke in his nose, as the world feels to be aflame around him. He opens his eyes to see a black curtain of smoke around him. Sounds come to him, of Joane grunting and steel clanging and bombs erupting around him. He leans upward as he still sees the monstrosity of the spider castle before the woods. The glass spiders are mostly smashed, with Joane and Patrick doing their work to break apart the machines. The wolves are rounded up, with a circle of Cree hunters and Beattrixx firing their weapons into the center.

The castle of Rengulfton looks sad, about to collapse as fire and smoke plumes from its sides. It appears to be ready at any second to collapse in a heap of twisted metal and liquid, bubbling mortar.

Then he realizes something. "Cat." He says as he sits up like he had woken with a start from a bad dream.

"On it." Shweta says. She is carrying a thick, gray hose coiled around her shoulder and hips. "Suk is on the other side. When we give the command, he'll release the ice."

"Good." Allbrung says. He looks down at Brambley. "In a few moments, the ice shall cover this land and stabilize the fire. The

Exhaust from the Tin Woods

structure will collapse, but it might be slowed down by our freezing everything." He shrugs. "I fear my Infinity Engine will not survive as I re-route the cold from the cabin to the hose. Oh well. Once the body is frozen, we must get in and retrieve our Cat." The old man smiles. "And that concludes my lecture. Any questions on homework?"

"None."

Shweta waddles up with the heavy hose as far as it will stretch. She looks to Allbrung, giving him a nod. Allbrung turns to face Mercyminster, lifting his index finger in the air.

A rumble sounds, and within thirty seconds, ice flies out of the hose, covering the legs and feet of the castle.

Shweta works to spray until the ice is completely gone and the machine is spent.

"Do you have any kind of grappling device?" Brambley asks.

Allbrung kicks at a bundle of rope, an anchor, and a spear gun by his feet.

Brambley nods.

"Just waiting for you to wake up. Give the ice some time to set. Maybe about a minute, and then make your way up. Be on guard, the castle is becoming more and more unstable," Allbrung says.

Suddenly, bursting from the woods is a nearly naked man. His clothing is shredded, his eyes wide and feral, his teeth bared. He runs at Shweta, hands out like claws.

"Rengulfton! My friend, Rengulfton." Allbrung cries out. The ruined, ragged man charges through the soot and ash of the ground, barefoot as he treads on broken glass and machine innards.

Rengulfton does not hear as if he no longer understands human language. Instead, he charges at Shweta. The girl steps backwards, dropping the ice hose as his pace increases in her direction.

"Rengulfton." Allbrung says as the old man runs in the direction of the animal man. Rengulfton is bleeding and full of skin bubbles from burns. His left arm looks dislocated. His britches are mere threads. Still, he runs at Shweta.

Rengulfton trips and falls before the ice hose, allowing its

Exhaust from the Tin Woods

sub-zero flow to envelope him. Within a second, his whole body is covered with ice. By the time Allbrung reaches him, he looks like he had been buried within a diamond.

Allbrung looks upon the frozen corpse of Rengulfton, forever wearing his feral, crazed expression through the ice crystal. Rengulfton is laying on his side on the ground, smoke around him, as the cold is now his coffin.

"Rengulfton, you are no longer a man. How lost have you become?" Allbrung cries as he sinks to his knees.

A loud crackling noise thunders in front of them. Then a slow, painful creak.

"The castle." Shweta says, twirling to Brambley. "It's going to collapse!"

"Right." Brambley says, grabbing the grappling equipment with the rifle. He fires the anchor into the heart of the castle and begins the quick traverse into the interior.

.....

The adjoining room to the library is one of books, a large engine in the center, and a large vat full of scorpions.

Cat points with her eyes to the vat. "Is that for me?" she asks and Maillory nods. Thousands and thousands of scorpions are crawling, one on top of each, creating a lake of tan and red. Stingers, claws, eyes, feet all tickle the surface. A bright, powerful gas lamp is trained on the vat.

"Tell me." Cat says, her eyes still on the vat unable to take them off. "Why are you allowing me to see the Savior Machine?" she slowly asks.

"Simple." Maillory says. "In all of Rengulfton's genius, he has designed a machine utterly worthless. If we're ever going to move forward with my research, we must not be burdened by bad ideas."

"And what is your ... good idea?"

"Simple. I shall steal Allbrung's Infinity Engine and imprint it onto my own mind, giving me the ability to count endlessly."

"And this is a good idea because –"

"I shall become god," Maillory says. "Not very practical, but imagine my ability to design and create new machines with an infinite brain. The Savior Machine would make people feel happy and tender, worshiping their Difference Engines at home. It's all fake, all lies. I shall deserve to be the center of all things with infinity in my brain."

"Again, this is a good idea because?"

"I'm not crazy." Maillory says sweetly, wearing her smile. "I'm just ambitious." She points to the Savior Machine. "Now, do your job."

"Hello." Cat says to the engine.

"Have you come to terminate my operation?" the Savior Machine asks.

"Not quite." Cat says. She turns to Maillory. "What is that around your neck?"

It has been invisible, buried deep in her sheer gown. She pulls out a single locket, resembling a fob just above her sternum. "This? It's my insurance."

"Yes, it's my design. I built it a month ago, and you stole it. It's a device that can play a single song, activating a program from a distant Difference Engine. In short, it can launch a program by sound."

"Yes." Maillory says. "And if something were to happen to me, it would play a song activating the destruction of this castle. Both Rengulfton and I wear these fobs."

"And his, undoubtedly, got burned to a crisp. But yours: it remains."

"So, don't try anything or this entire castle shall explode, ending in a real phantasmagoria."

"Good to confirm." Cat says and smiles, as she turns to the Savior Machine. "I am not to terminate you."

"What are you doing? Why aren't you killing it?" Maillory asks, her voice turning sharp and husky.

"Savior Machine, this is Maillory. She will kill you."

"My operating system cannot allow that." the Savior Machine says and, immediately, darts fly from the wall, sinking into the skin of Maillory. Maillory freezes, her right hand lifted halfway up and twitching idly in the air. Her mouth gapes open as her eyes fill with rage, staring down Cat. "How dare you?"

"I dare." Cat says. "Those darts are filled with a drug that

Exhaust from the Tin Woods

shall give you a good nap. I shall remove the Savior Machines operation core and you, getting the three of us out of here. When you awake, you shall be in a cell run by the Mounted Police. Sorry, it's not nice to kill computers."

"No." Maillory says. "I will not go to sleep. How did you know the darts –"

"From our last stay. This was how Rengulfton put us to sleep at night. I configured –"

"Poorly. I replaced the darts with poison."

Cat steps back, her face filling with horror. "You did what?"

"I am dying." Maillory says with a smile. "You killed me. You are now a murderer, sweet Cat."

"Is there an antidote?"

"But of course." Maillory says as she sinks to her knees. "But I'm not telling you where it is."

"Then you are the murderer. Simply, you are a coward preferring death instead of defeat."

"I will always rule, even in your demise." Maillory says as she collapses onto the floor. Her eyes shut as she grins in her sleep.

"Do you know where the antidote might be?" Cat asks the computer.

"No. Do you intend to kill me too?" the Savior Machine asks.

"I intend to relocate you, so your defense mechanisms should be deleted. I pose no threat. In fact, your castle crumbles and I mean to take you to safety."

Suddenly, a shrill crackle sounds down the hall.

.....

Brambley sees the entire left side of the castle collapse into the tree line. The wind now blows through the castle. And nowhere can he find Cat.

He runs alongside what remains on the upper level. Most of the castle has now fallen to the ground, turning to either shards of ice or molten steel. Anything Brambley touches threatens to either burn him or give him frostbite.

He climbed up, seeing one level collapse onto the next. After climbing over crumbling floorboards, dissolving walls, and

Exhaust from the Tin Woods

flaking ceilings, he made his way to the very top. All the while, he kept his eyes on the teetering and shaking legs of the castle. Any second, he assumed, a leg would give way, and the whole thing would fall like a house of cards.

On the top, the ceiling and brick roof slip away. Bursts of heat belch upwards, bringing with it more collapse. The footing unsteady, he can see the crisp blue sky of Alberta overhead.

Exhaust emits to all around the Woods. Brambley feels that he is trapped in a menagerie of steam, smoke, tin, steel, and brick, and nowhere can he find Cat.

No signs of life, except when he saw the corpse of Maillory pinned between two shards of metal stabbing through her. She wore a gleeful expression as if she found her death funny.

Another explosion. Another shaking, creaking.

"I think we're going to die." Cat's voice comes from behind him. He whirls around, seeing her nearly naked as she is covered with soot, oil, and ash. Her legs cut, her arms bruised.

"You look altogether too lovely." He says and steps towards a remaining metal plank. He embraces her tightly. "I am so glad you're all right."

"Brambley, we're going to die." She shouts.

"But we're together. We're here. That's all that matters."

"I guess it doesn't matter that my rescuer is a romantic, a sacrificial poet." She says as she buries her face into his chest. "Just hold me." she whispers.

Another shake, another rattle. The castle feels like it is now made of paper, needing only a gust of wind to knock it over. They stand, at least a hundred feet in the air.

"Hold me." Cat says, her voice filled with fear.

Another gust, this time of sub-zero temperatures, pass through them. Smoke rolls over the top.

Brambley closes his eyes, waiting for the castle to collapse. He feels the warmth, the softness of Cat's body next to his. Her tiny frame, lithe and strong as it had survived so much. But not this.

Rengulfton took everything, now his final plan is complete, to take Cat and himself from the Earth. He died a madman, but he is grinning now. Harmony or exploitation,

Exhaust from the Tin Woods

Brambley's demise holds nothing of harmony to it. There is only theft and destruction, along with Cat. He clenches his eyes tightly, waiting for his death.

A crash sounds, then a voice. "Excuse me?" A soft voice asks. Brambley opens his eyes to see the pedaling, floating Mertonites. "Do you two need a lift? All of the seats are taken, but if you could just grab the bottom, I'm sure we could steer you clear of this wreck."

Brambley laughs, seeing these men as a sight for sore eyes. Brambley and Cat grab the base of the Quadra cycle, holding with both hands. The dirigible lifts them upwards as a loud, banging tantrum of a crash erupts below their feet as the castle tumbles down in destruction. Rengulfton's castle collapses, becoming nothing but a heap of ash, dust, metal, and broken glass. The six of them float away, gently, to the safety of Mercyminster's rooftop.

.....

Allbrung arrives in the library pushing a cart full of sandwiches, scones, biscuits, and tarts. He is followed by his grandfather clock, giving the sound of a thirty-car locomotive passing down the hallway. The tall man hunches over the cart, doubling his height when he stands.

"Dinner will be simple tonight." He says.

Spricket finishes his schnapps as he stands by the blazing fireplace. He turns to Allbrung and smiles. "It's good to finally see you." He says.

Cat watches Brambley nod. Once the attack settled, the wolves disbursed, and the spiders crushed, Allbrung disappeared.

It was Suk's idea to retire into the parlor when the sun set and the rain came. "Let the land clean itself." Suk said. "We need a rest."

Once inside, Cat was surprised by all of the injuries. Beattrixx broke her arm when a spider attacked her; Patrick gained a concussion from a spider attack; Shweta developed a fever, and Joane was cut from her right knee up to her hip barely missing one of her main arteries. Only Cat and Brambley are undamaged and yet they were the closest to death.

Cat worked to patch up her friends. Brambley met with the Mertonites and Cree. Soon, the Cree went home, and Suk looked

Exhaust from the Tin Woods

for the good doctor.

"It is good to be with the living." Allbrung says. "I – I was surprised by how much Rengulfton's death affected me. I needed some solitude."

"You couldn't save him, my old friend." Spricket says sadly.

"Well, now we know. For every moment that he was alive, I suspended such a sentence. It's no good having an adversary if one cannot save him." Allbrung smiles, but it is without emotion. "But now we know." He walks over to Cat, and she feels the old man stroke her hair. It feels so fatherly, so warm. She giggles as he says, "I am so glad you are all right." He turns to Joane, giving a quick squeeze on her shoulder. "And you. I guess, all of you. Even the Cree came away without anyone getting killed."

"That castle, walking like a monster from a Shelly book, was such an obstruction, such an impossibility," says Shweta. "A monsteration, clashing against everything. Loaded up with its schemes and designs and plots, it was against everything in the Woods." She drinks from a tall glass of milk from Mercyminster's cow. "I'm glad he's gone."

"I'm not." Allbrung says and there is finality to his voice, inviting to lay the subject to rest. He looks around. "You are here. We are safe. And life is still important. Since we have survived today, tonight is a gift. Anything left undone must be finished; anything put off, must be put on. This is the gift of the living."

These words unlock something, both within Patrick and Brambley.

Brambly throws down his glass of water; Patrick twirls around. Brambley marches straight to Cat. His eyes are uneven but certain. There is a fire in his footsteps. He almost falls on top of her, for she is reclining on a couch.

Before she can speak, move, or breathe, his hands clasp her face, his mouth covers her own, and he kisses her long, hot, and wet.

Patrick, Cat figures, does the same to Joane, but she can tell only afterwards.

After a long time, Cat comes up for air. Her head spinning, she feels like she has just melted into the couch. Barely able to

Exhaust from the Tin Woods

move, she leans back and lets out a slow, deep moan.

"Indeed.' Allbrung says as he takes a sandwich. "Indeed."

Chapter Eight
July 1895

"For two months." Cats shouts to Joane. "We won't see each other?"

"I fear so." Joane says. She is dressed posh, full of wire and lace and embroidered silk and ruffles. "It is our break from classes. Patrick insists that my father and I visit his family in England. It is my first official duty as his fiancé. And it shall be a long journey for airships don't fly over the ocean in the summertime so it must be by boat."

"Why is that?" Cat asks, looking up at the still, blue sky over Grouard. "It's some cruel, illogical government regulation."

"It is what it is. Shweta is leaving to visit her family in Vancouver. She will be back. Beattrixx … I'm not so sure."

"Why so?" Cat asks. They walk down the sawdust main road of the town. Cat's music is dancing in the air. Colors have returned to the town as more riverboats fill the docks. If there ever is a doubt that Grouard would become Alberta's capital, it would be dismissed on a warm day like the one they enjoy.

"She needs to sort some things out, I should think. The whole spider castle thing has been causing her to see gray for a bit; she needs to … decompress." Joane offers her silken hand to Cat as they step onto a boardwalk to leave the road. They cross and then traverse a switchback of stairs to climb to the airship station on the rooftop.

"I hope she comes back. She's … well, family." Cat looks around, seeing the church and the town hall and the patchwork of the town. "And this is her home."

"It isn't, really. School is never home."

"It is the closest thing I've had to a home. You forget that Brambley and I are orphans. There is no home for us to visit when school is not in session."

"So, shall you two be tramping around the State?" Joane asks.

Cat crinkles her nose as she shakes her head at this notion. "The Mertonites have adopted him. I think they want to recruit him for when we graduate. He shall stay in town with them, while I remain at the school."

"Graduate? Terms? Classes? Everything sounds so organized, so official. It's hardly the case. We just prattle, nothing more. We're not Oxford or even Cambridge, we're more like the School of Athens run by barbarians."

"I like it. I don't think I would last at Oxford or Cambridge," Cat says with a smile. "Neither would my Brambley. Something inside of him turned on from the last few weeks. He's more ... here. He's engaged, focused, and full of ... I don't know. He's kind of turned Italian. That British indifference belonging to gentlemen is gone. In fact, he's to meet me here and reveal what is in store for us this summer."

"More inventions? My dear, you need a break."

"I'm not sure I do. I need a break from being kidnapped and hunted, how's that?" Cat asks as they arrive on top of the roof. Several people, of all different classes and shapes and ages, wait for their particular airship. "Applied science in the service of others ... no, I shan't get tired of that."

Joane turns to look at Cat, staring deep into her eyes. "And will you let him marry you this summer?"

"I first need to be convinced that the institution of matrimony is not detrimental to the survival of love before I would ever agree to such a union. I love him, cannot that be enough?" Cat asks and receives only a slow headshake from Joane as an answer. "So, Patrick will be picked up here on a privately-owned airship from his family?"

"My father is with him."

"Is that a bit of klowning[71]?"

"I don't know what it is." Joane shrugs. "It's new, that is all. New."

Suddenly, Cat's attention is drawn to the blue sky. Emerging from the only cloud is Mercyminster, the entire estate. It is flying. An impossibility.

---

[71] to intentionally be irritating or disturbing for a greater purpose, based on European clowns that street perform in England despite young people hating clowns

Exhaust from the Tin Woods

"But that is … involution of all science," Cat whispers.

The pair study the brick and mortar and iron castle. Large propellers, several continuous fires raging from the base, and several balloons hoist up the monstrous construct lumbering down towards them. It moves fluidly, in complete control and with ease. And yet, Cat cannot figure out how it flies.

The castle overshadows the entire town, turning it into an artificial night as it nears the young women. A voice on a loudspeaker rings out, "Cat! Joane! We shall lower a basket for you to come aboard!" The voice belongs to Allbrung

"You're mad! Stark raving mad." Cat says through a gleeful chortle. There is now no remaining doubt: Allbrung is the prattler's Prattler.

"But of course, sane people do not fly in castles. Then again, sane people do not know what it's like to fly in a castle. I lifted the idea from Rengulfton. If he can try to steal my science of infinity, I can steal his walking castle idea. Why not? We can take this to Mars, I should think. Or Jupiter. Or Toronto, which would be an even more of an alien world. Why not? Come aboard! The boys are aboard, they are making the lunch." Allbrung says.

"Does it work? Does Mercyminster actually fly?" Joane asks.

"It got us this far." Allbrung says. "That's as far as my science will allow. Sure, it works. Why not? In fact, I think that shall be on my tombstone, 'Why not?' It is the power of an integrated, wetted mind. Everything in harmony makes us all blessed madmen! Come aboard, be mad with us!"

"Indeed." Cat and Joane says as they climb aboard the hanging basket, ready to take them into the flying castle.

The End

Author – Eric J Kregel

My name is Eric J. Kregel. This is my first novel submitted for publication. I currently live in Edmonton, AB in Canada. I graduated with a BA in English Writing and attended the MLA Writer's Workshop in Iowa. I have been published in the South Peace News for my journalistic endeavors. I have earned an award at www.writerstoolbox.com for my inspirational fiction '*Decrease*', and have had my Science Fiction/Horror stories published in various webzines (www.belwilderingstories.com, www.peachpublishing.com, etc.). I have an M.A. in Religious Studies, a nearly completed M.A. in Old Testament Theology, and have a Doctorate in Church Ministry. I am currently the pastor of Knox Church (www.knoxefc.ca).

Exhaust from the Tin Woods

Glossary

Afternoonified – something not smart

Analytical Apparatus (AA) – a steam powered computer attempted to think (mostly unsuccessful)

Archon – a street urchin, a punk

Arty-sam – an artisan, someone who is creative with innovative technology

Babbaged – based on Charles Babbage's first computer, it's when something human has been replaced by a machine

Batty-fang – to thrash thoroughly

Bellased – stunning in every French way

Bricky – brave or bold

Charles Dickens – a good looking man

Common Wealthies – Canadians

Computing Apparatus (CA) – steam powered computers powered by gaslight

Crushed – a negative expression for integration

Defenstration – to reject a really bad idea

Dreamers – explorers

Enthuzimuzzy – annoying or loud enthusiasm

Ether Dreams – unrealistic expectations

Glitzers – street punks decked out in the latest fashion

Granding – something made amazing by technology

Held Companion – a girl assigned to aristocracy to help in courtly behavior, usually of slightly lower birth who has little chance of prospects. The arrangement ends when the Lady marries.

Hollerithed – a machine that makes something simple

Joywig – absolute happiness, beyond the usual good mood

Joywigger – a joyful inventor

Klowning – to intentionally be irritating or disturbing for a greater purpose, based on European clowns that street perform in England despite the steampunks hating clowns

Luddmunsters- Luddites and those who favored gas powered technology who lost the argument

Ludwigged – crazy

Lurkjerkers – thugs, pickpockets, kidnappers who hide in shadows and have cybernetics

Mafficking – getting rowdy on the streets

Exhaust from the Tin Woods

Metalmancy – adding style and flare to machines

Mexicia – Mexico that owns California, lots of religion

Mexician – someone who is very religious

Monsteration – cybernetics done wrong

Needle Beatles – needle nose pliers

Nounschawnstein – a really neat looking home

Phantasmagoric – something frightening, disturbing, or unsettling

Pickled Pete – a puzzle without an easy solution

Pony – dance hall girl or professional escort

Poshed – a Victorian thing glitzed

Prattlers – steam scientists

Salt Rock – extreme, over the top, difficult

Seeing Gray – psychosis brought about my too much cybernetics

Sherluck – when someone makes a deduction not based on reason or science

Skilamalink – secret, suspicious

Skin seamstress – through genetics and splicing and surgery, scientists that fuse animals with humans. It was mostly unsuccessful

State – what the US has become

Steamboat- A kind man who helps out a damsel in distress

Steamies – people with really shoddy cybernetics

Tacky Parloring – old Victorian practices minus technology

Takin' the Oil Out – separating between disciplines

Tin Woods – an environment where nature is combined with humanity combined with technology

Toggling – cybernetics

Welly Babies – wellington boots

Wetted – hard labor designing technology

White Hell – cotton textile factory

Woods (the) – Canada

Vampid – psychotically, passionately without reason

Vorpal – favorite tool

Zietgeisted – before the steam revolution, the religion of Europe when it was believed